THE 1st ASSASSIN

A UNIT 22 THRILLER

THE 1st ASSASSIN

A UNIT 22 THRILLER

MAINAK DHAR

Anecdote
Publishing House

Anecdote
Publishing House

Anecdote Publishing House
E-35-A, E Block, Gali No. 2, Ganesh Nagar,
Pandav Nagar Complex, Delhi - 110092

Published by Anecdote Publishing House

First Edition 2023

ISBN: 9788195890774

MRP: ₹ 350.00

Book Promoted and Marketed by Champ Readers Pvt. Ltd.
Edited by Amy Brantley
Layout and Cover by Damonza.com
Printed in India

Praise for The 1st Assassin

What made *The 1st Assassin* an Amazon bestseller?

"Breathtaking tale of espionage and conspiracy…This propulsive spy-thriller comes wrapped in a mixture of high action, deep intrigues, dark humor that will delight thriller lovers…crisp action, thought-provoking plot, and compelling protagonist will leave readers hungry for more."

—*Book Life by Publishers Weekly*

"Grab a bag of popcorn because you won't stop flipping through the pages…a gripping, action-packed thriller, this is a must-read…the most intriguing plot, with ingenious and mind-blowing twists… Coupled with a knack for painting a perfect setting, the author made me feel as if I was in the middle of all the action…Dhar incorporates a remarkably sentimental depth in his narration. This made me empathize and connect with the well-developed characters. There is action, thrills, suspense, and so much more in this magnificent piece of work."

—*Readers' Favorite, US*

"Dhar packs the plot with relentless action electrifyingly depicted—the book seems written for the big screen."

—*Kirkus Reviews*

"The author writes with clarity yet pulls you in as a reader. There's a great assassination plot going on, some interesting characters, and plenty of action to keep the pace moving quickly along. Definitely a fun and enticing read that keeps your attention."

—*Amazon Vine Voice review*

"The 1st Assassin is one of the year's top conspiracy thrillers."

—*Best Thrillers Book Awards*

Contents

As Always, for

Puja & Aaditya

EPISODE ONE

A CHESTFUL OF MEDALS

Here's some free career advice-when the man who could fire you says something that makes you angry, don't let him know you want to kill him.

Of course, I'm much better at giving advice than heeding it, which is why my boss was glaring at me, and the fat man in front of me was looking at me with the kind of distaste that would have been more appropriate if I had just thrown up all over his expensive Louis Vuitton shoes.

Louis Vuitton shoes? On a minister's salary? Worn by a man who never stopped advertising his humble background? In short, Manoj Kumar Pandey, the honorable Minister of State for Home Affairs was both stupid and corrupt, and unfortunately for me, I think I let my feelings show.

I had been long trained to keep a straight face, and when he walked up to me, shook my hand, congratulated me on winning all those medals, things had been under control. Then he held my shoulder, as if we were old buddies, and leaned into me.

"We need more men like you in Delhi. Real heroes, not just bureaucrats. Our government wants to crack down on anti-nationals and we need men, hard men, like you. Men who know who the enemy is and can take the war to them."

Till then, I had a smile fixed on my face. A smile I had long learned to reserve for stupid staff officers and bureaucrats. A smile which told them you were suitably obsequious and saved you from having to respond to the inanities being showered on you. My boss, Sean D'Silva, was peering on with pride, the kind of pride which you'd show when the neighbors admired your Doberman.

I could live with that; I'd learned to live with a lot worse. For example, I had learned to live with myself. More or less, other than the nights when I used to wake up dreaming of dead buddies, wanting nothing more than to put a gun in my mouth and end it all. Those nights were fewer now, but they still happened occasionally.

However, I couldn't live with the fact that a cretin like Pandey would disrespect men far better than him by saying what he said next.

"I have heard some details of what happened in that famous last mission, but you know, with all the secrecy you people in the Special Group love, I don't know it all and perhaps they will never reveal all that happened. They said all of you were heroes, but I said that I prefer heroes who don't get captured and killed by the enemy."

My smile disappeared, replaced by a look that many men had

seen, usually just before I killed them.

Pandey took a step back, his eyes widening in sudden alarm, my eyes boring into his. He was a big man, almost six feet tall, as tall as me, and he had at least twenty kilos in weight over me. The difference was that he only talked a tough game- of hard men and cracking down on enemies. Most of that extra weight he carried went into his ample stomach and his double chin. I had lived years among real hard men and had hunted other hard men like us for a living. Men who would have slit Pandey's throat and then sat down to enjoy a cup of tea even before Pandey bled out. Pandey's look of fear was soon wiped away, but I could see that quickly replaced by fury. He knew what had passed between us, and he was furious at having been shamed in front of his government lackeys by someone he obviously considered beneath his station.

Sean stepped in gently, coughing to get our attention, and breaking the impasse.

"Sir, we can get on with the briefing, if you don't mind."

Sean D'Silva had once been a policeman, but now he wore a suit instead of a uniform and rode a desk instead of a police car. There were others in that office who still retained some of the sense of duty, idealism, and stupidity that makes good men throw themselves into harm's way for what the politicians want, but Sean was smarter than that. He had learned that the way to a good pension, medals, and promotions was to play the system, and that included managing men like Pandey. So, he would take care of things and make sure Pandey was mollified, but that also meant that he would chew me out later. As he walked away with Pandey to the conference room, he glared at me, running his right hand over his bald head, as he did whenever he was angry or nervous.

The Doberman had just growled at the guest and perhaps pissed all over the guest's fancy shoes.

Bad doggie, me. I just hoped that fat fool knew that next time, I might bite his head off.

***

"I heard you made the fat bastard piss in his pants."

Salil Murthy's words sneaked out of his mouth between bites of kabab, and I couldn't help but smile not just at how much he managed to eat, but at the fact that no matter how crappy the day was, he would find a reason to smile. We were standing outside what was his snacking destination of choice, where he would stuff himself with kababs, away from admonitions about cholesterol and carbs that would come his way at home. Tahir Kebab Corner in Nizamuddin, tucked between shops selling mobile phones of dubious Chinese ancestry, offering driving lessons and a one-eyed tailor who seemed to always have a towering pile of clothes in front of him. Today we had come for kababs earlier than usual, for lunch, not just because I didn't want to hang around at work and have people look at me the way Sean had when word got out about how I had pissed off the minister, but because I wanted to get out with the one person in the office I could open up to.

Salil's background meant that he could empathize with some of what I was going through, and moreover, he never judged me. He would never look at me the way Sean and some of the other suits in office would.

"Salil, let's get back. The big bald man will be waiting to give me shit in the office."

The big, bald man of course being Sean, and the office being his corner room on the top floor in a drab, grey building in the Central Government Office complex in New Delhi. It offered a nice view of the Jawaharlal Nehru Stadium nearby, but Sean usually preferred to keep the blinds closed. He was sitting at his desk, poring over some reports when I came in, and to my surprise, he looked less upset than I had anticipated. He smiled as I came in and beckoned for me to sit down opposite him. My hopes that he was somehow in a good mood dissipated when he spoke.

"Sen, do you know why you still have a job here?"

When your boss asks you such a question, it's best to keep your mouth shut. I knew I wasn't there for my good looks, my skill at paperwork, or my ability to suck up to politicians, so I let him continue, curious to hear the reasons for my continued employment. He rifled through the file in front of him, and I realized he was reading my personnel file.

"You're not bad at what you do. In the six months you've been here, I suspect you could've done well, but you don't really care. You're happy to just coast along, doing the minimum."

With that ringing endorsement of my professional competence and motivation, he continued.

"It's not even the fact that you have a bunch of medals. Lots of heroes fade away and live in anonymity."

He looked at me to see if I had any reaction to offer. Maybe he was baiting me, hoping to get a rise out of me. Nope, as he said, I didn't really care, so I just looked straight ahead, and by now I was standing at attention. When a man in the line of work I had been in gets told off by his bosses, he takes it standing up like a man, not on his ass on a soft chair like a bureaucrat.

"It's not even that the big boss had a soft corner for you because he felt responsible for what you and your team went through and wanted to take care of you and your family."

Good to know someone cared, but clearly, he wasn't finished. Sean took a sip of water and then made a show of going through the files.

"You see, Sen, the reason you are still here is that people higher up didn't want the spectacle of a bona fide war hero committing suicide on their watch. Not just any hero, but someone who the media called the most decorated officer alive. Imagine the bad press if someone like that kills himself and the government gets told we don't take care of our veterans suffering from post-traumatic stress. And now you go and piss off a minister! I've read your psych evaluation. I have it here in front of me. Should I read beyond the part where it talks about a lingering sense of guilt and suicidal tendencies? The big boss may be humanitarian, but the others are just waiting for things to cool down, for people to forget the chest full of medals on that photo in the papers, and then you either settle down into how things get done here or you get pensioned off."

At least he was honest with me. I mean, I don't think I could have asked for more brutally honest feedback from any boss.

"Am I clear, Sen? As long as you are in Area One under my watch, you will toe the line. After that, do what you want. I've read that you're making decent progress with your therapy, so I hope it's just a matter of time before we part ways. Best for us all. If you can't handle the heat, you shouldn't be in the kitchen."

I looked down at him, feeling no anger, just pity. Here was a man who defined himself by the seat he occupied, who was less bothered about whether I actually did blow my brains out than the fact that if I did something on his watch, he would look bad. A man whose idea of leading people was to throw in inane lines like the last one he had just thrown at me- no doubt something he read in a book, written by someone who had also spent his life sitting on a seat, dispensing advice to others in an air-conditioned room.

"Am I clear, Sen?"

There was no way to respond to that other than to say yes. Not when you barely tolerate what you're doing, are barely tolerated by your boss, but have no real option. No, let me be clearer about that and try again.

I didn't hate what I did. If I took the time to be objective about it, I was surrounded by decent people trying to do their jobs, including a couple who were the rare bosses who actually did give a damn about you- including the big boss Sean had alluded to. In case you're wondering, Area One was the Pakistan Desk, which Sean headed as Joint Secretary. The big boss was the Additional Secretary, Srini Iyer, and our employer was the Government of India. To be more specific, the Research & Analysis Wing, or R&AW. In public folklore, filled with spies like James Bond; in reality, filled with some very smart people, and some lazy and political bureaucrats, not unlike any other workplace, except they didn't chase sales or revenue targets; they chased down those who would harm our country.

The real problem was me.

The real problem was the fact that I barely tolerated myself.

I once worked for the government, in another part of the R&AW not too many people hear of. I had been a part of the Special Group, a unit within the Special Frontier Force, what we used to call '22'. I had spent years riding into missions that never officially happened, killing enemies we never officially killed. Thcy gave me a bunch of medals, partly for doing my job well, mostly to keep my mouth shut. After my last mission, they wanted me to keep working in the office in Delhi, perhaps to genuinely help me, or perhaps to just keep me from being a PR nightmare if I did something stupid like blow my head off. On the face of it, it was all good. I had some people who cared about me, a job to do, people who depended on me.

The problem was managing to carry on when almost every single night after my last mission, I had been tempted to put a gun in my mouth and end it all.

***

"Ma, come on, have some cake."

She looked at me, a smile breaking out on her face as tears came into her eyes.

"When you were small, I would be the one pestering you to have cake. Perhaps this is my last birthday, so I'll do as you say, Major."

I wanted to scream, I wanted to cry, but I smiled and hugged her close to me.

"You're a soldier's mother and a soldier's wife. You made me brave all the times I wanted to give up, all the times I was scared. Now, you can't give up on yourself. So, soldier, have some cake and then we'll watch a movie."

We spent the next few hours sitting together on the sofa, watching her favorite movie. It must have been the tenth time I was watching it with Ma, but she never tired of the movie, or Sean Connery. It was the movie she had watched with my father on their first date, and for those few hours, she was transformed. Gone was the pain, gone was her complaining about how her hair had fallen out, gone was the talk of dying. She smiled, she laughed, and I sat there by her side, smiling along. When the title credits began, I had started singing at the top of my voice, till she reminded me, the way only a mother can, that I had many talents, but singing was not one of them, and that I was distracting her from admiring Sean Connery.

A few minutes later, I had tucked Ma into her bed and came into my room. I sat on the bed, looking at the wall around me. I don't think we had planned it that way, but it told the story of my life as I looked through the frames on the wall. There were photos of Ma and Baba before I had been born, him wearing sunglasses that I'm sure were stylish back then, but today's kids would make fun of; Ma with her long hair, which she told me had earned her the sobriquet of Rapunzel back in college; him in uniform in a snow-covered landscape, in Siachen or Kashmir or any of the many battlefields he had served in; then me joining the party as a chubby kid who seemed to never want to look into the camera; me with Baba, playing football; standing proudly next to him when I earned my Karate Black Belt. Then Baba faded out of the photos. There were Ma and me at his funeral, fifteen-year-old me holding her tight, now looking at the camera- no more the kid who was looking to escape, but someone who had to grow up much faster than he had planned, someone who now had to pretend to be in charge. Happier times followed- me joining the National Defense Academy; Ma standing next to me as I stood with the Sword of Honor awarded to the best officer-cadet.

Then came a board with all my medals. I had wanted to take it down. Ma had forbidden it.

Then the photos stopped.

All that remained were memories and nightmares. Ma no longer wanted to be photographed. Her hair was gone, her body wasting away, and she was fighting a battle tougher than any I had ever fought, against an enemy I could not protect her against. The continued government job and my medals meant she got the best health care the government could provide, but it was a battle that I could see her losing day by day.

I sat and wept, holding my head in my hands. I wept for the men who had lost their lives because of me, I wept for the fact that I lived when they had not, I wept because my breakdown had perhaps caused my mother's relapse. This was not her first brush with cancer. She had defeated it seven years ago, but when I came home, scarred, drinking every night, needing psychiatric help because the doctors said I might kill myself; her cancer had resurfaced. Her doctor told me that it was likely triggered by stress. Ma never said anything to me, she never blamed me. Instead, she continued to try to take care of me.

I looked up and smashed my hands against the sides of the chair. I had to force myself to become that fifteen-year-old kid pretending to be in charge once more. Pretending to be in control of myself and things around me for her sake. I cut down on my drinking; I forced myself to bottle it all up and show up at work when Iyer offered me a desk job in Delhi. I smiled when people thanked me for my service and congratulated me on my medals. I knew that I could not wallow in self-pity or deal with my demons when Ma needed me to be strong. It was for her sake that I had been clawing my way back to what and who I had once been, one painful day after another.

But when I was alone in the dark as I was now, all that was stripped away, and I saw myself for who I really was. A man who was afraid to sleep because he would dream of the two buddies who had been tortured and beheaded in front of him, and he had not done anything to help them. A man who was causing the death of the woman who had brought him up and had loved him more than anyone else in the world.

In my shoes, you would have occasional thoughts of blowing your brains out as well.

***

"Major Sen, how did you sleep last night?"

"Just fine, thank you. No dreams. I meditated before I slept and woke up with the alarm at five in the morning. Ran 10K this morning and went to the gym. I'm absolutely fine, doctor."

I had been taught many skills in my time in uniform but lying convincingly was not one of them. Doctor Hadap stared at me, as if boring into me, her glasses almost halfway down her nose. It was a look I had come to recognize well over the last few months. Then she smiled, as if willing to let go of this lie.

"Any recent suicidal thoughts?"

That was direct. I mean, if you're a doctor who is concerned your patient is suicidal, reminding him can't help, can it? But then, as I had learned, the good doctor had concluded that I was in denial and needed to confront what I was going through. She had also come to know me very well over the last eight months and over time, had decided that confronting what I had in my head was the best way of getting me to deal with them.

"No, doctor."

She wrote something down and smiled.

"Your boss gave me a call. Said you frightened some minister."

I couldn't help but smile as she continued.

"I'm glad to see you smile, Major. You've made huge progress. It may not seem so on a day-to-day basis, but you should be proud of what you've achieved."

When they had first told me that I needed to go to a shrink, I had scoffed at it. I mean, I could deal with my own issues, couldn't I? Ma had forced me to go when I had woken up screaming in the middle of the night once too often, and over time I had come to realize that my daily early morning sessions with Doctor Mugdha Hadap were perhaps one of the things which ensured I retained my sanity through the day.

"Now, I want you to tell me about your last mission. We've been working on this, and I think you're ready to go through it all with me. You've done really well so far, but so far, we've talked about it in bits and pieces. I want to hear it all from you in one go. I've got your most recent reports with me, and I've talked to your mother as well, and the progress from when we first saw each other is remarkable. However, it is important for both of us that you are finally able to talk about that last mission. You need to lay this to rest, and you may not think so, but I feel confident that you're ready to move on."

I didn't realize it at first, but my right hand was drumming on the table in front of me, and my heart was pounding. I had replayed those events in my mind a thousand times but putting them into words was harder than I had imagined.

'You know what happened, doctor. You've read the reports."

"Take it easy, take your time, but you'll feel so much better when you can talk about it. If you remember all our sessions, we said that you were truly on your way to recovery when you could talk about what happened. When you could face what you had seen and done. There's no rush but I think you are ready today. Go ahead and tell me."

So, I told her.

Me, Gurung, and Thapa. There had been three of us out that day. I was their officer, but in the line of work we were in, regularly putting our lives on the line for each other, we were buddies, the best of friends, brothers in arms. A bond that others who have not put on a uniform and gone into combat together can possibly relate to. We were in Kashmir, nearing the end of a deployment and then a short break before we were flown off to wherever the government needed to use our very special skills. A local informer had brought in news of an infiltration attempt from Pakistani occupied Kashmir across the Line of Control. We were nearby and were instructed to sweep the area and to call in reinforcements if we spotted anything. I'd been in the Kashmir valley for a long time over multiple deployments, and this wouldn't be the first time we intercepted jihadis trying their luck across the border. Recently there had been very heavily armed and well trained foreign jihadis coming in, proving to be more than a handful for the cops or the Border Security Force, and so I and my buddies were often called in to take the battle to the enemy or do recon sweeps to better understand what we were up against before we brought in heavier firepower.

We caught their trail after an hour and radioed in for reinforcements. We were told the informant had got some more intelligence about the terrorists meeting up with local contacts in a nearby village. Supposedly, a top terrorist leader was there. A man who was on America's Most Wanted list- someone who had masterminded many attacks in Afghanistan against US forces and then brought his terror to India. A man called Mullah Azam. We were asked to go and scout that village. I remember thinking that was a stupid idea. We were just three men, being sent into an environment we didn't know well, up against an unknown number of adversaries. The suit on the radio, sitting in his office in Delhi, told us reinforcements were being guided in locally by the informant, and in a rush to capture a high-value target, he told us to get eyes on the village as soon as we could.

So, we went in and were ambushed by over a dozen Pakistani Special Services Group commandoes who had come in with the militants- one of their Border Action Teams which would sneak in and try and ambush our boys. The battle was short and brutal. We got four or five of them, but we were outnumbered and outgunned, taken totally by surprise, and all three of us were wounded, with me taking a bullet in the left shoulder and shrapnel wounds on my back from a grenade that exploded nearby. That explosion dazed me long enough to not be able to resist when the SSG men came up and grabbed us. They dragged us across the Line of Control to a makeshift camp they had set up just a few hundred meters on the Pakistani side. I saw them work on Gurung and Thapa, torturing them with knives, taunting them, taking videos, boasting among themselves that this was the first time they had managed to get Indian Special Frontier Force men alive. Then, they beheaded both of them. One of them held up Gurung's head and spat in his face, talking about how these Indian dogs who called themselves special forces were not so special after all. I had been working on the rope they had bound my hands with. I had not been wounded as badly as Gurung and Thapa and had the ropes almost off when they came for me.

I was ready for one last burst of defiance and then an inevitable death when we heard helicopters. The SSG men stopped and then their radio exploded into life with their bosses telling them Indian helicopter gunships and drones were in the air and they needed to get away fast.

Some of the Pakistanis went off with Gurung and Thapa's heads, but the officer who had desecrated Gurung's body remained, along with two men. I think he wanted the trophy of the head of an Indian Special Frontier Force officer.

I had by then managed to untie myself, and when the SSG officer came up to me, knife in hand, I stood up straight. He froze as if he had seen a ghost. The idiots, complacent after what they had seen as an easy victory, had left Gurung's khukri lying nearby. I had trained with Gurung and Thapa and men like them for years, and they would joke that I must have some Gurkha blood in me for the way I managed to wield the khukri. I broke the SSG officer's neck, and then picked up the khukri and turned on the two remaining men. One of them had the fucking audacity to beg for mercy before I cut his throat.

Then I beheaded all of them. I walked across the LOC, carrying three heads, covered in blood, when my buddies found me. They would later tell me that many of the local cops with them ran when they saw a blood-covered demon carrying heads in front of him. I had become a demon, one fueled by rage at what they had done to my buddies. We went back and recovered Gurung and Thapa's bodies, but we never found their heads. The informant had deceived us, setting us up for money. It seemed he had been a double agent for quite some time, and the Pakistanis had used him to lure us in, hoping to score a spectacular victory against our forces.

A couple of days later, we got intel that he had gone into hiding and was trying to escape into Pakistan with Mullah Azam and a bunch of other jihadis. My wounds hadn't fully healed, but nobody could stop me from going out on that raid. We intercepted them not far from the LOC. My buddies were looking for payback and we took no prisoners that day. Some of the jihadis, seeing dozens of Indian special forces cornering them, tried to surrender by throwing down their weapons. They died where they stood. I found the informant and Mullah Azam himself. The intelligence guys had told us to try and get them alive, so they could pump them for information. I wasn't there to follow their orders and Mullah Azam made it easier when he tried to pull a gun on me.

I came back with both of their heads.

The ambush and what happened next never made the news. Gurung and Thapa were 'martyred in enemy action along the LOC'. I was given a bunch of medals for bravery in counter-terrorist operations, to add to the ones I had already earned earlier in Kashmir and Ladakh. Nobody mentioned the Pakistani commandoes we killed or the heads we brought back. Those were details too likely to upset the gentle sensitivities of the peanut gallery at home which cheers war on social media or from their living rooms as if they are watching a game on TV, while young fools like us kill, die, and watch our buddies die to fulfill their bloodlust.

When I finished, I was crying, and Doctor Hadap had her hand on my shoulder.

"It's okay to cry. It's better to let it all out. I have understood what you're feeling. The guilt of not being the one they killed, of having led your men into harm's way, of feeling that you are responsible for your mother's illness even if the doctors say that her relapse was likely brewing long before your mission."

My head was back against my chair, but my hand had stopped shaking. I didn't know if I would ever be cured of the demons that seemed to haunt me, but I'd settle for a few minutes of peace. I realized I had never cried when Baba had died and wondered later why that was so. Was it shock? When I used to wake up in the night, shivering, I would try and pull myself together, telling myself that I had to get my life in order to take care of Ma. I had driven myself hard, for duty, for family, but perhaps, I'd never really given myself the time to deal with the feeling I carried that those close to me died while I was cursed to live on. I was shocked when I first thought of killing myself. No, I was terrified. Cowards killed themselves, didn't they? What was happening to me? Doctor Hadap had taught me to accept what I was feeling, to realize that each year, more Indian soldiers killed themselves than were killed in enemy action. She told me about Post Traumatic Stress Disorder and how it could be cured like any other illness, with medicines and therapy. At first, I had resisted. I was a warrior, and warriors dealt with their issues without a shrink, but the night I had put a gun in my mouth and Ma had walked in was the last straw. I realized I wasn't in control and needed help, and I was glad I had been open to it.

Doctor Hadap was smiling at me as I looked back at her.

"Major, we have achieved a breakthrough. You never used to get this far before, and the medication and sessions seem to have really helped. We can see each other anytime you need me, but for now, I think we can reduce our frequency of sessions to once a week. Of course, you can call me anytime. Mr. Iyer will be incredibly pleased to hear of your progress."

"What does he have to do with this?"

She smiled again, the smile of someone who was not just an ordinary psychiatrist, but an officer in the Indian army whose job was to nurse back to health wounded warriors suffering from wounds that bandages and surgeries would never heal.

"He wanted you close not just because he owed you. He did, and a lot of people did, for all that you've done for the nation, but because he knew that you would really be cured when you had recovered enough to get back to doing what you were meant to do."

"And what's that, doctor?"

"Getting back in the fight, Major. Men like you were not born to sit at a desk."

***

I could see Sean stiffen behind me, obviously miffed that decisions were being made about me from well above his paygrade. Doctor Hadap must have worked fast because when I got to the office, there was a message that the Additional Secretary wanted to meet me in the afternoon. Sean and I were sitting in Iyer's office, and Sean muttered to me.

"Have you done something that's pissed off the boss?"

I had no idea what Iyer had in mind for me, but I knew that I hadn't done anything that would invite his ire, so for a change, I got to enjoy knowing that I had one up over Sean. It was immature, but I couldn't resist the next sentence.

"Sir, he called both of us. Maybe you did something to piss him off."

If looks could kill, Sean D'Silva was blowing holes in me with an RPG launcher. The door opened, and Iyer walked in. He was the polar opposite of Sean in many ways- a soft face, with thick-rimmed glasses which made him look more like a professor than a spy, and a gentle demeanor that put everyone around him at ease. Those hid a razor-sharp mind and the ability to be ruthless when needed, which made him perfectly suited for his job as Additional Secretary in the R&AW. I stood and saluted, which irritated Sean even more. I mean I never saluted him, and he didn't deserve it, but Iyer was no ordinary desk jockey like Sean. He had been there and done that- served in the army for a couple of years before being discharged after a training accident and then he had joined the Indian Police Service to rapidly rise in the R&AW hierarchy. In my last job, he had been my big boss as well, as the head of the Special Operations Command in R&AW, and he was one of those rare leaders even cynical, hard men like me were willing to follow.

"At ease, Major. Let's dispense with the formalities after all the years we've known each other. Sit down, Sen. And you too, Sean."

Another scowl from Sean. I had no idea what was coming my way, but so far this had turned out to be a rather good day, if only for the juvenile pleasure of seeing my usual tormentor get pissed off.

Iyer took off his glasses, toying with them in his hands, a habit of his I had long come to see as a precursor for sharing a mission. Usually, missions that put me in harm's way. That was the first warning sign.

"Sen, you're as physically fit now as you were as a young Lieutenant in the Paras, or when I first got you into the SFF. So, your physical fitness isn't something I'd even waste time checking. The question I had was about your psychological fitness. I know Doctor Hadap has been working with you a lot, and she's telling me that you're ready to get back in the game."

"Excuse me, sir, what game?"

Iyer laughed.

"Sen, you are not meant to sit in an office and grow old and fat and earn a government pension. I've seen you grow over the last six years you were in the SFF; I've seen your appraisals from your time in the Paras and I've seen you in this office over the last six months. I know that you don't have fun here. I kept you here because I wanted to see how we could help you recover from the last mission. We need men like you- who can think and who can act decisively when the time comes."

All that flattery should have told me that something was coming my way which would once again involve me putting my ass on the line for the government. I had no particular desire to do so and was about to say something when Iyer continued.

"How's your mother doing? You do realize you are not alone in looking after her. Your father was a hero, and you have more than done him proud. When a family has given so much to the nation, we must look after them. I've been speaking to some specialists and there are some limited stocks of experimental drugs that they would recommend. Nothing certain, but there have been trials in the US with a lot of success. Meet them and let them know if you'd be okay to continue."

I had talked to the doctors and had been planning on selling the old house we had in Kolkata to pay for the costs of the experimental drugs. With my salary, that was the only way to afford the drugs, but Ma had insisted we not sell that house as there were too many memories associated with it. Iyer must have seen the expression on my face and leaned forward across the table.

"Sen, the government will pay for the treatment. I've got it cleared."

I sat upright. I could do with help, but I didn't need charity. We may not have had much money, but my father had been an officer in the Indian Army and gave his life for the nation, and I had known a life where honor was something you could never buy, and you should never sell, no matter what the price. Iyer's expression softened.

"Son, nobody's doing anyone any favors. There's a critical mission we need you on and we need you to be fully engaged on it, reassured that your mother is in good hands. The government was getting some stocks to try out at our hospitals and when I sent in a request, with your father's record and what you've done, the ministry cut through the red tape and approved it immediately."

Sean thought that was a good time to cut in, perhaps to reestablish that he was my boss.

"Sir, what's this mission you need Sen on? Perhaps other officers may be more suitable for it."

Iyer put on his glasses and looked at Sean.

"D'Silva, this mission requires men with a lot of operational field experience, because we don't know where this may lead us. So, I'm getting Sen on it and Murthy in your team will liaise with him from Headquarters, and for a couple of months, they will be on a special task force that reports directly into me."

Sean looked like he had swallowed something particularly distasteful, but he knew better than to say anything in front of the boss. That way, he had better sense in managing his career than I did.

"Sir, what's the task force?"

"Sen, as you know, the US President is headed our way next month, and the diplomats, politicians, and bureaucrats are all excited, as they perhaps should be. If he does agree to a summit with Iran facilitated by India, that's a huge foreign policy coup. As you may imagine, all sorts of people aren't exactly thrilled with it- our friends in Pakistan, jihadis all over the place, to name just a few. But that's not what we need you for. There's been some chatter we've picked up that there may be a credible terror threat and the Americans wanted a joint task force to look into it. They're sending some of their guys, and we needed a team which included some intel types but also someone like you with operational experience."

I was many things, but I was not an intelligence agent by training or experience. I told him that. He had his glasses off again.

"The Americans insisted we have someone with recent experience in kinetic operations. Funny, how the Americans have fancy jargon for everything. We had only a handful of intelligence officers with recent combat experience and when we suggested your name, they lapped it up."

"Does this task force have a name?"

Iyer looked up at me, his eyebrow raised.

"Why? Do you have something in mind? The paperwork says something in typical bureaucratese about this being an inter-departmental cooperation team, but you can name it whatever you feel like."

I couldn't hide my grin.

"How about Unit 22, sir? Just for old time's sake."

Iyer couldn't hide his own grin and he nodded.

Sean wasn't willing to be ignored in silence so he thought this would be a good time to pipe in.

"I'm guessing sir that this is rather routine. You know, Sen, that name you came up with sounds very dramatic, but often these task forces are great exposure but little real work other than meetings. Should be just fine for you."

Iyer had his glasses back on and he glanced at Sean without saying anything. Then he looked back at me.

"This may actually turn nasty, so I can see why they'd want someone like you. You see, Sen, the Intelligence Bureau has a source which says this threat comes from a group led by a particularly nasty specimen, a Pakistani who made a name for himself by beheading hostages for ISIS in Syria and Iraq."

I could sense Sean stiffen behind me. He would not be pleased to know of this at the same time as me, but then the spooks operated on a strictly 'need to know' basis. The IB worked internal intelligence and the R&AW intelligence outside India's borders. The two did intersect when it came to Pakistan and its proxies within India, but the agencies often jealously guarded their sources and methods. I thought it was all bureaucratic nonsense which meant that men going into harm's way were often put at more risk while the bureaucrats fought over who should have which file or nugget of intelligence, but I was too low on the totem pole to have my opinion count for anything.

"Have I heard of this guy before?"

He looked up at me, and his smile was gone, replaced by a hard look. I saw now not the friendly mentor I had known but a former army officer and senior intelligence operative.

"Sen, he wasn't operational in Kashmir when you were there, so you haven't heard of him. Nobody's seen him since all his videos show him in a mask, but you do know the head of the family, in a manner of speaking."

"I'm sorry sir, I don't understand."

Srini answered with a grim smile.

"He's Mullah Azam's son."

***

EPISODE TWO

Bombs, Biryani & Bullets

"I think I'm going to enjoy working on this task force."

Salil Murthy's enthusiasm for his new project had little to do with the professional challenge or indeed the opportunity to break away from Sean's stifling orbit, if even for a short while. It had everything to do with the young woman walking towards us. I muttered under my breath.

"You're married, or have you forgotten?"

He smiled back as he responded.

"You're not, and I'm just watching out for your non-existent love life. Just being a good wingman, that's all."

I followed his gaze and looked at the woman walking towards us with long strides. She wore a dark suit that smoothened over curves that would otherwise catch any man's eyes. She was perhaps in her late twenties, almost my age. Her long, brown hair was pulled back behind her head in a ponytail. Her face was undeniably attractive, her tan complexion telling me there was some Indian, Middle Eastern, or perhaps Hispanic blood in her background, but it was her eyes that I noticed. There was no denying that she was extremely attractive, but her eyes told me there was much more to her than her looks. Her eyes were sharp, purposeful, and hard. All business. At the same time, her eyes seemed wary, darting from one place to another, as if assessing the landscape, watching for hidden enemies, as if afraid of being taken by surprise again. I had seen eyes like that before. I saw eyes like that when I looked in the mirror every morning.

"Salil, you don't want to mess with this one."

She walked up to us and shook hands with Salil first. Wearing a blazer and fancy loafers he probably looked like the boss, while in my jeans and sweatshirt I probably looked like the hired muscle.

"Morning, I'm Amy Khan from the Secret Service. We're going to be working together on the task force."

Whatever her looks, her accent was very American. I had spent some time training with American operators and had heard a couple of boys who spoke with the same Texan drawl Amy had. Salil introduced himself, throwing in all kinds of fancy acronyms, half of which I think I understood. Married or not, my so-called wingman was determined to make a good impression on our new American colleague. She seemed suitably interested, but by the way her mouth curled up a bit at the edge when Salil mentioned some memo he had written which had gone as far as the Pentagon, I suspected she was secretly enjoying his attempts at impressing her.

Salil beamed when she said that she had seen his background during her briefing and had actually read his memo on inter-service collaboration opportunities in disrupting terror networks. I had no idea if she had actually read it or was simply great at bullshitting. Salil didn't seem to care. From the expression on his face, he might as well have won the lottery.

I shook her hand next.

'Major Aaditya Sen.'

"What do you do now, Major? From the way your hand feels, I suppose you use them to break things versus typing memos. Your file was short on details but the guys in uniform seemed to think you were a mix of John Rambo and the Terminator. You don't look that scary in real life, not at all."

She smiled as she looked at me with a frankly appraising glance which totally unbalanced me, and I fumbled as I began to reply. I had spent way too much time among men trying to kill each other and then getting bored among old men in suits to remember how to say anything witty back to an attractive woman like her. Clearly, she had read the files that had been sent on the task force. I had skipped the mail when I saw it had been forwarded by Sean. Perhaps I should have read it and known a little bit more about this interesting new teammate of ours from America.

"I'm not entirely sure most of the time. I used to be in the army, but now I seem to hang around people with suits feeling underdressed, underqualified, and in present company, certainly underprepared."

She smiled, and I thought she should smile more often. That smile made me smile in turn, something I hadn't done a lot recently. I hadn't meant to flirt, but perhaps the good doctor had been right. I was getting back in the game in more ways than one.

Salil, perhaps feeling a bit left out of the conversation, butted in.

"Would you like some coffee? Sen is being modest about his skills. The office coffee sucks, but he makes the best coffee I've ever had."

I gave him an evil glance and then we walked over to my desk. Amy watched me while I took the coffee beans from a sealed pouch in my desk drawers, ground them using a portable hand crank coffee grinder, and then boiled water using a small electric kettle before pouring the fresh coffee out into three cups. As we walked back to the meeting room, Amy sipped her coffee.

"This is delicious. If the coffee here is always this good, I vote for having all our team meetings here."

"Coffee is a weakness I have. Even in the field, I'd carry my hand grinder with me."

She took another sip.

"That's true dedication to good coffee, Major."

"Just call me Aadi. I am dedicated to coffee, though it is an expensive passion to have. Each of those grinders costs a bit and I went through seven in my time in the field."

'Seven? What happened to them? You keep dropping them?'

I looked back at her and smiled.

"Four were destroyed by bullets, two were shattered by shrapnel, and one was taken by a jihadi when he fell off a cliff, holding on to my backpack. The idiot thought he'd take me with him."

There was a brief, uncomfortable silence. I realized that my words had taken me back to memories, some of which were fond and some which I wished I had not brought back. For a split second, I was no longer in the conference room. I was back in the valley, bullets whizzing past my head, Gurung and Thapa dying in front of me, Azam's head coming off his shoulders in my hand. Then I snapped back to the present and looked back at Amy and Salil, embarrassed. Salil knew all about me and he just patted me on the shoulder and went to get a refill of his coffee. What was interesting was the way Amy was looking at me. When I had come back from my last mission, broken and bitter, I would often catch people looking at me in a way that infuriated me. A mixture of pity, or even horror. There was none of that in Amy's eyes.

I saw understanding in her eyes.

We were soon joined by another American, and this one could not have been more different than Amy. I found myself looking up at an open, friendly grin on the face of perhaps the biggest man I had seen. He was easily six and a half feet tall, and while I would normally consider myself pretty well built, I suspect two of me could have fit into him side by side. Shaking his hand was like having your hand engulfed by a bear's paw. His voice was deep but gentle and he had a broad, open smile which showed his gleaming, white teeth, in contrast to his dark skin.

"Hi, I'm Donzel Bethune, a pleasure to meet you. I'm with the State Department. I heard you guys talking about your service days and I'd love to swap some war stories over a beer later. I was in the Marines for a while before I moved over to the dark side. I had read your file, but when I saw what you'd chosen as the name for this team, I chuckled. A man after my own heart- doesn't forget who he was in the field, even if he's now stuck in an office."

He didn't need to spell it out. Our new friend was in the CIA and while I had met my share of spies I disliked, he seemed one I could grow to like, with his honest, open manner. All four of us sat down in the conference room in the CGO Complex which had been booked for this introductory meeting. Given the various agencies involved, we would not have a permanent office. Instead, we would meet in our office or in the US Embassy depending on what we needed to discuss. A few minutes went in settling down and me pouring coffee for Bethune while we waited for our missing team member.

The door swung open ten minutes later and a thin man walked in, wearing a crisply ironed white shirt and black trousers, sharp eyes behind his glasses, and a thousand-watt smile below a thin mustache.

"Welcome to India. I am Ajay Pillai from the Home Department."

Why couldn't spies just say they're spies? Our new friend was from the Intelligence Bureau, but if he wanted to play cloak and dagger, who was I to bust his cover? Especially since he was a Deputy Director and reputed to be a fast tracker in the IB with all sorts of connections to the top bosses- both in his hierarchy and in the political arena. Scuttlebutt had it that his earlier posting as a Deputy Commissioner of Police in the Prime Minister's home state had done his prospects no harm. The fact that he was also supposed to be bloody brilliant and great at his work meant that he was someone whose stars were clearly on the ascendant.

As he flashed his smile and shook hands all around, I couldn't help but dislike him. I know it was grossly unfair to him, but the fact was that a political creature like him, chasing glory while sitting in his office, was the one who had sent me and my buddies into harm's way without vetting their information.

"Sen, you with us?"

I snapped back to the present and smiled at Pillai and took a sip of coffee to hide my embarrassment. When I looked up, I saw Amy looking at me, a knowing look in her eye. Bethune spoke up, rifling through some papers in front of him.

"So, what more do we know about this threat? We've all seen the combined dossier our bosses have pulled together. The problem is that we just know that this character goes by the name of Bin Azam. We don't know his age and we don't know what he looks like. All we know is that he's a nasty son of a bitch and that jihadi chatter indicates he's planning something when our President visits. But then these jihadis brag all the time."

Then Pillai proceeded to take out a laptop from his bag and hook it up to a projector. Salil was smirking and I was looking on in awe. I mean, you've got to admire a guy who has a PowerPoint presentation ready for any situation.

We were four slides through the threat matrix which by then was looking like a spider's web or the doodling of a particularly imaginative child when Pillai again caught me drifting off.

"Sen, do you have anything to add? Do you see any connections we may be missing?"

I wanted to slap him and wipe that condescending smile off his face, but I settled for sitting back, crossing my arms across my chest, and smiling at him.

"I'm just the hired muscle. Show me which of those bastards needs to be killed and I'll get to it."

Pillai looked at me, panic flashing across his face for a second.

"Sen, that is not the mandate of this team. We are meant to assess threats and direct them to the right channels. In fact, when I heard of the name you had for this team, I thought it may send all the wrong signals…"

Amy cut in.

"Relax. He's just messing with you. Now, what I can gather is that we can summarize the situation by saying that there are about three dozen different groups and individuals who have the motive, means, and opportunity to strike when the President is visiting. We just have no real idea who, when, and where."

Everyone laughed other than Pillai, who seemed to take it personally, and began to mutter something about intricacies of intelligence work. Amy continued, with a slightly apologetic tone, perhaps realizing that inadvertently she'd put Pillai on the spot.

"I'm sorry if I sounded flippant, but really for me, as the representative of the Secret Service, the whole thing hinges on how credible the threat against the President is. Otherwise, it's unfortunate but true that both our nations live with terror threats all the time. How credible is the threat against the President?"

Pillai seemed to be hesitating, and Bethune, perhaps coming to the rescue of a kindred spook, stood up, and when a man of his size stands up, everyone shuts up.

"Look, Pillai, I've been in this line of work a long time, and I know how important it is to safeguard sources and methods, but we do need to know whether we're dealing with the general nut jobs and jihadis always out to make a name for themselves, or something more. Can you share more?"

I could see a determined look in Amy's eyes.

'I'd go a bit further than that, Mr. Pillai. A threat to the US President is not a trifling matter, and my bosses will lean hard on me to understand the nature of the intel that leads us to conclude this. Otherwise, every day, there's some nutcase out there making a threat against the President on social media. Can you tell us more about how you got this intel so that we as a task force can be on the same page and get a calibrated view of this threat?"

Pillai seemed to fidget, making me realize that I really didn't like him much, not just because he was a bureaucrat, but because he clearly didn't want to share what he knew, despite us being on what was supposed to be the same team. At the same time, I got a renewed appreciation for Amy. She was far from being just a pretty face. The way she had stood her ground and stood up to Pillai took real guts. Bethune saw that Amy was clearly not comfortable with Pillai's reaction, and he gently chipped in.

"Well, Mr. Pillai?"

Pillai, who stood perhaps a foot shorter than Bethune, looked up at the hulking American.

"Mr. Bethune, I will need to get authorization to share that."

Bethune leaned down towards him, perhaps not realizing how intimidating he looked.

"Mr. Pillai, I agree with Amy. We cannot act as one team if

the right hand doesn't know what the left hand is doing. If you share with us more of the intel you have, then we can combine it with what we know and form a plan of action."

When it came to a physical shoving match, Bethune may have been able to squash Pillai like a bug, but when it came to whose stubborn bureaucracy was stronger, Pillai would win hands down.

"I do need clearance and while I understand where you are coming from, to disclose specific sources and methods is something I need to consult my superiors on. I am sorry. We will meet again the day after tomorrow to review what we have. Till then, goodbye."

With that, Pillai walked out of the room, PowerPoint slides, mustache, and all. No sooner had he left than Salil piped up in a passable imitation.

"Sen, anything to add? Do you see any connections we may be missing?"

Amy laughed, Bethune looked uncertain as to whether laughing would be a breach of protocol and I just got up and shook my head.

"Let's get the hell out of here and get a drink."

***

"Welcome to India!"

Salil was drunk, and he perhaps didn't realize that this was the third time he was raising the same toast. Bethune, who got drunk way faster than you'd expect such a tank of a man to be, was grinning and they emptied their glasses and ordered one more round.

"You don't drink a lot, Major."

I looked across the table at Amy, who had been nursing a Coke for the entire time we had been at Salil's watering hole of choice for the night, Ek Bar in Defense Colony. He had said something about it having authentic Indian cuisine with which to welcome our American guests, but I suspect it was just the closest bar to the office.

"And you don't drink at all."

"Touché."

She raised her glass in a toast.

"To the soldiers who have drunk so much to forget that they'd rather not drink anymore."

I touched my glass to hers.

"I think these two are going to get even more happily drunk here. Do you mind if we get out for a walk? My shrink had advised me to avoid loud music, dark places, and too much alcohol. Staying here would mean I violate all three of those."

She smiled, gathered her coat, and joined me outside. There weren't too many people about, and the few that were scurried past bundled in their sweaters and jackets. The Delhi winter in December did that to you. Amy seemed to notice and smiled.

"I was born in Texas and spent my early years there, but then spent a few years in Minneapolis. This is practically summer weather for me, compared to Minnesota. You not feeling cold, Major?"

"I grew up in whatever place my father was posted to, including some stints in Kashmir, and then spent most of my adult life in places like Kashmir and Ladakh. This is positively mild weather, with the added perk that nobody's shooting at me. And please call me Aadi, all my friends do."

She told me what it was like to grow up, the daughter of a second-generation Indian immigrant, a doctor, who had married the daughter of Irish immigrants, a doctor herself. Her parents had set up a successful medical practice, but she had always been afflicted with wanderlust and felt cooped up living in one city all her life, and so joined the army.

She took out a cigarette and lit up, a bit to my surprise. She caught my glance.

"Hope you don't mind my smoking?"

"No, not at all. Just figured someone who nibbles on salad for dinner and doesn't drink alcohol would steer clear of cigarettes."

Actually, I did mind, because the smoke was distracting from the very nice perfume she had been wearing, but I wasn't about to bring that up.

"Bad habit, I know. One I picked up in Iraq when we got blown up or shot at way more often than I would have liked."

I was genuinely surprised.

"What did you do in the army?"

She had a look on her face I knew well. Ma told me I got that look at times. The slightly vacant, faraway look of the combat vet who is remembering things no person should have to remember.

"I did a tour and was assigned to a Combat Support battalion, accompanying Green Berets near the Syria border. Supposedly there to help establish better relations with the locals- get the women and children to open up to us more than they perhaps would have with only the men around and help train the Iraqi special forces. The enemy didn't get the memo that we were not supposed to engage in combat. Was scared out of my mind when they first hit us. Can't forget the first time one of our guys died in front of me. Unlike you, never did any shooting or killing, but saw enough carnage to last me a lifetime of bad dreams. Can't say I ever got used to it but managed to survive and came back and applied for the Secret Service."

She had been so lost in her story that she never noticed that the cigarette had burned itself out almost to her fingers and she threw it away with a jolt of pain and irritation.

"I know what you mean."

She looked at me with genuine surprise.

"Bethune told me about your record. You're supposedly one of the most decorated Indian army officers alive. He said you were a genuine hero, and when someone like Bethune says that about someone, it means a lot."

I looked her straight in the eye.

"Those medals don't mean I wasn't scared, they don't mean I still don't have nightmares about the men I lost, or that I wouldn't give all those damned medals back if my men could come back."

We stood there for a while. I would be lying if I said that I didn't feel some attraction towards her. With someone like her, any man would be lying if he said he wasn't, but it was more than that. I felt something I had not felt in a long, long time.

I felt connected.

Trust Salil to come ruin it all when he careened into me as he came down the stairs with Bethune.

"Donzel and I realized our birthdays are the same."

That was a big coincidence and I looked at the big American.

"Really?"

He was drunk, but still a few degrees more sober than Salil so he looked at me a bit sheepishly.

"Well, the year's different, and so's the month, but the date is the same."

Salil cut in.

"See what I mean? We're practically twins."

After dropping Salil home, it took me only about half an hour to get home. I had called Ma to tell her I would be a bit late and when I came home to our small apartment in Mayur Vihar, I had assumed she was asleep.

I was in the middle of pulling a crumpled t-shirt over my head when she walked into my room.

"Someone is in a good mood today."

I looked at her standing in the doorway to my room and rushed to her, hugging her.

"You're the one smiling, Ma. It's been a while since I saw that."

As we sat down on my bed, she stroked my hair, the way she

used to when I was a kid.

"I could say the same about you. I'm smiling because I see you smile. What happened at work?"

I tried to put it into words, but it was complicated. It felt like I was useful again. Like I had something to do where people valued me. Like I was finally among people who understood me.

"It's not just the work, Ma. On the way home, I got a message from the hospital that they've got the experimental drugs they had mentioned. They are okay to stop the chemo and start on those as early as next week."

Her eyes narrowed in confusion.

"How? I hope you haven't decided to sell the flat."

I held her hands.

"No, Ma. The government's picking up the tab."

"That's a lot of money. What brought on this generosity?"

"They need me to be part of a team for a while and wanted to help. Plus, I guess all those medals need to be of some use sometime. Seems the ministry approved it as soon as Srini brought it up with them."

I could see the relief on her face. I could only imagine the hell she had been through with the chemo, yet as I got up, she held my arm.

"I've been a soldier's wife and a soldier's mother for way too long. When the politicians seem to be too generous, chances are they're going to send you into harm's way."

"Come on, Ma, the only danger I face is falling asleep in

meetings."

As she was about to walk out of my room, she turned to me.

"Is she very good-looking?"

I turned towards her; the shock perhaps apparent on my face.

"I know you better than you know yourself. The first time I saw that look on your face was when you had that crush on that horrible Malini back in school."

"She wasn't horrible."

Ma grinned and I realized what a stupid response that was and I laughed as well. It felt good, to have laughter in this house after so many months. Ma came towards me, and I hugged her.

"Just be careful, will you?"

"Of the government or the girl?"

She laughed again.

"Both."

***

After checking Ma into a very fancy private room where the doctor said they would observe her for a couple of days, I kissed her on the forehead.

"Ma, I'll be back at night after work."

"You don't have to spend the night here. You have work every day. There are so many nurses here to take care of me."

I winked at her, earning a playful slap on my shoulder with my response.

"The nurses are why I want to be back here."

She smiled and kissed me on the cheek.

"That's the boy I haven't seen for so many months. Welcome back, Major Sen."

When I entered the office, Salil pulled me aside.

"I hear Aunty's in good hands. What a relief, man."

"You can say that again. It's still a long battle ahead, but at last, I can see some hope."

"It's not just her, though. You look much better."

We walked into the conference room to find Amy, Bethune, and Pillai waiting for us. Amy smiled and I sat down next to her.

"What have you done today to piss Pillai off?"

She laughed as she passed me the coffee.

"I have no idea. He's been like this ever since he walked into the office."

Pillai coughed to get our attention.

"Mr. Bethune, I gather that your bosses decided to go over my head and request for the disclosure of our source."

Bethune had his hands out in front of him in a defensive gesture.

"Hey, no offense intended. Our President's life is at stake, and we are one team, right? So, someone at the Agency above my paygrade went ahead and rattled a few cages. If it's any consolation, I didn't ask them to do so. I was happily waiting for you to let us know, but someone up there was impatient and wrote a message."

Pillai passed around a sheet of paper.

"Well, here are the details. My source is a small-time travel agent who used to launder money for gangsters and eventually got contacted by jihadis, who wanted to get his help and use the cover of his operation to get them in and out of the country. A bit of a bastard, but our bastard."

"What's the specific intel he gave you? How did he get info on a plot of this sort and the involvement of big fish like Bin Azam if he hangs out with small-time gangsters and jihadis?"

Pillai looked at Amy.

"Good question. He stumbled upon some information about guys traveling into India to try and conduct a hit on a high-value target. He had no specifics, but he heard Azam's name being mentioned. It meant nothing to him, but we connected the dots. In one of his videos, Bin Azam talked about killing the US President, and we know he's here in less than a month for the Republic Day parade. It could have been bluster of the sort these jihadis love mouthing on their videos, but you never know."

Bethune wasn't totally convinced.

"So, this intel is less conclusive than I may have expected. You guys turn Delhi into a fortress during your Republic Day parade and with POTUS here, our guys will be all over the place. That's not to say we should get complacent, but even if there was a real plot to target POTUS, if we shake the tree hard enough, they may realize it's too hard a target and abandon their plans."

"What did you have in mind?"

"We follow the trail to see where this travel agent of yours got his info and we take it from there. First, we shake him down to get any information he's holding back. I'm not comfortable just relying on what he chooses to tell us and assuming that's all he knows."

Pillai shook his head.

"Azfal is a crucial asset of ours. I've cultivated him for a couple of years and while his business supposedly comes largely from arranging group tours for Haj pilgrims, he had been managing travel arrangements for drug smugglers for years. When militants approached him to work for them, he couldn't refuse, because he realized he'd endanger his family, but soon after that, he approached me, saying he was a patriot, and it didn't feel right to help these militants. I've been looking out for him and also getting whatever info he can get without blowing the fact that he also works for us. By now, he's got connections and leads to several militant networks which have helped us pre-empt many attacks. As far as we know, none of his jihadi contacts know anything about his connection to us. If we push too hard, we'll burn him and lose him as an asset."

Amy leaned forward.

"That's a risk we would be more than willing to take. If there is any credible intelligence about a threat to POTUS, then we need to act on it."

Seeing Pillai and Amy once again in a pissing match was not my idea of fun, so I cut in. Plus, if I really admitted it, I wanted to help Amy out, and I suspected my interests were not purely professional.

"This Azfal knows you, Pillai, but he has no idea who I am."

Pillai scowled.

"Right, so R&AW agents beating down his door will be any less damaging than Americans going in guns blazing?"

"He's a small-time travel agent who does business with shady people. We can go in pretending it's an income tax raid. I'm quite sure it won't be the first time he's been raided by the tax people. We get access to documents and hopefully learn more about his contacts without scaring him about Americans at the door or warning any of his militant contacts about his connection to you."

Pillai was about to say something and then held back, looking genuinely surprised.

"That's not a bad idea, Sen. Not bad at all. He has been raided before and once or twice, he actually called in favors with me to stave them off."

Bethune nodded and had a grin on his face.

I had never imagined I could come up with an idea that the spooks would appreciate and get Pillai and Bethune to shut up. Imagine that. Pillai soon however threw a wet blanket over my plans.

"Sen, it is a good idea, but R&AW has no jurisdiction to go knocking down his door."

I didn't say anything, but Salil told me later that the thought bubble above my head read in all caps- WHAT THE FUCK? Trust bureaucrats to think of jurisdiction and paperwork when there was real work to be done. Pillai clearly missed that thought bubble as he continued.

"I'll get the Income Tax people to pull together a small raid this evening. There will be no warning given, and they'll go in and seal the place. I'll then send in a couple of my men undercover to recover what material they can find and also put in bugs and hidden cameras so we can monitor what happens there when Azfal's jihadi friends come calling. I'm sure Azfal will be calling me for help, and I'll pretend I helped call off the tax people by pulling strings on his behalf. Hopefully, we get the info we need, and he feels he owes me even more."

I wasn't happy, but then there was nothing I could do about it. Officially, at least.

Over lunch, Amy seemed to have her share of concerns as we sat in the cafeteria.

"This Azfal is the only lead we have. We can't afford to blow it."

I stopped eating and looked at her.

"Don't you trust Pillai and his jurisdiction and clever plans?"

She had an exasperated look on her face as she answered.

"Pillai and Bethune can spend their time in pissing matches on who pulls rank over whom but in among all the men with their big egos you seem to have forgotten that the security of the US President is my job!"

There were only two of us sitting at a corner table and I could see a few heads turn to look at us. Amy lowered her voice.

"I'm sorry. I shouldn't have snapped at you. You don't realize just how much pressure is coming my way from Washington.

It's not your problem and I have no business taking it out on you."

"Hey, no offense taken. I can be a jerk, I realize that and to be honest, I have little appreciation or idea of what people with real jobs do. I've been here in Delhi for just over six months, and my boss barely tolerates me, which tells me I still haven't figured out how to do any work in the real world."

She smiled and I found myself thinking, not for the first time, that it felt good to see her smile and also felt good to know I had made her smile.

"You seem to have done okay. When the Agency works with anyone, they probably run your background so well they know you better than you know yourself, and Bethune told me you're a bona fide hero. He didn't share details and I didn't ask, but he just said your record and ops would make most SEAL teams jealous."

I took a sip of my coffee as I replied, trying hard to put the bitterness out of my voice. I had no business taking out my issues on Amy.

"They gave me a bunch of medals, that's all. I don't feel like much of a hero. I did what I had to, and often didn't do it well enough. I lost men, good men, whom I shouldn't have. Sometimes, I wonder if it would have been better if I had died and they had a chance to get back to their families."

I realized that despite myself, I had let my feelings show and I began to apologize when Amy placed a hand on mine. Her touch was warm, calming and as she looked at me, I saw no sympathy, just genuine understanding in her eyes.

"You forget that I was there, with men like you, in Iraq. I never killed anyone but saw what these men were made of and what they did. Some of them were young and brash, bragging about kills, but the best of them, the ones who got the job done, the ones who really kept everyone together, the ones who never claimed to be heroes, they were the real heroes. I've seen the pretenders and the real ones, and you're the real deal."

I tried to change the subject; not sure I was ready to share more of myself with anyone.

"Your job can't be easy. I mean, taking a bullet for the President if you have to? No offense and I don't usually judge people by their tweets but he is pretty out there at times."

She laughed out loud.

"Let's put it this way, protecting him is something I have to do and it's not about the person, it's about what they stand for, what the office of President, our democracy, our ideals, stand for."

I smiled at her, as she withdrew her hand, suddenly rcalizing that her hand had still been on mine. I realized that I wished she had kept it there longer.

"You're an idealist, Agent Khan."

She smiled back.

"As are you, even though I'm sure you'll deny it. Just be careful, and just call me Amy."

"What do you mean? This should be pretty simple. They go in flashing Income Tax Department badges and get hold of his computers and documents, scrub them and return them after Pillai pretends to run interference on his behalf."

She folded her arms, looking straight at me.

"You haven't been around spooks as long as I have. I've been in Washington three years now, and I wish things were as simple as when I was a simple grunt. They have their own games with their secrecy, turf battles, and need to know bullshit. That usually means their looking good is a priority versus the mission itself. Plus, why do I get the feeling that you have your own plans for tonight?"

I looked down at my plate. Damn, was I so transparent to everyone? Clearly, I would have made an unbelievably bad spy. Or Poker player for that matter.

"Salil was telling me he was surprised you took it all so quietly, with you not being allowed to go on an op which was your idea. He also mentioned something about you being a troublemaker. So, I'm assuming you won't sit typing out reports while Pillai puts his plan into motion."

I made a mental note to give Salil shit for ratting on me to Amy, but then he was probably doing that to have an excuse to strike up a conversation with her. Couldn't blame him. I looked at Amy.

"Let's just say that my boss didn't want me on this job for my looks, good behavior, or ability to produce amazing inter-departmental memos. He trusts my judgment and I have a hunch about this thing- and not a good one."

***

"Sen, why did you get a firearm issued without my permission?"

I really didn't have time for Sean and his bullshit, so I snapped back, in what was probably a severely career-limiting move.

"I got the big boss's approval."

That shut him up. To be absolutely clear, I hadn't done all the paperwork, telling myself I would do it the next day, but I had called Srini and told him I thought the shit was about to hit the fan, and Pillai and his IB clowns would likely mess it up. Srini had once been a good soldier but being part of the bureaucratic system for so long meant that he couldn't resist an opportunity to have his agency show up his IB counterparts, so he told me to do what I thought needed to be done. Whether that included issuing a firearm and showing up in the middle of a raid where I had been told not to go was a minor detail I had not gone into with him.

I was wearing a coat over my t-shirt and was sitting on a worn-out plastic chair at Shahbaz Biryani Corner. The place was run down, but to be honest, the biryani in front of me was surprisingly good, perhaps one of the best I'd had. However, I hadn't come there for thc food. Sitting at my table, facing the road, I had a clear line of sight to Azfal's shop, which was just over a hundred meters down the road. We were bang in the middle of a slum in the Nizamuddin area, and as I looked around, I thought that Pillai might be a good spy, but he was terrible at tactics and I was happy I was there to see how things unfolded, and perhaps lend a helping hand when needed. To be fair, I doubted Pillai had spent the years I had spent in places like Kashmir. I was there over an hour before the income tax raid was to happen, and I could already tell that it was likely to fail. It was a Friday evening, I was within a stone's throw of at least four mosques I could see, and the area was already crowded with young men loitering around after prayers. A posse of government officials coming in would be spotted instantly and I had no doubt someone like Azfal would have contacts who would tip him off. I had asked around about Pillai, and to be honest, my initial assessment of him had been uncharitable. He was supposed to be an honest and capable officer, but I doubted he had ever led a raid into such an area on a Friday evening. I had, many times in the Kashmir valley, and knew how messy things could get. It started with slogans, moved on to stone-pelting, and before you knew it, some joker was taking shots at you with a Kalashnikov.

I heard the loud and increasing roar of motorcycle engines. Hearing them was not what made me sit up and take notice. It was normal for the young men to leave for their homes on bikes, which were lined up outside the mosques. What was not normal was for four of them to ride in together, as if in formation. When you've done the kind of work I have done for years, you spot things others won't. The four men were riding in a pretty smart tactical formation. Two ahead, and two flanking them behind and to the side. Gave clearer lines of fire if they got into trouble and they could engage enemies without risking hitting each other. They were wearing faded and stained kurta pajamas like most of the youth around, but they were all wearing pretty similar lightweight jackets with the front open. It was a chilly day, but unless these were four buddies who shopped for clothes together, wasn't it more natural for at least one of them to wear a sweater or a jacket of a different design? Wearing jackets with the front open would have made the chill of the wind uncomfortable, wouldn't it, given they were on their bikes? Why would they not zip them up? Revealing the stained and dirty kurtas underneath could not have been a fashion statement. Then their shoes. Good quality sneakers with solid soles, and the familiar swoosh on the side. If not the real Nike, then at least passable imitations. Not a single slipper or flip flop among them, unlike most of the other young men around.

All innocuous observations and perhaps all coincidental, but you didn't live long in my line of work if you banked on coincidence. Good sneakers helped you get away fast if you needed to, and light jackets with the front open were great for drawing a concealed gun fast if you needed it. I should know, I had made the same choices.

The four stopped their bikes in front of Azfal's shop and one of them knocked on the door. When it opened, three of the men went inside and one stood outside, facing the street. If you're four friends overcome by religious fervor and have come to book tickets for your Haj pilgrimage, you don't leave a lookout outside the travel agent's office. If these were jihadi buddies of Azfal's then this was monumentally bad timing. The income tax officers on their way for the raid in half an hour would be in deep shit. I paid for my Biriyani, which I had to regretfully leave half-finished, and began to walk towards the shop, my eyes glued to my phone as I walked. Just another guy forwarding WhatsApp jokes, except I was walking on the other side of the road from the shop and through my peripheral vision was keeping a watch on Azfal's suspicious customers. The window on the side of the store closed as I came closer. Another warning bell. Why would Azfal want to get so cozy with his new customers? I was now bare feet away from the shop and stopped, raising the phone to my ear, and got a good look at the guy outside the shop. He was young, very fit, and was looking straight at me, as if telling me to bugger off. His eyes were rimmed with kohl and he seemed to be chewing on something- gum or tobacco. Pretty decent-looking guy, other than the long scar down the side of his face. I was guessing he hadn't got that from a shaving accident. I should know. I had similar scars on my body from when I had been cut by knives.

He raised his head subtly, a wordless message telling me to fuck off. Instead, I walked straight towards him. I could see him tracking me as I walked closer, putting my phone in my pocket, but before I did that, I sent the message I had been typing while I walked. A message to Pillai which told him things were very wrong here and he needed to hold off on the raid and wait to hear back from me.

The man in front of me kept looking at me and I walked right up to him and raised my voice.

"Aren't you Iqbal's nephew? I met you at Munaf's wedding. I think you were the one hogging all the dessert and took the last slice of Black Forest cake. I was standing right behind you and hoping you'd take something else and leave it for me. You remember, we joked about that?"

I walked up to him and hugged him. He was thrown totally off balance. I think the last thing he expected was a random stranger walking up to him talking of weddings and cake and then hugging him. By then I had achieved my objective. To get a closer look and understand what the nature of Azfal's visitors was. In hugging him, I had patted around the side of his jacket and confirmed that my newfound friend was carrying a gun. He gently pushed me away.

"I don't know you. You've got the wrong guy."

I did my best to first look surprised, and then suitably apologetic.

"I am so sorry. You so looked like him. I feel so stupid. I'll get on my way."

That was mission accomplished as far as I was concerned. Azfal was with some armed jihadi buddies, which made me wonder if all he did was book tickets for them, and how much of a reliable source he was for Pillai. Also, the fact that his armed buddies had shown up just ahead of a planned raid was sending up all kinds of alarm bells about the timing. But that was all I had in mind. Go away, maybe order another Biryani and then contact the team to debrief them on these curious developments.

That was when I heard a sound most people would not have noticed, but one I couldn't help but react to. In the movies, a silencer supposedly magically makes a gun silent. In real life, it doesn't work that way. Those in the business don't even call it a silencer, we call it a suppressor. Sure, it suppresses noise, but if you know what it sounds like, and you're close enough, you will hear a noise. The real benefits in a firefight are less that it makes a weapon magically silent but that it significantly reduces muzzle flash making you less easily visible to your enemies. If you remember your science from school, light travels much faster than sound and the guy you're shooting at will see the muzzle flash before he hears the shot. Also, for long-range sniping, sound suppression is helpful. Up close and personal, it reduces the sound, but you do hear a very audible pop. My jihadi buddies afflicted with wanderlust who had come to a travel agent carrying guns would generate easily over 70 or 80 decibels if they were packing handguns with suppressors. That's as much as a blender or vacuum cleaner next to you. What I heard was most definitely not a blender or vacuum cleaner. No, Azfal and his buddies were not having a housecleaning party or making smoothies.

I knew what the sound was, and clearly, by the look in my eyes, the guy in front of me knew that I knew. That meant he began to reach under his jacket. As I saw his hand close over his gun, instinct and training took over. My left hand snaked out, holding his right hand against his body, while I leaned in, smashing my forehead against his nose. He staggered back and I bent my right arm at the elbow, parallel to my body, and then extended it, moving my left leg forward to give added momentum and put my weight behind it. The ridge of my right palm connected with his nose, and I heard a crunching noise. Nose broken, bone shards likely working their way back into his brain. If not dead, the man was stunned into unconsciousness, and I grabbed him in a hug. The whole thing had taken a couple of seconds, and unless anyone was paying really close attention to us, we were just two buddies who liked to get all touchy-feely and were hugging each other again. I moved him back towards the door and settled him on a chair next to it. That left his three buddies and Azfal inside. The door was unlocked, and I opened it a bit, my hand inside my jacket, on the gun which was in a holster on my left side. As the door opened, I saw a man lying on the ground, presumably Azfal, because the three young men I had seen go in were gathering documents and files and putting them into a large backpack.

Life had been simpler in the army. I would have gone in, and started shooting, and asked my buddies to cover me. If the enemy was too entrenched or the likelihood of casualties too high, then I'd have called in air or artillery support. Here, I was all alone, with no support, and if I started blasting away, even if I managed to take down all three men inside, the mob outside would begin gathering and I might be in a pretty difficult situation explaining what had happened when they suspected me of killing one of their neighbors. That indecision almost cost me my life when one of the men turned to look at me, raised the gun in his hand, and squeezed off two shots. I dove back out the door, my back to the wall. I had been hesitant to engage in a firefight out here, but now all bets were off. I was better off taking my chances with the mob outside than sitting there waiting to be shot by the men inside.

The tactical situation was hardly in my favor and how I wished for the good old days when I would have rolled a grenade inside. I had no grenades, so I did the next best thing. I took a shoe off my dead or incapacitated buddy sitting on the chair outside, parted the door, and flung it inside. Two suppressed shots rang out. Then I had my gun out, flicked a little switch on the left-hand side of the slide, stuck my gun inside the gap, and fired away, moving from left to right at what I thought would be knee height. Three little trigger presses. Three little loud buzzing sounds. That was all.

The Glock 18 is a masterpiece of modern engineering. Packing 17 rounds, it has sometimes been called the most dangerous handgun in the world. I don't know about that, but it is a piece of work. It can fire on semi-automatic mode, activated by flicking the little switch I had, and in that mode, which I personally liked to call Beast Mode, it fired bullets at a rate of 1200 rounds per minute. It was akin to carrying a little machine gun in your pocket. The recoil was significant and firing one-handed meant I knew my rounds would travel up with each burst, but within a couple of seconds, seventeen bullets had been sent at the three men at a speed of over 1000 feet per second. I waited a few seconds, put a fresh clip in my gun, and opened the door. Two men were on the floor next to

Azfal, lying in expanding pools of blood. Where was the third guy? I heard a door open and close in the back of the shop. As I walked in, I saw something on Azfal's body, and when I came closer what I saw stopped me cold.

He was wearing an explosive vest.

I heard a bike start outside and I ran out, to see the fourth man sitting on his bike, hosting the backpack on his shoulders. As he began to ride away, he turned and smiled at me.

For a man who had just had three of his buddies killed, he seemed to be an in awfully good mood. That was when I saw the mobile phone he held in his right hand.

Shit. I knew from experience that explosive vests, jihadis, and mobile phones in one sentence never led to happy endings. I began to run away from the shop as fast as I could as he pressed a button on the phone and sped away. I was still running when the vest on Azfal's body detonated, and the whole world seemed to explode around me.

Then there was darkness.

***

EPISODE THREE

ATHITI DEVO BHAVO

If death and the afterlife meant spending time in heaven with an angel that looked like Amy, perhaps it wasn't a bad deal.

That was my first thought when I woke up to see her leaning over me, holding my hand.

"Thank God you're okay."

I smiled, not just because I was happy to see her and happy to be alive, but perhaps because I was still a bit dopey from whatever the doctors had injected in me.

That happiness and hopes of spending eternity in heaven with an angel who was an Amy doppelgänger disappeared when behind her I saw the scowling face of my beloved boss, Sean.

Amy moved aside as he walked up to my bed.

"You have fucked up even more than I would have thought possible of you, and that is saying a lot."

Maybe I was in hell.

The doctor came to my rescue, shooing everyone out of the room, saying I needed to be under observation. She stood a foot shorter than Sean, but I was amazed at how efficiently and quickly she managed to get him out the door. I flashed her a look of gratitude and then she left, saying she would be back soon. In the meanwhile, the nurses would check how I was doing.

A couple of hours later, she was back. By then, I had recovered my senses enough to know that I was alive and well, other than a sore spot on the back of my head where something had hit me, and presumably knocked me out. I had also figured out that I was in the same hospital as Ma.

When the doctor came back in and began to look at some papers on a clipboard in her hand, I raised myself to a sitting position.

"Are you feeling okay, Major Sen?"

"Yes, doctor. I'm fine. Can you please do me a favor and let me know when you can how Mrs. Sen in room 618 is doing."

"That's in the cancer wing. Is she related to you?"

"Yes, she's my mother. I never got to check in with her today and she might be worried about me. If it's not too much of a bother, please let her know I'm ok and will get to see her very soon."

She smiled.

"I'll do that. You seem to be fine and can leave shortly."

"Thanks, and please don't tell Ma anything about me being blown up in an explosion. Mothers tend to overreact to such things."

She smiled and left the room.

That night, I didn't go home but went straight to Ma's room. Her doctor had said that she was responding well to the new medication with no major side effects, and I just sat next to her, watching her sleep. I still remembered her as the strong, vivacious woman who had lost a husband and then brought up a son single-handedly, on a teacher's salary, and never flinched when he said he would follow in his father's footsteps and join the army. When I had come home wearing the maroon beret of the Paras, she had cried, saying my father had always joked with her that while he was a career infantryman, his son would do one better and join the elite Paras. Then came my move to the Special Frontier Force a few years later, a unit operated by the R&AW. Originally set up to create havoc behind Chinese lines in the aftermath of the 1962 war and gradually growing to be a clandestine unit which worked in the shadows, going on missions that most people didn't hear of. I had been part of the sword arm of the SFF- the Special Group. That stint had seen me go to Ladakh, spend time on the Chinese border, cross into Tibet, go on multiple deployments in Kashmir, go across the Line of Control into Pakistan Occupied Kashmir- missions I could never tell Ma or anyone about. Missions that never made the papers, and all I got were a bunch of medals, some lost buddies, and nightmares that stayed with me long after I stopped. I would disappear for days, months, and then when I came home, she would simply tell me that she had been praying for my safety, and as importantly, praying that I always do my duty.

Yes, she was my mother, but she was not just another mother. She was a soldier's mother. She had made me who I was, and now I saw her lying there, her hair gone, her cheeks sunken, her veins prominent in her thin arm which had a drip attached to it. She was fighting her own battle and I was the one praying for her. Having been tempted to take my own life in past months, now that I had come face to face with death once more, I realized I wanted to live. Not for myself, but to be there for this woman who had been there for me all my life, even in my darkest moments.

I held her hand and put my head down on her lap. My back and head were sore, I had just killed men and narrowly escaped being killed myself, but as I sat there by Ma, I closed my eyes and slept better than I had slept in many, many years.

***

The next morning, after chatting with Ma and reassuring her that I was okay and that the small cuts on my face and hands were the result of a minor traffic accident, something she no doubt didn't believe, I left for work. When I reached there, I found Salil standing outside my room.

"Dude, you don't want to go inside."

"Look, I saw a bunch of stuff there which people need to know about…"

I never got a chance to finish as he showed me a memo on his phone. I scanned it and after the first couple of lines learned that I had been placed on leave till a fuller investigation could be done into the events of the previous day.

"On leave? Has Sean finally decided to fire me?"

Salil shook his head as if marveling at my naïveté.

"You clearly haven't been in Delhi long enough with bureaucrats like him. He is not going to make any decision, so that just in case you come out smelling like roses, he doesn't look stupid. That is the skill of people like him, a skill you and I will never learn. Take the credit when you can, but never take the hard decisions, get others to do so. If the decisions work out well, you can take credit for nudging others to look into it. If they don't work out well, you can blame others who actually took the decision. So, a committee will look into this and write a report. Till then, you chill, get paid, and don't go to the office unless you want to get chewed out."

I have never been good at listening to instructions and it was too late to begin now, so thirty minutes later, I walked into the big conference room. When I opened the door, I saw a couple of people I had never seen before. In addition to Pillai, Amy, Bethune, and Srini, there was a thin American in a dark suit who was probably a spy, given he sat next to Bethune. Maybe his boss, maybe someone from the US Embassy for all I knew. There was a fat policeman sitting next to Pillai. Some Delhi Police bigwig, and then there was Sean, looking at me with a mixture of disbelief and disgust.

"Murthy, take a seat. Sen, I believe you've got the memo. Please excuse us."

As I said, I was bad at listening to instructions, so I stood my ground.

"Sir, I saw some things there that you should all know about."

He gritted his teeth, and I knew he was trying hard to not explode in fury in front of his boss.

"What I saw was a mess unlike any in recent times. An

explosion in a busy area, four men killed, and a dozen bystanders wounded, and you in the middle of it all, when you had no reason to be there, carrying a gun, which you fired without any authorization. I think you have done more than enough. Please excuse us."

I just stood there. I mean, Sean couldn't physically throw me out, could he? There's something to be said for being shameless and stubborn. Srini got up and gestured to me.

"Sen, come in and sit down. We are debriefing on what happened yesterday, so you can fill in the gaps."

I walked in and sat down in a seat that just happened to be next to Amy. Pure coincidence, just a random choice of where I might sit. Okay, to be truthful, there was an empty chair next to Sean, but if you had to choose between sitting next to Sean and Amy, I bet you would have made the same choice I did. Amy smiled at me, and I smiled back, but then Srini burst my bubble.

"Sen, don't get too comfortable. After this meeting, Sean and I need to debrief you more fully in private and then you can proceed on the leave you have been sent on."

The cop got up and took the floor, preceded by his considerable belly.

"Our initial investigations show that of the four dead bodies, two suffered multiple gunshot wounds from 9MM rounds consistent with the weapon Major Sen discharged. One body, the one flung outside the building, had suffered blunt trauma but no gunshot injuries, and the fourth body, which we believe to be that of Azfal Khan, was badly mutilated by the explosion, and we believe he was wearing the vest that was detonated."

Pillai picked it up.

"Here is the working hypothesis the cops have so far. Maybe they weren't even jihadis, but gangsters whom Azfal had borrowed money from or cheated in some way. That doesn't explain the suicide vest, so the other theory is that Azfal was working with jihadis all along and they were planning something when you interrupted them. It all ended spectacularly, but Sen, if you had just waited for the raid, we may have captured them."

I had not said anything yet, but I looked straight at Pillai.

"They would have massacred a handful of income tax officers accompanied by a couple of cops carrying ancient weapons. One of the men shot Azfal before I interrupted them, so they were certainly not working together. Azfal never detonated the vest, by the way. Dead men don't do that. The guy who got away did that remotely with a mobile phone. Gangsters don't do things like that- trained operatives and terrorists do."

There was a stunned silence in the room as I continued, telling them what had happened. I could see Pillai's face fall. Perhaps Pillai was one of those rare intelligence officers who cared for his sources as human beings. That made him rise more in my esteem.

"What the hell happened in there? Why would they kill Azfal?"

That was a good question which Srini had asked, and I had no idea, but I had some hypotheses.

"Maybe he was in on their plan, whatever it was, and was chickening out. Maybe they found out he worked for Pillai and wanted revenge. I don't know, but the guy who escaped took a bunch of documents and hard drives with him, so they were not there just to pop him but to cover their tracks. Makes me believe that Azfal was indeed part of their plans and they perhaps realized he was sharing information with Pillai and needed to be shut up."

I couldn't help adding the next bit as I looked at Sean.

"I know I was there without authorization, but I'm not a bureaucrat. I've been trained to use initiative and adapt to the tactical situation, and I'd have preferred to not have anyone dead, but at least now you know more than just having to scrape up Azfal's remains from the floor of his shop and wondering why he decided to blow himself up. Also, these guys were not just random gangsters. They demonstrated pretty savvy tactical thinking and were carrying suppressed guns, which isn't common and certainly not available to just any gangster in India. Whoever they were, they knew what they were doing."

He didn't say anything, but Amy cut in.

"What we're not clear on is what this means for the investigation into the supposed threat to the President. Why would Azfal bring up Bin Azam otherwise?"

Bethune had been sitting quietly across the table from me, looking at me intently. His hands were steepled under his chin, and I could almost hear the gears spinning in his head. He seemed about to say something when the man next to him, the man in the dark suit who had not even introduced himself to me, said just one word.

"Misdirection?"

He got up and began pacing the room, with every eye on him.

"Maybe Azfal's buddies were planning an attack and bringing up something like a plot against the US President and involving big fish like Bin Azam would get all of us distracted while they did their operation. For all we know, they knew Azfal was working for Pillai and used him to feed us wrong information. The planned attack may not even be against the US President, but something totally different. Something you guys would not look at while you chased down leads on a supposed threat against our President. We have our own assets and information and nothing we have points to any credible threat against the President."

Of all the things I'd heard that morning, that made the most sense, except for one minor detail, which I pointed out.

"Why would they shoot Azfal?"

The man stopped and looked at Pillai.

"Just how much of a player was he? I gather he just arranged tickets and shuffled money and made some money from all sides. Maybe they paid him to feed you the information about the plot against the US President and maybe he knew too much about their plans, so they wanted to pop him and tie up loose ends before they went live. They may have planted the suicide vest to make it look like Azfal was just another jihadi wannabe who blew himself up by mistake. Wouldn't be the first time."

Once again, that was very sound logic, and it was hard to disagree with that. A staffer knocked on the door and passed some papers to Srini. He glanced at them and passed them around, and he shared the news as the papers made their way around the table.

"Looks like we have ID on the men Sen killed. This is an IB report that just came in. All three were known jihadis- two fought in Kashmir and one supposedly had wanted to go to Syria. Our teams raided their homes and scrubbed their social media accounts, and just over an hour ago, they found a video one of them made and kept on a laptop at his home. A video pledging allegiance to the Islamic State and promising an attack in Delhi. Probably they had planned on releasing it after their attack. This guy had several videos from Bin Azam on his browser history, and while there's no direct evidence that Azam was in touch with them, they could have been inspired by his messages. Wouldn't be the first time that wannabe jihadis got radicalized watching people like Azam. That probably explains them mentioning Azam and perhaps his video about the US President to Azfal. We also found messages from them to Azfal on WhatsApp, threatening him to keep his mouth shut about the help he had given them in terms of arranging tickets. Looks like they were a local jihadi cell and found out about Azfal being cozy with the government and bumped him off before they carried out their attack so he couldn't finger them afterward."

Bethune smiled at me.

"I think we need to cut the major some slack. Looks like he may have disrupted a terror strike and saved many lives. Also looks like the plot against our President may have been a red herring and we can gradually wrap up our work here."

It had been a while since anyone had praised me for anything and I couldn't help but appreciate how Bethune was helping get me off the hook. As everyone filed out, and Srini told me I could get back to work, I noticed that the man with Bethune was staring at me. He hadn't said a word and never introduced himself.

Bloody spies.

Sean glared at me and as he walked past me, he whispered.

"I still want a report into the disciplinary lapse involved in checking out a gun without appropriate paperwork and permissions."

Asshole.

That left me and Amy and I was feeling happy, relieved, and reckless. Just having escaped with your life and your job can do that to you.

"Amy, when I'm done with filling forms and trying to mollify Sean enough to keep my job, mind if we catch up for a drink tonight?"

She looked at me, an appraising look in her eyes.

"Are we celebrating anything?"

"Your President seems to be safe. Perhaps there's no threat against him. You can celebrate that. I'll just celebrate being alive and still having a job."

She smiled, nodding.

Maybe it wasn't going to be such a bad day after all.

***

"You're leaving tomorrow morning?"

I guess it was hard to hide my disappointment at the news Amy had shared. The beer I was sipping suddenly tasted sour and I toyed with the dumpling on the plate in front of me. I guess I should add acting to the list of things I suck at because Amy held my hand.

"Hey, are you okay?"

I hadn't even realized it, but my hand had been shaking. She held it tight.

"You okay?"

"Yeah. I'm fine."

I wasn't so sure of that. I had killed three men just a day ago, one with my bare hands. At that time, I had reacted with training and instinct, and to save my own life. The day had gone on in a blur of meetings and reviews, but now finally it was sinking in. I had killed many men, and to be honest, they deserved it. However, the act of killing someone had brought back all the memories of my last mission. I bunched up my hand, making a tight fist.

I was a soldier, dammit. I was trained to do this shit. I don't know if Amy read my mind, but she always seemed to know what I was thinking.

"Aadi, you don't need to pretend to be a hero in front of me. Not pretending makes you even more of a hero to me."

I just looked at her, into her eyes. Hell, I was attracted to her, that was for sure, and I could see in her eyes that she wasn't exactly beating me off with a stick. If anything, her hand was still on mine. That thought got me even more pissed off as I thought of her leaving the next day. I looked up and smiled at her. I mean, what had I realistically expected? But I had hoped for more than one dinner date. I thought I had spotted something between us, but then perhaps that was just wishful thinking.

"I'm fine, just that I was hoping to get outrageously drunk and then show you around my city."

She grinned back.

"The folks up above seem to be more comfortable that there may not be an imminent threat against the President and so they want me back."

That did surprise me. I was certainly biased because I would have wanted to spend more time with Amy, but the speed at which the Americans seemed to want to wrap things up was surprising.

"Who's decided that this task force may not be needed anymore?"

"People well above my paygrade."

"Like the guy with Bethune? Who was he?"

"Some Agency bigshot. I don't know him. But let's talk more about things that are more fun to chat about. What makes you think we can't get drunk and do outrageous things? My flight is at eleven tomorrow morning and it's not as if I have anyone special back home I need to FaceTime or chat with later tonight."

Hold on, had she just said what I thought she had just said? To be honest, early on in our professional relationship I had sneaked a glance to see she wasn't wearing a ring but being available and being interested are two very different things. And she hadn't called me Major or Sen. I was totally being an adolescent with raging hormones, but it had been a while since I'd been with such an attractive woman who showed signs of interest in me versus being around men shooting at me. My frame of mind was not helping, making me reckless. When you face death and kill other men, you realize just how tenuous your hold on life is, and then you realize all the things we put off for later or hold off on because we'll look silly or because we don't want to face rejection, are things you will likely regret not doing when you're lying there, breathing your last, knowing you'll never get a chance to do those things ever again.

I squeezed her hand back and she didn't withdraw it.

"Amy, I should warn you that I'm even more irresponsible when I get a few drinks in me."

She smiled back.

"That's the part of you I actually like. If I wanted to hang out with boring bureaucrats, I would be elsewhere."

It was beginning to look like my day was about to get even better when my phone rang.

It was Salil.

I ignored it and asked Amy more about what it was like growing up, compared to my nomadic upbringing, when every couple of years would bring a new posting for my father. She had hardly begun when my phone rang again.

Salil again.

"Maybe you should get that, Aadi."

I picked up the phone.

"What?"

"Geez, what the fuck's with the grumpiness? You in bed with

her?"

"Fuck you."

"Ok, I guess not. Well, I found something you may want to know about."

"Tell me, esteemed colleague, what have you found that I need to know now so urgently."

"The cops combed through the ruins of Azfal's place, and they found a piece of paper that your jihadi pal missed stuffing into his backpack before he vamoosed, and which wasn't incinerated after the explosion because it had slipped outside the back door."

That got my attention.

"Does it say anything useful?"

"No clue. Just says RA205. Analysts have filed it away, and may never get to it given the case seems closed, but thought you'd want to know?"

"Why do you think I'd want to know?"

"Because you stick your nose in stuff others ignore and that sometimes leads to things. Now get on with your date."

I hung up, not sure if Salil had just complimented me or insulted me, but I was intrigued. I told Amy about what he had said.

"Could be code, a locker number, a room number, literally anything."

"Maybe something will come to me if I sleep over it."

She sipped her drink.

"I thought you were going to be getting me drunk. Your plans changed?"

A few drinks later, we were back in her hotel room, kissing and helping take off each other's clothes. Things went by in a bit of a haze, considering I might have been liberal in my interpretation of what 'a few' drinks meant, but before long we were in bed. We talked for a long while, as Amy felt the scars that I carried on my body, scars that came from a life led in harm's way while wearing my nation's uniform.

Then, I discovered that this was a particularly good day indeed.

I woke up in the middle of the night, covered in sweat, breathing hard, shaking, my mind still foggy from the dream I had of Thapa without his head, asking me to get his head back. Amy sat up and held me from behind. I tried to get up, ashamed of my behavior, but she held my hand and pulled me back onto the bed. This was the first time I had shared my bed with someone after my last mission, and it had been a few years since my last serious relationship, and the only person who had seen me so vulnerable, so damaged, was Ma. What would Amy think of me? Some hero, who wakes up screaming and shaking at night?

I held my head in my hands.

"Amy, I'm sorry. I'm still more messed up than I might appear."

She just held me from behind, stroking my hair.

"Tell me what's bothering you."

It had taken Dr. Hadap months to get past my defenses, past my denial. Somehow, sharing my darkest fears and secrets with Amy seemed natural. I told her about that last mission, about living with the guilt of being the one to survive when I felt I should have been taken and my men should have returned to their families. I told her about the guilt of leading them to their deaths, the guilt of bringing back Ma's cancer with my self-destructive behavior. When I turned around and looked at Amy, I saw an expression in her eye I had never seen before. We had been attracted to each other, had shared what no doubt would have been a one-night stand, but for the first time, I saw a look of pure empathy in her eyes. Tears were filling her eyes and she held me tight.

"I can't imagine what courage it takes for you to be so strong for everyone around you when you're dealing with all this. I can just tell you that perhaps you don't see it, but today everyone was in awe of you. They may call you reckless, but they all secretly want to be you."

"That doesn't help me sleep any better at night, with all the stuff in my head."

She smiled and kissed me.

"I know something that might work. It's worked for me in my darkest nights."

As I lay down, she stroked my hair and sang. A soft, lilting song, which I was sure I'd heard somewhere before, but in my sleep-fogged mind, I couldn't immediately place it. Soon I found myself drifting off to sleep, and my last thought before sleep overtook me was that it was just my rotten luck to meet someone like Amy only to be fated to be separated from her.

***

I dropped by to check on Ma the next morning and before I left, she said just one thing.

"I just hope she ends up with a happier ending than that Malini."

Trust mothers to figure everything out about you. Well, there was no happy ending I had in mind for Amy and me. She would fly off to Washington in three hours and then perhaps we'd be in touch on social media, and eventually, she would get busy with her life and I with mine, and over time we'd move on. Perhaps we'd both look back fondly on the time we shared. That was about as happy an ending as I had any right to expect. Chances were that the moment she got on that plane, she would forget all about me. I drove to Amy's hotel, and she was mildly surprised to see me there.

"Thought I'd drop you at the airport."

"Shouldn't you be at work?"

I held the car door open for her.

"I have the memo asking me to go on leave. I never got the memo asking me to come to the office. I think I should wait for proper paperwork versus just acting on verbal instructions."

She got into the car and kissed me. This ending was already looking happier as we drove to the airport, chatting about various things, but mostly avoiding what would happen when she got on the plane. Fair enough. We were both adults, and with the kind of jobs we did, what did we expect, a happily ever after ending? We were mature enough and honest enough with ourselves to be happy with what we had shared. As we reached the airport, I parked and walked with her to the departure gate.

"Aadi, it seems like you want to make sure I get on that plane."

"I just want to make sure I get to spend every minute I can with you."

She stopped, her smile gone, replaced by a glint of sadness that flitted across her eyes, and then the smile was back. I knew what she was feeling. In that second, I had felt the same, perhaps I had a similar look in my eyes as well. For in that second, I had imagined what life would be like with someone like Amy in it. Someone I could be myself with, laugh with, love, without any pressure to be anything or anyone other than who I was. That was of course replaced by the cold, hard facts of what we did and just how far apart the trajectories of our lives took us. A Secret Service agent in the US and someone like me could never realistically have a relationship that lasted unless one of us gave up life as we knew it, and it was way too early in our relationship for that, and I knew we would never get the time to see if our relationship ever became anything more.

She kissed me again and I held her tight, whispering in her ears to stay in touch. In turn, she told me to not blow myself up the next time my curiosity got the better of me. As she began to walk towards the gate, I happened to glance up at the board near the gate which listed the arrivals and departures.

Then I froze.

Amy had turned around to wave at me, and she stopped on seeing the look on my face. She walked back towards me.

"Aadi, what happened? You look like you've seen a ghost."

I pointed at the arrivals board.

"RA205 is not a hotel room number, a locker number, or

any sort of code. It's a flight. Nepal Airways flight 205 from Kathmandu to Delhi, and it lands in about thirty minutes from now."

She let go of her trolley and held my right hand with both of hers.

"What are you thinking? You have that look in your eyes which means you're going to be up to no good."

"Amy, it's the most obvious answer. Azfal was a travel agent and Pillai mentioned he used to arrange passage for jihadis. Maybe he was getting in jihadis for their operation from Nepal. The Pakistani Inter-Services Intelligence had all sorts of networks in Nepal once upon a time. I'm sure they still have connections there."

I called Pillai next and told him what I had seen and the connection I made.

"I can't do much by flashing my R&AW card at the airport, but can you get the IB guy stationed here to pull a few strings and get passengers coming in on RA205 screened? No small kids, no old men or women, other than that, everyone should be fair game."

"All this based on something scribbled on a piece of paper."

"A piece of paper left at the site of the murder of an informant, who was killed by professional hitmen. If they were covering their tracks before a strike, maybe they were expecting help to come in from outside. You did mention the three dead men were known jihadis, and you know better than me how Nepal has been a conduit for jihadis in the past."

He was still silent.

"Sir, do you want to take the risk that a terrorist comes in on today's flight and we miss him? So close to the US President's visit?"

He quickly agreed. Maybe my stint in an office in Delhi had taught me something after all- how to push all the right buttons on a bureaucrat. Call him 'sir' to make him feel more important, and then make him worry about losing face in front of his bosses.

Within minutes, a young, competent-looking officer wearing jeans and a coat came up to us.

"Major Sen? I'm Ankit Sharma, the SIB officer here. Pillai Sir briefed me. What do you need?"

I told him, we exchanged numbers and he was off. Amy was still standing next to me, and I could see that she was busy messaging someone on her phone.

"Amy, aren't you going to miss your flight? Get going."

I could see a twinkle in her eyes.

"And miss all this fun?"

"What do you mean?"

Then, she was a Secret Service agent again.

"Major, we all came together to avert a supposed plot against the US President. Last evening, we thought it was all over. Now, it isn't that clear. I have a professional obligation to see this through. I messaged my bosses and they're okay for me to hang around a bit longer till you check this lead out."

Then she was just Amy as she grinned.

"Plus, I've learned that hanging around you tends to make

things pretty exciting pretty soon."

***

Sharma had done well in the limited time he had. A section of the airport before Immigrations was closed off and all passengers from flight RA205 were being shepherded there. The story was that they were being checked for a new virus. With all the chaos everyone had seen through the COVID pandemic in the recent past, the mere mention of that was enough to ensure that the airport authorities did whatever we wanted, especially when Sharma waved around an impressive-looking document from the Health Ministry, which no doubt Pillai had managed to rustle up in record time.

Many of the passengers were cranky, a few resigned, but they really had no choice. There were 127 passengers on board that day and I was standing on the sidelines with Sharma and Amy while he coordinated with the airport staff. Two doctors were checking for fever, taking swabs, and asking all sorts of irrelevant questions, buying time for a young man Sharma had called over to check each passenger's details on a laptop he had to see if the passenger showed up in any of the terror databases India had. Amy was doing the same on her laptop.

Four guards of the Central Industrial Security Force, which provided security at airports, were standing by with their rifles hanging loosely by their sides. Just in case things got ugly and my hunch was correct. We had let the crew go, along with four old passengers in wheelchairs. Then we prioritized quickly screening mothers with young kids. As time wore on, I could see everyone's enthusiasm flag almost in direct proportion to the increasing agitation among the passengers. Once the women and kids were gone, some of the younger men were letting their feelings be known in no uncertain terms. Our methodology was hardly perfect, as a terrorist would likely not be traveling with his real passport, but Sharma had proved to be very competent and imaginative. While we could not get conclusive proof unless we were up against the world's stupidest terrorist who was traveling on his own passport, we were putting the group under severe stress and maybe someone would snap. The reality was that most shooters who took part in terror attacks in our backyard were not sophisticated James Bonds trained in elaborate fieldcraft. Most were boys from humble backgrounds, brainwashed and trained in the field, and sent out to do the one thing they could do well- kill people. They were good trigger pullers, but likely had little training in escape and evasion or in withstanding interrogation. That was what made me and my old buddies different from the jihadis we met. They knew how to fight and die for their cause- indeed, many of them signed up knowing they would likely be on suicide missions. We knew how to kill them, get away and stay alive. That was why we wiped the floor with them whenever they met the Paras or SFF in the field.

Amy walked up to me.

"Forty-five passengers left. Of them, nine are American backpackers. Should I scan them fast- they'll show up easily on our federal databases."

"Good idea. They're the ones swearing the most anyways. Let's screen them and get them off our hands."

The Americans grumbled as they were called up as a group, but some of the young men were sufficiently distracted at seeing Amy nearby that they went peacefully without more drama.

A few more minutes and there were 21 passengers left. All young men. All from the subcontinent. Sharma came up to me.

“Twelve have Nepali passports and the idiots just thought of telling me now that they are a bloody football team. Their documents seem legitimate and they’re playing in some tournament tomorrow. I called the Nepal Embassy and they vouched for them. They were in the newspaper yesterday and only now did they show me their picture. Idiots.”

I grinned.

Nine passengers left. Six Indians, two Nepalis, and one Bangladeshi businessman who was so overweight that the only way he could be a terrorist was if he sat on someone. We screened the Bangladeshi first and he checked out. He walked on, wiping the sweat on his brow with a handkerchief.

Eight left. By then, the doctors were trying to hurry things up, two of the CISF men had disappeared, ostensibly on toilet breaks and everyone was beginning to think this had been a very bad idea.

Six passengers left. All Indians. Two were students at a prestigious Delhi college and dropping names of influential relatives who worked in the government. They were painful but they checked out and we sent them on their way.

Four left.

Amy nudged me.

"Looks like my bosses will chew me out and I'll have to catch tomorrow's flight and hope they are sympathetic and reimburse the flight cancellation charges."

When she got no response, she nudged me again.

"Earth to Major Sen. You there?"

No response. While everyone had been getting bored for the last few minutes, I had been watching a young man. For the longest time, he had been sitting quietly, reading a novel. Trim, tall, wearing glasses. Dressed in comfortable jeans and a sweatshirt. He could just have been a student or a young corporate type coming back from a trekking holiday in Nepal. Except as time wore on, I was beginning to sense a change in his body language. I had asked Sharma to check him last and as the third last man was waved through, the young man got up. I knew nothing about catching criminals and I had never been a detective, but I had spent my whole life around men who had been soldiers and I knew what I was looking at.

A soldier standing up, impatient at the delays.

His arms were locked behind him. His legs splayed apart. His chin up. Defiant, dominant, and trying to contain himself. He had been trained very well, but I was guessing he had been trained as a soldier, not a spy. He had done well to conceal himself so far, but now I thought I had him. I whispered to Amy that we had our guy.

"Are you sure?"

'Only one way to find out.'

I walked up to the man and took his passport. Right behind me was a sign put up with a rather good-looking woman, her hands folded in greeting, welcoming visitors with a slogan printed below her in Sanskrit.

Athithi Devo Bhava.

The guest is God.

I had no interest in the divinity of the young man in front of me, but there were many other things I was curious about. His name was Surinder Raina, or so his passport said. Born in Kolkata on the 7th of May. I looked the man straight in the eye.

"What a coincidence. I was born in Kolkata and on the same date and year. Imagine that."

He smiled, though I sensed a nervous twitch. That didn't clinch the deal. Most people would be nervous meeting authorities after being made to wait for three hours at the airport.

"Are you by any chance related to Varindar Raina? I knew him in college. Great guitar player."

"I'm sorry. I don't know a Varindar."

I had spoken in English and his response had been in English. The English of someone who can barely get by in the language, not someone who has learned it for years. That didn't mean anything, but I persisted in English. If that was another added factor that made him uncomfortable, maybe he'd slip up. I was making stuff up, trying to buy time to think of something, and also clearly pissing him off. That was okay. Men who are pissed off make mistakes.

"Bangla te kotha bolte paro?"

I had just asked him if he could speak Bengali, not an unreasonable request of a man supposedly born in Kolkata, whose address on his passport was a Kolkata address and whose passport had been issued in the same city. The passport was legit. Amy and the IB guy had reaffirmed that but that didn't mean the young man in front of me was that guy. His blank expression told me he had no idea what I had said. Even if he couldn't speak Bengali, for someone who had lived in Kolkata for most of his life, that was a strange reaction.

"I'm sorry if I'm bothering you. Let's shake hands and I'll be on my way."

He couldn't refuse to shake hands and as I felt his hand in mine, I felt the callouses on his palms and the gnarled and thickened knuckles. A manual laborer? Not dressed the way he was. A martial artist, who he might well be. Or a soldier. I should know. My hands were just the same, and by the expression in his eyes, he knew he was not shaking hands with a desk-bound immigration officer. I still had nothing conclusive, no clinching evidence. I could let him pass and wonder if I had made the right choice and when the next terror attack took place, wonder if I had let go the guy behind it.

Only one way to find out. My time in the Paras and the SFF taught me many things, but a couple of important lessons were that when in doubt, trust your instinct, and when you have to act, be bloody decisive.

I lapsed into Urdu, a language I and my buddies had picked up in the Kashmir valley, given that was the lingua franca of so many of the jihadis we encountered.

"Did they train you on AKs or did the Pakistani bosses let you play with the M-4s some of your jihadi buddies are bringing into the valley recently?"

His eyes widened and he tried to pull his hand away. No such luck as I had his hand firmly in mine. He brought his head forward to head butt me, not the smartest choice since he was wearing glasses, but I guess he was out of options. I had anticipated it and moved towards him, jabbing his face with my left fist, putting my whole weight into the blow. His glasses shattered and he screamed in pain as he staggered back. I let go of his hand and took a step towards him, bringing my right arm up to elbow him in the face and then took another step, crossing him, and then I turned, holding his left hand in a lock as I brought him down. He squirmed and resisted, and I increased the pressure, hearing a pop as I dislocated his left shoulder. He screamed but tried to turn, enduring what must have been excruciating pain, to bring up his right hand to strike at me. Brave, well trained, but way out of his league. I was trained to kill, not to arrest people and it was good that the CISF men ran in, guns pointed at him and held him down. Had he resisted, I would have killed him, and he was going to be much more useful to us alive.

***

"How's our guest doing?"

Srini had just walked in along with Sean and I realized our cozy team meeting was going to get very crowded. Pillai, Amy, Salil and I were there, and as Pillai got up to greet Srini and respond to him, Bethune walked in together with the man of mystery who had been with him in the last meeting. To complete the party, then in walked the cop, who this time, perhaps realizing I was no longer in the shit house, introduced himself as Deputy Commissioner Niladri Banerjee.

We all sat down and then Pillai got to work.

"As you know we apprehended a young man at Indira Gandhi International Airport yesterday. Our boys have been interrogating him all day and all night."

This was the moment when I'd realize whether I was going straight back into the shit house. If the guy whose shoulder I had dislocated and roughed up ended up being a professor of geology with a speech impediment, there would be hell to pay. Perhaps, realizing what was going through my mind, Amy squeezed my hand under the table. Pillai was looking straight at me, and for an absurd second, I was transported back to being a kid in college holding a girl's hand under the table while the lecturer droned on about Socrates and I was caught out by the professor. I wondered if Pillai knew I was holding Amy's hand but then he did something exceedingly rare.

He smiled.

"Major Sen here seems to have scored quite a coup. The young man is singing like a canary after our boys began persuading him to share more about himself."

Yup, being threatened and then roughed up in a darkened room did that to anyone.

"We have also run some of the background info he gave, and it checks out. His real name is Munaf Khan, and he's from a small village near Muridke in Pakistan. Local tough, got into trouble and was arrested several times, and then discovered God and purpose when he came across some local boys who had come back from fighting in Kashmir. He wanted the swag and the glamour, and he went to the Lashkar boys. They told him they needed to wait for clearance from their bosses, but some men came to his place in a few days and told him he was in. They weren't the Lashkar recruiters he met, but he assumes they were also Lashkar. He was taken to a location he does not know, seems he was blindfolded for most of the journey, was trained for a few months, and then told he was being prepared for a special mission."

Bethune leaned forward.

"Pillai, does he have anything to do with a plot against the President? We had discarded that as a possibility, but with the flight number in Azfal's shop and now this guy we picked up, do we think that is a real possibility?"

Pillai shook his head.

"He says he was told to make bookings online for a cheap hotel, but not actually check in or stay there. He was to go to Old Delhi Railway Station and wait in front of it, where he would be given further instructions. He does say that he was told it was a special mission which would make the 26/11 Mumbai attacks look like child's play."

The man next to Bethune spoke for the first time.

"That could be an attack against a domestic target or indeed, could be against the US President. That suddenly puts this back on our radar. Bethune, get your men to help in any way they can. Pillai, the first principle of interrogation is to offer something close to the truth and make interrogators think you're cooperating. That way you can hide some crucial information. He's talked about a big mission, but not what it was. I would press more and see what else he knows. How much have you leaned on him?"

The man was clearly CIA if he was ordering Bethune around

and some big shot if he was asking Pillai such questions. 'Leaning on' someone meant things far bloodier and messier than what those innocuous-sounding words indicated, things like bones broken and fractured. I didn't know how far Pillai and his men would go, but Pillai looked at the American and then around the room.

"We can go further but we will need authorization. Also, if he was trained by Lashkar e Taiba, it is unlikely they would strike against the US President. They're trained and paid for by the Pakistani ISI. Why would Pakistan want to strike against the US in such a brazen manner, and that too when your President is visiting the subcontinent?"

Bethune chipped in.

"If there is a potential threat to the President, I would strongly request you go further. My government would be happy to intercede with yours if needed. It could be anything- rogue elements in the ISI or Lashkar but given your earlier intel on a threat to the President, we cannot disregard the possibility that a threat remains in the light of this capture."

The man next to him just looked at Pillai and spoke with the authority of someone used to having the last word.

"I would strongly advise in favor of enhanced interrogation."

When someone in the CIA said those two magic words, what came to my mind were waterboarding and torture of Iraqi detainees at Abu Ghraib. I still remembered the photos and videos that had exploded onto the news and social media. I knew Pillai and his boys wouldn't go that far- we did a bunch of things, but gratuitous torture wasn't on the list. However, I knew now that the young man I had captured was going to have an unbelievably bad day ahead. Pillai made a couple of calls and we waited. Bethune was looking at me and when I caught his eye, he just nodded at me and mouthed the words.

"Good work."

I was once again getting a bad feeling about this. Unlike the movies, no terror group launches strikes of the sort Munaf was bragging about with one terrorist being flown in. These guys are for the most part foot soldiers, relatively competent at what they do, but no Carlos the Jackal or Terminator. There was no way he had come in alone. If anything, with the four men I had encountered at Azfal's shop, whoever was orchestrating this was putting way too many resources behind this for it to be just one guy.

"Pillai, have you checked if he was alone or if there were others with him?"

"He doesn't know. At least he hasn't said anything yet, but my boys are still working on him. Why?"

"Something doesn't feel right. This guy is not a highly trained sniper or demolitions guy. He's a trigger puller. Useful, but he can't pull off any meaningful attack all on his own, and why would Lashkar or whoever sent him invest so much to get him here? There are plenty of jihadi wannabes who can fire an AK around inside India. There have to be others coming in."

Bethune was looking at me with an intensity I had not seen in him before.

"Major, you have shown some amazing initiative and instinct, and they have all proven right so far. If you're feeling that something's not right, I'd be inclined to trust you."

I smiled at him. Getting praised for what I did wasn't all that common around here and I have to admit, it felt good to not have everything I said questioned. Srini and Pillai's phone beeped at about the same time, and I gathered that whichever political bosses they had asked permission from had gotten back. Srini spoke for both of them.

"We have clearance to notch up the interrogation efforts. It may take time, so let's adjourn. We'll check on the target and also Sen's theory of multiple attackers."

Pillai made the call. I heard him say to use all means necessary. We all knew what that meant. There was nothing noble about torturing a man, and I had seen two of my own buddies tortured and killed in front of my eyes. I took a deep breath and closed my eyes. Amy once again sensed what was going on in my mind and leaned in close to me.

"Aadi, there's nothing else we can do. If this man is who he seems to be and he's here to launch an attack, learning more about him and his plans will save a lot of innocent lives."

We took a break while we waited to hear back from Pillai's men. Salil, Amy, and I grabbed a coffee in the cafeteria.

"You doing okay, Sen?"

I looked back at Salil. How would I explain to him that being a man who was trained to inflict violence on others did not make one a man who enjoyed it? The night before, while I slept with Amy's head on my chest, I had tossed and turned, dreaming of my men being beheaded and me cutting off someone's head. Those dreams had stopped for a while, but the events of the last couple of days had brought them back. I had woken up, covered in sweat, and Amy had held me as I tried to sleep again. She knew what I had been through, and she knew who I was. The fact that she was with me despite all that made me love her all the more.

"You okay, Sen?"

This time it was Amy who spoke up for me.

"Have you ever killed anyone?"

Salil shook his head. He had been in the National Security Guard for a couple of years but never taken part in an active operation.

"I haven't either. So, I can't know what Aaditya's going through, but I know that having good friends around helps."

Salil looked at her for a while and then at me, understanding dawning as he realized that Amy and I had gone far beyond being colleagues on the same team. He downed his coffee and patted my arm.

"You need anything, I'm there. What do you reckon Pillai's men will find out?"

"If they lean hard enough on the guy, he will spill whatever he knows. What I can't figure out is who the man of mystery with Bethune is. Amy, who is he?"

She shrugged.

"Some guy who was sent in as a subject matter expert. Calls himself Smith, but I'm sure that's not his real name. Some spook from the CIA, no doubt, and with such people, it's safer not asking too much about who they are and what they do."

As we got back into the conference room, my mind was whirring. I didn't know much about intelligence operations, but I knew a fair bit about infiltrating shooters into enemy territory.

"They would have all come in from Nepal. Maybe some of them are already here, maybe others are coming in. Think of it- a bunch of young men, being sent behind enemy lines, into what for them is unfamiliar territory. Too risky to open up multiple ingress routes. They would have found one route they thought was reliable. Pillai, you said Azfal was an old hand at this, and I bet he used to help with drug runners in addition to jihadis, and Nepal is a well-known route for that. There was a good officer at the airport called Sharma. He can help us with checking out passenger manifests for the last few weeks and also tracking new arrivals from Nepal."

Pillai was looking at me, perhaps wondering if he should go with my judgment. That was when his phone rang. I could see his face turn ashen as he processed what was being said. When he put his phone back in his pocket, he looked at us.

"Seven."

Srini looked up sharply.

"Excuse me. Seven what?"

"Despite all our efforts, he says he really doesn't know what the specific mission was, but he says he heard one of his trainers say to someone that seven assassins were being sent on this mission."

***

EPISODE FOUR

Thrice Is Enemy Action

I was having a good Sunday for a change. While Pillai and his associated spies and cops did their investigating, a task in which I had little role to play, I slept in late, and I was sitting on Amy's hotel bed, watching her type away furiously on her laptop. To be honest, it wasn't her typing or her work I was watching too closely. I was idly admiring her silhouette as she sat there in her sports bra. She must have read my mind again because she said over her shoulder.

"Major, get those dirty thoughts out of your mind and take a shower. We don't want to be late in getting to the hospital to meet your Mom."

I kissed her on her neck and would have gone further had she not pushed me away playfully.

"My bosses back in Washington are asking how long I should stay here. Seems Bethune has already sent in a memo saying there doesn't seem to be conclusive evidence of a threat against the President but that we should stay a few days more till the investigation is complete. Everything so far looks like there was a real terror plot, but it may have been a localized jihadi strike supported by Lashkar or the ISI, and Azfal was helping bring the shooters in. Should I tell my bosses that I want to come back sooner because I need to be saved from your advances?"

"Tell them you are needed here forever."

She looked at me and I half regretted what I said. Was I ready to commit to anything more than we shared? Was that even possible given our careers? I think similar thoughts went through Amy's mind as she quickly changed the subject.

"Go on, you need a shower."

When I had told Amy more about Ma and that I couldn't spend the day with her because I needed to be with Ma, she had asked if she could come along. Perhaps unwittingly, we were deepening our commitment, and perhaps that wasn't a very smart thing to do, because there was really no feasible long-term future we could share, but if something felt so good, it was hard to let something as minor as logic come in the way.

An hour later, we were sitting in the hospital cafeteria with Ma. The doctors had pronounced her well enough to come out of her room on a wheelchair, and she was taking a break from treatments while they ran scans and tests to see the progress being made with the new drugs. As Ma chatted with Amy like an old friend, I sat around, feeling a bit out of the loop. Amy leaned in towards Ma and whispered something and they both laughed. It was wonderful to see Ma laugh but I couldn't help but feel that the joke was at my expense. It had been a while since I'd been seriously involved with someone, and I had always hoped that when I found someone special, she would hit it off with Ma, but now I wasn't sure if their hitting it off so well was a good idea.

"Aadi needs someone like you. A beautiful, sensitive woman who can shoot as well as he does."

Amy laughed and I just looked at Ma, wondering once again how she read me so well. No, Amy's shooting accuracy wasn't important, but what she did made her appreciate the world I lived in and what I'd been through. With her, I didn't feel the need to hide my old scars. Indeed, being with her seemed to help heal them.

"Lost somewhere, Major?"

Without realizing it, I had just been staring at the two of them, and my eyes were misting over. I had been through so much, Ma had been through so much, that it was almost overwhelming to sit with her, and not talk about my issues or her illness, but find something, and someone, to be happy about.

I took Amy's hand in one hand, and Ma's in the other.

"Nothing. Everything's perfect."

As we walked back to my car, I turned to Amy.

"Thanks."

"For what?"

"For being you. For being there."

She kissed me, earning a disapproving look from a passing nurse, but I didn't care.

At that point, my phone rang.

It was Srini, and he sounded troubled.

"Sen, you need to come into office now. We have some developments we need to update all of you on."

That did not sound too promising.

***

The suspense in the conference room was killing all of us. Srini was there along with Sean. Both looked like they had eaten something particularly distasteful. Bethune sat in a corner, saying nothing and Salil joined us, grumbling about being called in on a Sunday. A man I didn't immediately recognize came in and closed the door. Despite it being a Sunday, he was wearing a suit. Either he always was dressed to make a good impression, or just worked way too hard.

"I'm Mahesh Shukla, Joint Director Ops from the IB. I'm here to replace Pillai."

Replace Pillai? What was going on here?

Shukla sat down with a loud sigh.

"Nasty business, this. We don't do things like this and it's really unfortunate things are the way they are, but there is a silver lining to this, isn't there, Mr. Bethune?"

I wanted to say that I, Amy, and Salil seemed to have no idea what the hell he was talking about, but I waited for Bethune's reaction. His huge hands were steepled under his chin, and the contemplative giant responded.

"I and my men did get a chance to see all the transcripts and we also had a man sit in on the questioning, and as far as we can tell, this man Munaf knew of nothing about a plan to kill the US President. I personally met him with an associate for a while to cross-question him. If anything, on further questioning, he seemed to indicate that he and the others were being brought in for another mass-casualty strike like the Mumbai attacks. So at least we don't have an attack on the US President to worry about. That's about the only positive thing I have to say about what has happened over the last day."

I couldn't contain myself.

"That's good news, isn't it? We seem to have disrupted their network and I guess it is a matter of time before we track down the others. Shouldn't we be relieved that you believe there's no threat to your President?"

Shukla turned to me.

"Munaf died early this morning. Early diagnosis is that he died of a heart attack perhaps caused by the torture he went through. Imagine if that gets out to the media. A Pakistani national beaten to death by our IB boys!"

"Sir, with all due respect, he was here on a terror mission, not as a tourist. He admitted as much."

Shukla's exasperation showed in his response.

"We are a democracy! We don't just pick up men and torture them to death. Pillai has been placed on administrative leave till we fully investigate this, and the government now has to do some serious damage control. He was asked to take enhanced interrogation measures, not beat a man to death! We need to make sure the media doesn't pick this up and then we need to figure out how we communicate this to Pakistan and get the body back to his family. I suspect we'll make up a story about him being killed in an encounter, but no matter how we try and spin it, it's going to make the government look bad."

Shit. Pillai was the one who knew the most about Azfal and the investigation. With him out of the picture, we were seriously hobbled.

"What happens with the investigation?"

Shukla had a bunch of papers in a folder before him and he briefly flipped through them, seeking security in the stamps and signatures on them that only a veteran bureaucrat would.

"There is no reason to believe there is any threat to the US President. Bethune himself is attesting to that. The man who was picked up seems to be a Pakistani national trained by Lashkar and when he was questioned along with Bethune and his colleague, he seemed to indicate their agenda was not a strike against any specific VIP target but a mass casualty attack. So, the joint task force as it currently stands is disbanded. The remaining terrorists, if they are already in India, will be tracked down. We are on the job. If they have not yet come into India, our enhanced measures at points of entry should dissuade them and disrupt their plans."

Shukla got up and left and I took a deep breath. What the hell was happening?

Bethune got up and came up to shake my hand.

"Major, it's a shame about Pillai, but I'm sure he'll be okay once they establish that Munaf perhaps had some pre-existing medical condition which may get him off the hook with your government over time. You've done some great work, and it looks like our time together will be coming to an end soon. I know there are still some loose ends to take care of, but I'm getting a very clear direction from my superiors that we believe our role in this is close to being wrapped up."

He looked at Amy next.

"Amy, I think we need to get back stateside. Let's wait a couple of days to ensure no more surprises emerge from the Indian investigation and then we can go back."

Things were moving way too fast, and it wasn't just that I realized that Amy was leaving much sooner than I had hoped. The government seemed very keen to close off any broader investigation of Munaf's death. The IB would clean up I suppose, and Bethune couldn't care anymore what happened now that he was convinced there was no threat against the US President. With everything that had happened, nobody even seemed to be asking what Azfal's death had to do with Munaf and the terror plot he had mentioned. With Pillai tainted, Azfal was just a source of his who had died in a dispute with fellow jihadis.

Amy and Bethune left and while I couldn't say anything in front of the others, I messaged Amy that I needed to meet her in the evening.

When just Srini, Sean, Salil, and I were left in the room, we all sat down.

"That was a lot of excitement for a couple of days but looks like this Unit 22 business is behind us."

Coming from Sean, who had done nothing but sit in his office, that was a bit rich, but I didn't say anything. I was still processing everything that had just happened.

"Sir, we still have six terrorists perhaps out there. Shouldn't the US team be more involved? Who knows if they actually were after the US President?"

Srini gave me a compassionate glance.

"Sen, they will still very much be in on the intel but with Munaf's death, they are washing their hands off this team. They want us to take the blame for it."

"That's nonsense. I think Bethune or the guy who was with him were the ones who brought up the idea of leaning on Munaf more heavily. He was the one who brought up all that enhanced interrogation nonsense."

Srini sighed as he sat down.

"That's how this line of work goes. Plausible deniability. They will say the Indians beat the suspect to death- no way would the CIA want to get its hands tainted with any more revelations of torture. We will of course hunt those six remaining terrorists down. Doesn't matter whether they were after the US President or not. Bethune and his bosses will not and cannot be seen to be involved in this anymore, and whether I personally like it or not, and whether I think it to be fair or not, Pillai is the one who will take the fall."

I walked out of the office; a bit dazed by the sudden turn of events. Just a day ago, it felt like the investigation was moving in a way that seemed under control. Now Pillai was out of the picture, Unit 22 was disbanded, and whatever else happened with the investigation, I was out of the loop and would go back to sitting at a desk, looking at intel reports, and putting up with Sean. While the Americans washed their hands off this and the Indian government tried to clean things up, the terrorists would be out there, waiting to strike.

To top it all, Amy was going to leave very soon.

***

"Packed your bags?"

Amy looked at me from the corner of her eyes.

"Not yet. The flight's in two days, and I don't have a lot to pack. You did come to drop me off at the airport once. You do remember that, don't you? So why so glum?"

"Yup, but then I got my hopes up of you staying longer."

She threw a pebble across the pond, and we watched it skip across the surface of the water.

"It's not like we need to write letters and wait months to hear back. I'll call when I reach America.'

"Will you be here with the President?"

She shook her head.

"No idea. They won't tell us who's actually coming till later, but he has his protective detail for overseas visits, with agents much more experienced than me."

Now it was my turn to send a pebble skipping over the water, but given my distracted mood, the pebble skipped once and then sank to the bottom. We were sitting by the side of the lake at the Old Fort complex, a place I would often come for my jogs when I was younger.

I was about to say something to Amy when my phone rang.

It was Pillai.

"Sen, we need to meet right now. It's urgent."

That was a strange request.

"Sure, where do you want to meet? Where are you right now?"

"Doesn't matter where I am. Let's meet at Bahrisons bookshop in Khan Market."

That was even stranger. What was going on with Pillai? I looked at Amy and wondered if I should tell him she was with me when he preempted me with his next strange request.

"Come there alone, and make sure you are not followed."

I mean, if someone followed me, it isn't as if I'd necessarily know. I was a soldier, for God's sake, not some Hollywood secret agent, but I just agreed and told Pillai I'd meet him in ten minutes. When I told Amy what was up, she was as puzzled as me.

"Just sit at the Starbucks and have a coffee while I meet him. He sounds really stressed and insisted I come alone. He got screwed at work today so he may just be worked up over that, but I have no idea why he'd reach out to me of all people. I didn't even think he particularly liked me."

A short while later, I was inside the venerable bookshop and saw Pillai standing in a corner, his head covered by a beige cap and his face almost buried in a copy of a biography of Ian Fleming.

A spy reading a book about a spy, who became famous for writing novels about a spy.

This meeting was weird enough without this last touch of the bizarre, and as I approached, Pillai closed the book and looked up at me.

"Read any of the James Bond novels by Ian Fleming?"

"No, seen some of the movies though. Lots of gunfights and attractive women. Fits my definition of award-worthy cinema."

He just nodded silently and as I came closer and smelt him, I realized he had been drinking, not one glass of wine with lunch, but some serious drinking. What was Pillai up to?

"Sen, perhaps you're wondering what you're doing here?"

No shit, Sherlock. But I didn't say that, of course. I just nodded as he leaned conspiratorially towards me.

"Have you wondered why you were put on this task force? On this Unit 22, as you call it."

No, but I was sure he was about to tell me.

"You had no investigative background, a brilliant military track record, but barely competent as per your bosses in Delhi in learning the ropes of doing a desk job. Yet you got into such a high-profile task force. Amy is in the Secret Service, but there are many others there with more experience and law enforcement backgrounds. Her only qualification seems to be that she's of part Indian origin. Not the best qualifications to be put on a task force investigating something as serious as a supposed plot against the US President. Both of you are novices in over your head."

Now that he had crushed any delusions of grandeur I had, where was he headed? He looked straight at me with an intensity I had not seen in him before.

"Azfal was a good man. I knew him for two years, and while he had committed his share of crimes and worked with us for money, I believe he was a patriot who didn't want to help jihadis harm this country. Do you know his wife called me today? He knew he was in a dangerous line of work, so he had a will ready- most of what he owned of course goes to his family, but he made a big donation to the National Defense Fund. Does that sound like a man who would be helping jihadis?"

I had no idea what to say as he continued.

"I should have trusted my instinct, but things were moving so fast. My boys worked over Munaf, but they know their jobs. There is no way he died because of torture. Our doctors inspected him, and he was healthy. No way did he suddenly have a heart attack and no way did my boys hurt him so badly that he died."

"What are you trying to say, Sir? I'm sorry but I really don't understand."

He gave an exasperated sigh.

"Don't you get it, Sen? This whole thing has been set up from the beginning. A task force with people on it who should not be there. Azfal being taken out just before we were going to stage the raid. Munaf dying in custody. What do you think is common to all of those?"

"The plot we were investigating?"

He waved his hand in a distracted manner.

"Of course, but that's the superficial similarity. The moment I got intel about the likely threat to the US President, I let our intel community know and of course, we then immediately reached out to our counterparts in the CIA. Don't you get it? What's common to all of these are the Americans."

"What?"

I was sorry, but I had blurted that out. Of course, the Americans were involved. It was their bloody President who was supposedly in some terrorist's sights.

"They want this investigation to go away. Don't you see how quickly they want to wrap this up? Bethune and the other CIA guy, that strange bird called Smith whom you saw in our meeting, met Munaf along with our boys and soon after that, he has a heart attack. A coincidence? Azfal is targeted just before the raid, and other than us, who else knew about it? The Americans!"

I could see that Pillai was pissed off about the trouble he was in, and perhaps right in blaming the Americans for distancing themselves so that the shit splattered only him, but this was taking conspiracy theories too far. To top it all, Pillai was drunk, and that hardly did a lot to enhance his credibility.

"Think about it, Sen. I have no idea if there was a plot against the President they want to minimize or if they have some other agenda, but these are not just the ravings of a drunk, disgraced officer."

Ouch, so he had read my mind. He leaned towards me and grabbed my collar.

"I've been in the IB for twenty years. Twenty damn years. I am good at what I do and just because they want to make this investigation go away and me to fade away doesn't mean there aren't people out there who will help me, young men and women I've trained. This afternoon, one of them reached out to me saying that they had evidence of an intrusion in our servers over the last few weeks. Someone had likely got into our internal comms. We can't prove anything, of course, because it was done in a way that we can't trace it back, but jihadis and their ISI masters cannot hack into our servers. The IT guys said that the best they could make out was that someone used one of our own files to get a back door into our system. Only the Americans and Chinese could perhaps do it, and the only ones we shared intel and files with regularly and especially recently are the Americans. With the US President coming and everyone talking about this great new alliance, nobody wants to entertain that theory. We swept all our phones and upgraded the encryption on our phones recently. For the computer servers, once I heard of this, I got the IT guys to put in a major security upgrade which they say will protect our servers against similar intrusions."

I gently held his hand and took it off my collar.

"Sir, why would the Americans do this? Do you mean to say the American government would ever sanction something like this?"

He laughed an eerie cackle that had nearby customers looking at him in some alarm. He dropped the book he was carrying, and it hit the leg of a man standing close to us, browsing the shelves. I picked it up and handed it back to Pillai, apologizing to the man with a slightly embarrassed smile. The man just nodded at me and walked away. Pillai seemed to have ruined his mood for book browsing.

"Son, you are very naïve about how the world works. The CIA does all sorts of ops the government may not even know about or sanction. It may have nothing to do with the senior political leadership in the US government."

"What do you want me to do? Why are you telling me all this?"

He looked at me with a smile and winked.

Because you're not part of the system at heart and I think

you can still have an open mind. Also, because you're a troublemaker, who pokes his nose into things he shouldn't and because you seem to be on rather friendly terms with Agent Khan, so maybe you can be closer to what our American friends are doing and thinking."

Shit. Did he know about me and Amy? I tried to keep a straight face.

"What do I do?"

"Just listen. Just observe. Especially Khan and Bethune. See what else they say and do and let me know."

He tapped the book in his hand.

"Ian Fleming once said that once is happenstance, twice is a coincidence, but thrice is enemy action. We've had the attack on Azfal, Munaf's death, and I'm sure they will strike again, something that will make it clear what the nature of the enemy is and what they intend. Remember, my boy, in this business there will be no more coincidences, what comes next is enemy action."

***

"What did he say?"

I caught myself as I was about to reply to Amy.

Was that drunk, crazy spy getting to me? No way Amy was involved in any of that shit. No fucking way.

But then a small voice spoke up in the back of my head.

What the hell do you really know? You spent your life in a

cocoon of people in uniform who lived, fought, and died by simpler rules, with none of the intrigue, cloak and dagger bullshit that people like Pillai lived with. I had seen what happened at Azfal's place, and those four guys had felt like trained operators, not everyday jihadis of the sort we'd come across in Kashmir, who would grab their AKs and spray and pray, hoping to hit something. Then there was Munaf's death. Easy to believe that Pillai's boys had been too rough on him, but…

"Hey, are you okay? Where are you lost?"

I looked back at Amy's eyes, and I mentally abused Pillai for screwing with my mind. Why did I agree to meet him in the first place?

"It's nothing. He was drunk and blabbering about how unfair things are."

"Don't blame him. Feels like he's been left holding the bag. Hey, are you still pissed off about me leaving so soon? We still have a couple of nights."

She smiled as she said the last few words, and I cursed Pillai again for spoiling my mood. He had really gotten under my skin. I figured that the best way to get him out of my system, and out of my mind, was to spend time with Amy. I held Amy's hand.

"I guess it's just been a crazy couple of days. We do have a couple of nights…"

That was when Sharma called.

"Major, I know Unit 22 is disbanded and all, but Pillai Sir asked me to tell you if I found anything. He recruited me and taught me everything I know, so I owe him."

"What have you found?"

"We've been looking at all the passenger manifests coming in from Nepal and getting our teams to scour for any leads near the Old Delhi station. As you may imagine, there are hundreds of young, single males who have come in from Nepal who could be suspects and we were eliminating which of them have already flown out."

"That sounds like that could take a lot of time."

"It does. Bloody mind-numbing work, but we've had the teams on it non-stop. The good thing is the records are computerized. That makes it much easier and faster, and one of our analysts spotted something interesting. Four other young men had flown in from Nepal over the last two weeks who had their passports issued on the same day by the same passport office in Kolkata."

I sat up straight.

"We looked some more, extending our search another week back, and we found a total of six passengers who came in from Nepal with their passports issued on the same date at the same passport office. I'm sure if we keep looking, we will find the seventh assassin as well."

"That's brilliant."

"Wish I had thought of it. Pillai Sir called me early this morning to tell me to run those searches. He hypothesized that the passport looked genuine, so someone may have influenced a local passport office to get booklets. So, now we know who these six are, or at least their covers."

"How do you track them down after that?"

"We've got our network chasing down every small hotel in the Old Delhi area. Munaf was supposed to wait at the Old Delhi station, so a reasonable guess is they were going to be put up near there. If they're staying with some local sympathizer, then it's much harder to track them down, but there's a chance they may be at a hotel. Now we wait."

He was about to hang up when I remembered what Pillai had told me. That old spy had made me paranoid.

"Sharma, who knows about what you've found out?"

I heard him laugh before he replied.

"Major, you are getting into the whole spy business, I see. The reality is pretty mundane. Analysts file what they find, I scan it and what I think to be actionable gets bumped up the chain. So, email reports would be going out to my bosses, up to Shukla, and given the nature of this investigation, to your bosses at R&AW."

No Americans. At least Pillai wouldn't be stressed about his supposed American conspiracies anymore.

"Thanks. By the way, why are you telling me all this? I'm off the investigation."

He chuckled.

"Pillai Sir said that you are a good sort of troublemaker. I saw you in action at the airport, Major. We would never have got that bastard if you hadn't acted on your instincts. He asked me to run by you what we learn because he told me you will likely be able to put yourself in the shoes of trained commandoes behind enemy lines and help with what they might be up to without the filters the men in offices will have. I will let you know if we find anything else."

Amy was staring at me when I hung up.

"What was all that about?"

"Sharma, telling me about how they're looking through passenger manifests to figure out who the other terrorists are."

"And?"

I told her what he had found. She smiled and placed her hand on mine.

"I think they have it all under control. Now, why don't we go and get some time to ourselves."

***

When I was awakened by my phone buzzing, my first panicked reaction was that the hospital was calling about Ma. I had felt guilty about not spending the night at the hospital and had told Amy that I would leave before she woke up to be with Ma. We had checked in on Ma and had dinner together and she had been in great spirits. The doctor had said that she was responding very well to the medication. It was too early to declare success, but in his words, he was cautiously optimistic. After months of despair, that was the best news I had got in a long time. Ma, Amy, and I had celebrated with me smuggling in some of Ma's favorite chocolate which we shared.

I was relieved to see that it was Sharma calling and not the hospital. That quickly gave way to confusion as I saw the time. Why the fuck was he calling me at two-thirty in the morning? Not wanting to wake Amy up, I walked to the bathroom and closed the door.

"Can't sleep, Sharma?"

"You bet, Major. We have the bastards."

That woke me up fast.

"You've captured them?"

"Not yet, but we know where at least some of them are. A beat Constable shaking down some of the local auto drivers found that they had noticed single, young men coming over the last few days and going to stay at the Hotel Du Ramanna in Old Delhi. Just a kilometer from the station. We checked with the hotel, and we have matches on four of their passports. Four of them are staying in a couple of rooms at the hotel, on the top floor in adjacent rooms they had requested- well away from the main street. The hotel owner is a good man, a retired cop, and we just told him these four may be wanted in a criminal case, so he's keeping it quiet till we get the cops there."

"So, go get them."

"Wish it were as easy as that, Major. We have started the process of getting approvals. We can't go in guns blazing in a crowded neighborhood without due approvals. From the kind of men you've bumped into so far, these are likely to be highly trained and armed terrorists. They'd wipe out a regular police force blundering in, trying to get them. We're getting the NSG organized for a raid but with elections coming, our political bosses tend to get very sensitive about operations in minority-dominated areas without being fully briefed. If something goes wrong, or there's collateral damage, they will go ballistic. We're getting the ministers up, but I wouldn't bet on us getting clearance till dawn. Till then, I'm getting our IB boys to watch the area and coordinating with Delhi Police to have a team ready. We've also got an NSG team on standby."

Life outside the military was much too complicated for my liking. I'd have gone in with my buddies, kicked down the door, and taken down the bastards who had thought they could waltz into our country with fake passports and kill innocent people.

"You do realize they may be striking tomorrow if four of them are together and if they've figured that their buddy Munaf is not showing up. If they suspect he's been caught, they may advance their plans."

"I kind of figured that, Major. Pillai Sir would have probably got things moving faster but Shukla is a creature of the system and after what happened with Pillai Sir, they are all going to play it by the book.'

I couldn't blame him for being snarky. Something was beginning to bother me. Something Pillai had told me.

"Sharma, I assume that all the info you passed up the chain goes through your computer systems."

"Obviously, Major. I can't call every officer personally."

It was almost three in the morning and the man was stressed out and frustrated, so I didn't blame him for snapping at me, but I needed to know something.

"Do me a favor, Sharma. Call your IT guys and ask if the security upgrades Pillai wanted have been done already."

"At this time of night?"

"Yes, right now."

"Is this important?"

I didn't have time for this shit.

"Yes, it is. Please do it."

He called back within five minutes.

"Major, that upgrade is happening a week from now."

I gripped the phone hard.

"We need to act now. We can't wait till morning."

I told him what I had in mind.

"Major, this is nuts. I'm willing to go with your judgment, but this could go wrong in a hundred different ways."

"I get that, Sharma, but I don't think we have the luxury of time. If we don't get there, someone else will get to them first."

***

"I don't have a gun. I'm not a field officer."

I could sense that Sharma was spooked. I didn't blame him. It was good enough for me that he trusted me enough to come into the heart of the Jama Masjid area at four in the morning.

"Don't worry, she does."

He looked at Amy, and she smiled. When I told her what was going on, leaving out the part about my suspicion about Americans hacking into the IB system, of course, she insisted on coming. I would have refused, but she had her gun in the hotel safe, and there was no way I was going to get approval for taking a gun at this time, on an unauthorized mission. My personal licensed handgun was in a safe, where it had been placed when I began therapy, and the safe deposit vault it was housed in wouldn't open till morning. I hoped we wouldn't have to use her gun, but if things went really bad then we would be wise to have some firepower.

The plan was simple. Amy and I would go in and ask for a room for the night. A young couple, after a night of partying, looking for an unobtrusive place to shack up. What Sharma's local sources had told us while we were driving was that a couple such as ours would hardly be an unusual sight at the Hotel Du Ramanna. Once we checked in, then we would get eyes on the rooms where the four men were staying, tail them when they left, and then if we still hadn't got approvals, as soon as they were outside the hotel, provoke them into revealing their hand. I had a bogus official-looking letter which Sharma had rustled up with his usual efficiency which said that I was some official checking for illegal migrants, and we had reason to believe these young men were not here legally. At that point, they would likely try and make a run for it, in which case the IB guys and cops were around in force to take them down. It wasn't exactly due process and I'm sure some human rights lawyer would give me hell for it, but they would never find out. Worst case, they would shoot me down and get away, but I was trying not to think of the worst cases.

As we walked into the lobby, I whispered to Amy.

"You should not be here. Just please stay far away when I approach them in the morning."

"I'm the one with the gun. So, you may well want me close if things go to hell."

Hard to argue with that.

"Won't you get into trouble with your bosses?"

"Maybe you're rubbing off on me."

She smiled as she said that and put her arm through mine as we walked up to the counter. A young man in a faded t-shirt and days-old stubble greeted us and wordlessly took the cash I offered as half advance payment and went back inside the small cabin behind the counter. I took a look around what passed for the lobby. There was one new-looking sofa and another which looked like it had seen better times. Either that was part of the design strategy or they had run out of money to get two new sofas. The most striking part of the lobby was a large fish tank, and I was curious to see if it was there for purely decorative purposes or if there really were fish in there. I walked up to peer inside when the man came up behind me, coughing to get my attention. Amy was looking at him, slightly pissed off, but I guessed he wouldn't give her the key.

"Room 411, on the top floor as you requested. The lift doesn't work, so you'll have to take the stairs. Oh, and no loud parties, no drugs, and no cats."

That was curious.

"No cats, or no pets in general?"

Amy was nudging me to get going, but I was genuinely curious.

"The boss likes dogs, but no cats."

I guess he didn't like fish either, because the tank had none inside. Armed with his extremely specific instructions and our room keys, we began to walk towards the stairs. The view was probably crap whatever floor we were on, but we had specifically asked for the top floor because that is where Sharma had told us that our unwanted guests from Nepal were staying. As we reached the stairs, two men came down them. Both were wearing leather jackets, their heads covered by caps and as they passed us, I noticed both were wearing leather gloves. It was pretty cold, but you don't see too many people wearing leather gloves in Delhi. Then, the sense of déjà vu. Once again, young men who seemed to be always shopping together or were bound together in friendship due to shared sartorial tastes. The last time I had encountered such young men, Azfal and three of them died and I nearly joined them wherever they were headed in the afterlife.

"Hey, what's the time?"

One of them looked back on reflex and then he seemed to stop and stare at me for a second before quickly turning away. I had seen that face before, and very recently.

Where?

Both of them were now hurrying out the door. Amy was pulling on my arm.

"What's wrong?"

Then it struck me.

Bahrisons.

The customer who had been next to Pillai and me. The one whom I had made eye contact with when Pillai had dropped the book. I kept looking at him but shouted out to Amy.

"Call Sharma and tell him he and the cops need to get those two men. I'm going after them."

The young man turned and saw me start after him. Then, he grinned at me and both of them set off sprinting with me in hot pursuit. Both turned left and I was just behind them. They were fit and fast, but then I hadn't been sitting at a desk all my life, and I was sure I would run them down. In the middle of the night, with not a soul around, all I could hear were the sounds of their feet on the gravel and of my own footsteps and breathing. Up ahead I saw a public toilet lit by a single streetlight nearby, with a garishly painted pink door covered with the painting of a rather morose looking lady in a blue sari and open urinals next to it, presumably for men who either didn't deserve the privacy or because budgets had run out before the door could be installed. Both of the men stopped and turned, reaching inside their jackets.

Whatever they had come to do at the hotel, they must have figured their job for the night was over, and they had put their guns into their shoulder holsters. Getting your hands into a shoulder holster past a jacket, when you've just come to a halt from a few hundred meters of flat out sprinting, takes time, and the little time they took was what saved my life, and gave me the time I needed.

They had their weapons and I had mine.

Amy had asked me why I was wearing the old, tattered jacket I had chosen. Not for the fashion statement it made, but for its bulk and length. Both helped conceal the scabbard at my waist on my left side, which contained a khukri. Gurung's khukri. When I had gone to meet his father, a retired soldier, at their home in Dehradun to pay my respects and apologize for letting his son die, he had heard what I had done and told me to keep his son's khukri. He told me that I had done well to avenge his son and his son would have wanted me to keep his beloved khukri.

That khukri, all sixteen inches and nine hundred grams of it, came out in a smooth motion and without changing my stride or grip, I continued bringing it up in an upward arc as the man in front of me began to point his gun at me. I had heard of Gurkhas who would take off a man's head with one strike of the khukri. I guess I wasn't as accomplished as those men were, but when the sharpened blade met the man's wrist, it sliced almost all the way through it. The man looked in shock as the gun fell from his hand and blood spurted from his mangled wrist, which now lay flapping open at an obscene and unnatural angle. As I got a good look at his face, it was my turn to be shocked. I couldn't be sure, since it had all happened so quickly, but I thought he was the same man I had encountered at Azfal's place, the one who had got away and detonated the vest. That second's delay almost cost me my life as I saw the other man out of the corner of my eye, bringing his gun into play. The second guy, who had been the distracted book buyer at Bahrisons, had his gun almost pointing straight at me, and I was a second away from having the suppressor screwed onto the barrel of his handgun be the last thing I saw before I died.

I didn't have the luxury of time to try and disentangle the khukri from the first man's hand and swing it around to attack the second man, so I loosened my grip on the khukri's handle and turned towards the second man, taking a long stride forward with my right leg, grabbing his right wrist with my left hand and moving my left leg forward past him. We were almost cheek to cheek, his gun arm pressed against his body by my left hand. He was strong, and my left hand was my weaker one, so inch by agonizing inch, he began to move his hand out from under my grip. He wanted to grapple. I had no such desire. I head-butted him and then brought my right hand up to join my left and took a step back with the right leg, my leg moving in a clockwise direction, my hands twisting the other way. My leg was acting as the fulcrum, transmitting not just the strength of my arms, but my whole body weight into the point where I twisted the gun away from him.

See, even simple soldiers can pretend they know a bit about fancy physics.

At that point, I was offering my friend three choices. One, hold on to the gun and be rewarded with a broken finger or more. Two, let go of the gun. Three, try and follow my movement, in the process unbalancing himself and opening him up to having his legs swept out from under him.

Of course, as my dumb luck would have it, he seemed to have gone through the same kind of training I had, because he did none of those three things, but added a fourth option into the equation, by letting go of the gun and immediately moving on to the offensive. He stepped towards me, trying to sweep my left leg with his right. I saw it coming, but a fraction late, and even as I raised my leg to dodge the arcing motion of his leg, he caught my foot and sent me staggering back.

The gun had dropped between us, and as I saw it, I noticed that something else had fallen from the man's pockets in the melee.

A bunch of purple or burgundy booklets. With some gold lettering on top.

Passports?

I didn't get a chance to get a closer look because the man saw what I saw, and then he made a most curious choice. He looked behind me, and perhaps saw or heard Amy coming up, gun in hand, since I could hear her in the distance, screaming at the cops to follow her. But he didn't go for the gun. He grabbed the passports and ran. I was about to grab his gun and go after him when his friend grabbed me from behind. The man was well trained, dedicated to whatever cause he served or just loved his pal who was getting away, because despite having his right hand almost hacked off, and no doubt in severe pain and having suffered shock and blood loss, he tried to hold on to me and pull me down. I turned in his weakened grip and kicked him in the groin, sending him doubled over in pain. His friend had gotten away but I'd at least try and get hold of this man and whatever intelligence he could provide. Instead of going down for the count, he grabbed my legs with his left hand and tried to wrestle me down to the ground.

Did these guys never give up?

I took a wobbly step back as if stumbling, and that seemed to give him confidence that he had me as he let go of my leg and tried to grab the khukri lying near his feet. I had seen it first and as soon as he went for it, I grabbed his mangled right hand and brought my elbow down on his half-severed wrist. The man screamed louder than any man I've heard scream and stood up, grabbing at his hand.

Then his head exploded.

Standing a dozen feet behind him was Amy, gun in hand.

"What the fuck, Amy?"

She turned on me in fury.

"That's some way to thank me for saving you."

'Saving me! He had half a hand left and I would have captured him.'

She came closer, taking a look at his body and then back at me. Her voice lost its edge.

"I'm sorry. In the darkness, all I saw was that he had a blade in his left hand and that he was raising it towards you."

A bunch of cops arrived, together with a man flashing an IB badge. Standing near a dead body in the middle of the night was a good way to get shot by cops in the darkness who'd mistake us for terrorists, so I shouted out who I was and flashed my badge. The IB guy walked up to me.

"We know who you are, Major. Sharma Sir sent us your photo, saying that if things went to hell before we got involved, you'd likely be in the middle of it and there'd be dead bodies all around."

I grinned but then something he said struck me.

"Bodies? There's just this one guy here and one who got away."

Now it was his turn to be puzzled.

"I was talking about those four dead guys in the hotel back there, who have all been shot dead."

***

"So, you sliced this guy's hand with a khukri you were carrying, which by the way is illegal, and then you fought the other guy. All alone, taking an insane risk. Till Ms. Khan shot one of them dead and the other got away."

I somehow got the feeling that Sean was less interested in debriefing on what had happened than in laying the blame on me for screwing up. I had been there for three hours, not getting a minute of sleep after the events in Old Delhi, and I was tired, irritated, and fast losing patience with Sean's repeated needling.

"What were you doing there, Sen?"

Shit. I wasn't sure it was such a smart idea to tell them about my clandestine meeting with Pillai or the intel Sharma had given me. Shukla was in the room, and I was sure I would get both of them in trouble if I mentioned all I had learned, so I was being a good soldier and trying to see how long I could keep the tale going without involving them. As it turned out, Pillai was a good man, in addition to being a good officer, and Shukla suddenly glanced up and called Srini and Sean over. When they came back to me, Sean's expression told me that he was pissed off at not being able to get me into deeper trouble. It was Srini who took up the debriefing.

"Pillai just wrote a mail outlining the intel he had given you and that he had called you late at night about what was happening at the hotel and asked you to have a look. He will have to bear whatever repercussions come his way for going against official protocol, but to be entirely honest, I can't say we're unhappy with the outcome."

I sat up straight. Pillai had clearly taken the fall for Sharma and me, but Srini seemed to be not too displeased at what had happened.

"The four dead men had all come in from Nepal. They all had on them fake Indian passports issued by the same passport office in Kolkata. We are yet to identify who they are, but I won't be surprised if they were terrorists like Munaf, sent on the same mission. We found AK-47s and lots of ammunition in their rooms, so they were not here for a vacation. That now takes off the table five of the seven terrorists who supposedly came in on their mission."

All three of them seemed to be pretty happy with the outcome, but I was bothered by several things.

"First, they get to Azfal before we do, then Munaf has a heart attack, and now these guys get to the terrorists and kill them before we get there. Who was the guy Amy shot?"

Shukla looked at some papers he was carrying.

"We don't know yet. Maybe there was some falling out among jihadi groups?"

I didn't buy that for a minute.

"They were very well trained. To the level of special forces if I were to guess, not ordinary jihadis who've been taught how to load and fire an AK for a few weeks and then sent on their date with martyrdom."

Shukla shrugged. I guess he was happy that the number of terrorists out there was steadily being whittled down. But it wasn't just the nature of the men I encountered, but the more basic fact of their timing. How were they always a step ahead of us? Even if Pillai was right about the Americans having compromised our servers, I had spoken to Sharma only on the phone.

Then I sat up straight as if I had been jolted by an electric current.

Amy.

She had shot the man when I could have captured him alive.

She knew precisely what I had been planning.

Had I let my silly sentimentality get the better of me, and not fully trusted Pillai when he had turned to me for help?

Shit. Should I have taken Pillai more seriously? Sure, I was attracted to Amy and I thought we shared something special, but how long had I known her after all?

At that point, Srini looked at his phone and dropped it on the table, and stepped back, shell-shocked. I had never seen him react to anything like that. Shukla's phone was buzzing and when he saw it, I saw his mouth open as if he was going to say something, but no words came out.

What had just happened?

Srini sat down on the chair in front of me and closed his eyes as if trying to come to grips with something. When he opened them, he looked straight at me.

"Pillai has committed suicide. He hung himself at his home. His wife had gone to drop his son at school, which is near their home. When she got back, she was planning to have breakfast with Pillai like they always do. Instead, she saw him hanging from the ceiling. Perhaps the pressures of the last few days got to him."

Sean chipped in with the worst timing possible.

"What a terrible coincidence."

Boss or not, I turned and snarled at him.

"It's no coincidence. It's enemy action."

***

EPISODE FIVE

Rakshas In A Bottle

I was ten years old at the time and had come home, my lips bruised and bloodied. Ma had thrown a fit about me getting into a fight again, and when Baba had come home, he had not even waited to take off his uniform. Instead, he had asked me to come out with him for a walk. I still remember the chill in the air and the chill I felt inside which had nothing to do with the weather. We were in Srinagar and winter was just around the corner. Baba was in a field posting, where families normally didn't accompany officers. Ma and I had been in Delhi and had come to visit him during the school holidays. We walked for a while, and in the small community that was the army cantonment, word had clearly got around that the junior Sen had got into another scrap. Two soldiers running nearby stopped to salute Baba and gave me a grin as they passed.

"What's the story this time?"

I turned to look up at Baba. He was smiling, but his eyes were hard.

"There were two bigger boys and they were picking on my friend."

He chuckled.

"I think Ma's told you enough times not to play the hero. So, you just saved your friend? That's all that happened?"

At that point, I realized that he knew all about what had happened and there was no point in lying.

"No. I got them off him but then when they hit me, I got angry."

"And you beat them so badly one of them is in the hospital."

I hung my head.

He held my shoulders and asked me to look at him.

"Son, there is nothing wrong in standing up for your friends. I would expect nothing lesser of you. However, you need to keep your temper in check. Remember the story of the genie in the lamp? Well, think of your body as a lamp or perhaps a bottle. When you lose control of yourself, what comes out is not a helpful genie, but a terrible rakshas. You know what that means, right? The ancient name for a demon. It makes you hurt others and most of all, it hurts you. So, keep that rakshas in check and keep it inside that bottle. We had talked about those karate classes. We'll get you started. It's not just about learning to defend yourself, but about learning discipline and self-control."

I soaked in his words.

"Baba, when you're fighting the enemy, do you still keep the rakshas inside?"

I saw a strange look in his eyes that day. One I did not fully understand. I understood it many years later when I saw the same look in my own eyes when I looked into the mirror. Baba had smiled and spoken with a gentle voice.

"Every soldier has to let that rakshas out in combat. The problem is putting it back inside."

Now, many years later, I was struggling to keep that rakshas inside. I was sitting at home, my gun and khukri on the table in front of me. It had taken a considerable effort of will to leave the office, go and meet Ma and try and pretend that all was well. Then I had picked up my gun from the safe, made a detour to a liquor shop, and then come home.

The first two visits had been a good idea. Meeting Ma and seeing the progress she was making helped settle me a little bit, though when she asked about Amy, I had to try and not let my feelings show. Given that whoever was behind the killings hadn't hesitated to stage the suicide of a senior IB officer, getting my gun was a good idea as well.

Getting the bottle of absinthe had seemed like a good idea, till I opened it and poured myself a drink.

I had just one glass, diluted with cold water and ice, and I realized it had done nothing to improve my mood. Going back to Baba's words, the rakshas in the bloody bottle of absinthe was now inside me, working its way through my bloodstream, transforming me into a rakshas. Having a drink with close to 80% alcohol content does that to you, but then I stopped at one glass. I had not picked absinthe because I particularly liked it or because I wanted to get drunk. Absinthe is an interesting liquor, made from the flowers and leaves of Artemisia absinthium, otherwise known as grand wormwood, together with green anise, sweet fennel, and other herbs. It also has a chemical compound called thujone, which is supposed to be a hallucinogen.

See, even simple soldiers can pretend they know a bit about fancy chemistry.

But it wasn't the alcohol's chemical composition or even taste I was interested in. I had picked what I thought would have the highest alcohol content of all the options I could find. Higher alcohol content means faster and longer-lasting combustibility. In other words, it burns very well and for a longer time. But more on that later.

If only Dr. Hadap could have seen me now! Slightly high, with a loaded gun and a khukri in front of me. She would have signed me on for daily therapy again, afraid that I had once again become suicidal. She need not have worried. I had no interest in killing myself, but I so wanted to kill the bastards behind Pillai's death. I didn't particularly care for Munaf or the four men who had died in the hotel. They were jihadi scum and whoever had killed them had done the world a favor by removing them from the gene pool. If anything, they had saved us some time, effort, and ammunition. Those five bastards had come to embrace martyrdom, except that they would have taken many innocents with them before they died. I didn't even care much for Azfal. Yes, sure he might have been patriotic if one were to believe Pillai, but at the end of the day, he was a small-time crook whose lofty ideals had never come in the way of helping drug dealers, criminals, and even jihadis.

But Pillai's death rankled. I didn't for a minute believe he had committed suicide. He had been in the hunt till the very end. They had sidelined and disgraced him, but he had reached out to me, to Sharma, giving ideas, nudging us, warning me, still trying to help, still trying to serve his nation. He had been a good man, and a good officer, and now he would be remembered as nothing more than a disgraced officer who had committed suicide.

I walked to the kitchen, pouring out some of the absinthe into a small glass, and then doused a cotton cloth in the glass, before rolling it into a thin wad that would just fit into the mouth of the bottle. I put the cloth into the bottle, leaving a couple of inches sticking out. Then I walked back to the living room and opened my gun case and lay it on the table in front of me. My trainers in the Paras had drilled into me the importance of taking care of one's gun. It was not just a practical necessity, but the ritual of disassembling, cleaning, and then assembling the gun was in itself calming, even therapeutic. For men who lived lives punctuated by short bursts of extreme violence and chaos, anything that brought routine and order was welcome. I took the gun apart, cleaned it, and then put it back together. Ordinary civilians in India had to make do with the mostly junk pistols churned out by the Indian Ordnance Factory for civilian ownership but being in the army had its perks. I could own the good stuff under a provision called Non-Standard Pattern Weapons- bureaucratic speak for the fact that we could own weapons and bores prohibited among civilians. In my case, that meant a Glock 17, just like the one I had carried as my service weapon in the Paras and SFF. Like the Glock 18 I had used at Azfal's shop, but without the 'beast mode'. I loaded three clips with rounds and inserted one clip in the handgun.

With the khukri in the scabbard at my waist, the Glock in a shoulder holster, and the two spare clips in my pocket, I was ready to wage war.

The problem was that I had no enemy I could wage war against. Not yet. That's what was driving me crazy. No, the problem was that perhaps I did know the enemy, but I couldn't get myself to face it. My phone rang again and once again I ignored it. I looked at it to see thirteen missed calls from Amy. After the incident at Jama Masjid, she had been spirited away by her Embassy folks and I had similarly been whisked away to my office for debriefing. She had kept calling me since afternoon, but I had ignored her calls.

What the hell did she expect me to do?

If she was part of the American plan to derail the investigation and played a role in Pillai's death, did that make her the enemy? Could I shoot her?

I banged my fist hard on the table, cracking it. On top of all my other issues, now I'd have to explain to Ma when she got back why I had broken her favorite center table. I wondered if I should have another drink, but then realized that it wasn't alcohol I needed; it was an enemy to strike out at. I had felt this way before, when a jihadi ambush on a nearby base had killed a buddy. We had spent two days fidgeting, swearing, raging, waiting to be given the okay to take the fight to the enemy. The difference was that this time, there was nobody who was going to point the enemy out for me. I knew who the enemy was but couldn't bring myself to confront it.

The doorbell rang. It was close to midnight and while I was

expecting company, I had not expected them to ring the bell. When I opened the door, still carrying the khukri and gun on me, the person who stood there visibly shrank back in alarm when I began to reach for my gun.

It was Amy. Behind her was Salil.

***

"What the fuck is wrong with you?"

Amy had just continued to gape at me, but Salil had shouted at me, pushed past me, and made me sit down.

"Sen, put those weapons away. You're freaking us all out."

Amy sat down on a couch opposite me, her hands folded in her lap, looking at me. I could tell she had been crying.

Salil sat down next to me.

"What do you think you are doing?"

I told him everything Pillai had told me, except that I wasn't looking at him, but straight at Amy. Her eyes widened as I told her Pillai's suspicion that the Americans had been sabotaging the investigation and then I came to the point.

"Amy, you knew everything we were planning last night."

She flinched as if I had slapped her.

"Aadi, you can't possibly think…"

I interrupted her, raising my voice.

"I don't know what to think anymore. Pillai's dead, nobody seems to want to know what is actually going on and how am

I supposed to trust you, after all, after everything we…"

My voice trailed off as I didn't know how to put into words all that we had shared.

Wordlessly, Salil got up and stood near the kitchen door while Amy came and sat next to me, putting her hand on mine.

"I've been worried sick all day about you, trying to see how you were doing. My hands have been shaking all day, do you know that? I had never killed anyone before and every time I close my eyes, I see that man's head exploding. All I've been trying to do all day is to talk to you, to meet you, to make sure you're okay, and to have you tell me that I'll be okay."

I looked at her eyes and took a deep breath. I was furious, but this was Amy, close to me, the same Amy whom I had felt so connected with. Salil spoke up.

"Sen, get a grip. If she was part of some secret American plot, why would she call me right after her debriefing happened, asking me to get her to your house because she wasn't sure she was in a condition to take a cab herself? Why would she be here now, alone, with us?"

He made sense. Too much sense. I wanted to have a simple, visible enemy to lash out at, and he was making it complicated. He came and stood in front of me.

"I'm pissed off as well, after hearing what you told me, but it's not Amy. You said that Pillai told you the server may be compromised. Maybe someone intercepted the messages Sharma sent up the chain about the four men in Jama Masjid."

"So, who is it?"

Amy tugged at my arm.

"I don't know, Aadi. But if the man you fought was the same guy at the bookstore, then it's clear someone is orchestrating this. All I can tell you is that I know nothing about it. I was as surprised as everyone else when I was asked to be part of this task force."

"How well do you know Bethune?"

Her eyes widened.

"I met him for the first time here at the Embassy when I flew in and was told he was an old subcontinent hand who would lead this effort for the US. Could it be him?"

Salil had been pacing across the living room.

"There's nothing to be gained by speculating. It could be Bethune, it could be someone else at the CIA, or it could be someone else altogether. Go and tell it all to Srini. He'll do something with it or at least he'll have the seniority and credibility to be listened to by our big bosses who will hopefully put an end to this madness."

"I would have told Srini, Salil, but today, there was no time for all that. Everyone freaked out over Pillai's death."

"Do it first thing tomorrow."

Just then, I felt something. It's hard to put a word to it, but it's that animal instinct that tells a veteran combat soldier he will be in danger. I had felt it several times when I had been serving in uniform. It had always served me well and saved my life on several occasions.

"There may be no tomorrow, Salil."

'What do you mean?'

I turned to Amy.

"Who knows you're coming here?"

She seemed puzzled.

"I was at the Embassy and then went back to the hotel. Bethune called me asking if I was okay and if I had packed for my flight. I told him I was coming to check on you..."

She stopped in mid-sentence as I picked it up from there.

"The guy who was at the bookstore knows what Pillai told me and also knows I got a good look at him last night. If they've been setting this all up, they probably are tracking and bugging your phone, or at least having you followed. They know you're here, whether or not Bethune is in on it. They probably know the relationship we have, and they may well assume that I have told you what Pillai told me since you were there last night with me."

"What does all that add up to, Sen?"

I looked up at Salil.

"My friend, what all that adds up to is the fact that if Pillai was right, and if my instincts are right, then they will come for me tonight. I was preparing for that. But now that Amy is here, they will take out both of us before we can tell anyone else what we know or suspect. One more suicide. A lover's tiff gone wrong. An accident. I'm sure they can cover it in any number of ways."

Salil began to protest.

"That's taking it too far..."

"Salil, I need you to leave right now. Go out the door, take the elevator downstairs, pause in front of the building lobby for a while as if you're checking your phone or something.

Basically, make your departure obvious."

"What are you talking about?"

"I suspect they want me and Amy dead. They have no reason to believe you know anything, and they wouldn't want the mess of an added body here. Plus, I see no good reason to widow Bharathi or orphan Vihaan."

He was staring at me.

"You want them to come for you? You're mad."

"My friend, they will come for me, whether I like it or not. Let them come when I am ready for them. Now go. Take the alcohol bottle in the kitchen. Cover the opening so anyone watching thinks you're taking a bottle of alcohol with you."

"What the hell are you talking about?"

He cringed when I spoke again. Gone was my friendly tone. In its place was my command voice- the voice all officers use when getting ready for battle when there's no time for double-guessing orders.

"Salil, there's a bloody Molotov cocktail I've prepared in the kitchen. That bottle of absinthe. Get it and the lighter next to it. I was planning to use it myself, but this may be a better plan, with the added benefit that I don't have to risk burning down my apartment. Take it with you, wait a couple of minutes and then light it and throw it at something that will burn big and bright. Those garbage cans next to the parking might do nicely. Got it? Now get the fuck out of here."

I had named our little team Unit 22 as a nod to the time I had served in the SFF, but I had never imagined I would be getting back into combat, not on any border, but in my own apartment. Salil had been gone just a few minutes when we heard a slight, ringing noise outside.

***

"Tripwire."

Amy, having served in the military, knew what I was talking about, but still didn't register why I would say that sitting in my apartment. I had assumed they would come for me. Part of what had left me conflicted was wondering if Amy would be among them and if I could kill her. I had guessed the man I had grappled with, the book shopper, would be among the men who would come for me. Call it instinct, or call it knowing how he would think, because I guessed he was a man like me. Someone trained for war, someone who went to war not for the fat fools who ordered the missions, but for the man next to him. That camaraderie had been evident in how the other man had sacrificed himself to let this man get away, and now he would want revenge. When his masters ordered the hit on me, he would not let anyone else get the job. In his shoes, I wouldn't have either. I had guessed correctly that they would not take the elevator. I lived in a solidly middle-class colony in Mayur Vihar with my neighbors an eclectic mix of old, retired government servants or young couples starting out their careers who had rented their apartments from old, retired government servants. That meant a bunch of old people and very young kids who would be on the elevators. It was now one in the morning and the elevators would likely be abandoned, but a bunch of young men coming for me would not risk taking the elevator, bumping into residents, and arousing suspicions. Living in a society full of nosy, retired couples and young parents whose kids played with each other meant that everyone knew everyone and a bunch of strange, young men visiting at night would be remembered.

They would come up the stairs and there would be many of them. They knew who I was and even if they surprised me, they would know that I would not be taken easily. The housing society I lived in had a security guard, a fat old man who sang well, but otherwise would be useless in case of any real threat. I doubted they would kill him but evading him would be easy since he was prone to wander off for long bathroom breaks. They would likely try to make my death look like a suicide. Given my history, it would be a convenient and plausible excuse. Maybe they'd say I killed Amy in a rage brought on when she tried to reason with me.

The one silver lining was that Ma was in the hospital and I didn't have to worry about her being in harm's way, so I had been preparing for them to come. My early warning system had been a thin wire stretched across the top stair one floor below mine, attached to a toy alarm clock I had picked up in the evening. I had unscrewed the bulb on that floor's staircase, and whoever was coming for me, not expecting tripwires or ambushes, would likely not notice the wire, and put the noise down to some kid's toy left lying on the floor.

We had, by my reckoning, one minute before they got to my door.

"What do we do?"

Amy had rushed into the kitchen and come out, looking rather ridiculous holding a knife in her hand.

"Have you ever stabbed a man to death?"

"No."

"Then, put that away."

Her face was a mixture of determination and fear.

"Aadi, what do we do? I don't even have my gun on me. They took it after the shooting, saying I'd get it back when their inquiries were finished. How can I help?"

I was no longer Aaditya. I was once again a soldier in a combat zone and my mind was working overtime as I thought of the correlation of forces and how we might prepare. My voice, when I spoke, surprised Amy. Later she would tell me she hardly recognized me. I don't blame her. As I said, then I was no longer her Aaditya. I was an officer preparing for combat.

"Amy, you need to call for help. Say there's a fire in progress in the society. Don't mention anything about an attack or a robbery. The cops will take forever getting themselves ready. The fire station is ten minutes away and a fire engine will come sooner. With the fire Salil starts, more residents will likely call as well."

She had her phone out but then stopped.

"What good will a fire engine do?"

I snapped back.

"Just do it, and then take cover behind that large sofa over there."

I handed her my gun. I would have preferred to keep it myself, but with Amy there, I couldn't leave her defenseless.

"I don't think they intend to use a gun. Too noisy and will

make it difficult for them to get away or to stage a suicide. But if they get me, fire away. Protect yourself."

At that moment, I realized that if Amy was in any way part of the plot, she could shoot me. I was putting my life in her hands, and she knew it. She took the gun and smiled at me.

"So, you trust me?"

I smiled back, my voice betraying my emotions.

"No, stupid. I love you. If you have to shoot me, go ahead. Worse ways available for me to die tonight."

Her eyes glistened as she held the gun tight.

"What about you? Don't you need the gun?"

"I'll be okay."

She gently touched my arm.

"I'm scared, Aadi."

I looked at her.

"It's okay to be scared. Just remember that we are going to make these bastards feel a fear that's far worse than anything you may be feeling now."

Then I grinned.

The rakshas was coming out of the bottle.

***

I had turned all the lights off. Let them think I had gone to bed with Amy and would be naked, defenseless, and unprepared when they came for us.

I heard the lock turn. That took no great expertise. I was sure the men who had come for me would have the ability to pick locks in their repertoire of skills and be through the old-fashioned lock on my door in no time. The door began to open, letting in bright light from the corridor outside. Normally, the society only turned on two of the four bulbs in the corridor outside. That evening I had turned on all four, paying the electrician a small tip, saying I was expecting guests and wanted the place bright. All part of my planning. They couldn't see me at all in the darkness, waiting by the door, but I could see their silhouettes clearly, lit from behind by the lights in the hallway.

Three men.

Enough to take me down if all of them were trained to the standard of the book buyer, and if they managed to take me by surprise.

Not nearly enough when I was lying in wait for them, Gurung's khukri in hand.

The sensible play would have been to stab the first man and close the door, perhaps bar the entry of the others, and buy time while help came in the way of cops. But I was not in a sensible mood.

As I said, the rakshas was out of the bottle.

The khukri came slashing across the first man's throat as he entered my house. A single, swift stroke, delivered in silence, without me breaking cover of darkness from my position just behind the display case next to the front door. He grabbed his neck, making gurgling noises, blood spurting from the cut, his brain perhaps starting to process that something was very wrong with his body. The two men behind him perhaps didn't even register what had happened as he slumped to his knees.

Some fool I met once, a pretentious American officer I met during a training exercise, had looked at some of my men's khukris and said that while they seemed fearsome for slashing, they didn't seem to be good at stabbing. Fool. If only he had seen me now, for it's not whether a khukri can be used for stabbing or not, it's where you choose to stab that makes all the difference.

After slashing the first man's neck, I had brought my hand across my body in a circular motion and brought it straight up towards the bottom of the second man's jaw. At the same time, I took a step towards him and grabbed his head with my left hand and pushed it down towards the khukri now coming up at him. The blade entered the soft tissue below the jawbones, and I kept pushing up. I didn't know if he would die instantly, but from the way his body slumped into mine and the amount of blood gushing over my hands, he was out of the fight. As I pulled the khukri out, the man in his dying spasms, grabbed my hand, knocking the khukri out of my grasp.

That left man number three.

The book buyer. Standing there, looking shocked and rather stupid holding a garrote in his hands. So, the plan had been for his pals to subdue me, and he would have strangled me. Perhaps then dangle me up as they had done with Pillai. That must have sounded like a good plan when they made it, but now here I was, covered in blood, looking indeed like a rakshas, standing over the bodies of his buddies, grinning at him.

'Hello, motherfucker. Time to die.'

To his credit, he was fast. Faster than I would have liked. The garrote was gone, dropped in a jiffy, and he was going for what was no doubt a gun under his jacket. My khukri was gone, stuck in the face of the guy at my feet, and I wondered whether I would get to him before he brought his gun into play. That was when the fire brigade came to my rescue. Loud sirens shattered the quiet of the night and my attacker, as well trained as he undoubtedly was, was but human, and for a split second, he was distracted enough to turn his head to the side.

I had a decision to make. Go for him or dive for the khukri. He was skilled in unarmed combat and there was no guarantee I would prevail if I took him on unarmed while he had his gun. So, I dove down for the khukri as he brought his gun towards me.

For the second time in two days, Amy came to my rescue, and this time I was incredibly grateful. I had no pretensions of being able to take this guy alive. When someone like me tangled with someone like him, one of us would die. And this time, it looked like I would be the one dying. Amy knelt, holding the Glock in a two-handed grip, and fired three shots. All hit the man center of mass, one in the stomach, one slightly higher up, and the last near the neck. He stumbled back, still trying to get his gun towards me.

God, this was a tough fucker to kill.

Amy solved that problem by firing one last shot.

This one hit the man in the head.

***

"What the hell were you thinking, Sen? That was a bloodbath at your apartment! Add to the carnage from the previous night and you're leaving a trail of dead bodies all over Delhi. Pandey called, asking if we had a problem with a rogue officer."

I had no sympathy for Sean and his issues with his political bosses. In fact, at that moment, my blood was still up and if Pandey or some other minister had entered my apartment after the fight and lectured me, I would have cut him to ribbons with the khukri. I smiled as I thought of Sean seeing me, blood all over me, khukri in hand. I bet he'd piss in his pants.

"Sen, do you find something funny? Am I cracking jokes here?"

I looked up at him and he stopped. He saw the same look Pandey had seen. I was no longer the docile, quiet office dweller Sean had come to expect. The rakshas was out of the bottle. The pet Doberman had turned out to be a wild wolf.

"Sir, with all due respect, you have no fucking clue of what's going on. I'll speak only to Srini. I'd given him a call with some requests, and I need to meet him in person. And get Amy here. She needs to be here, not with the Americans."

"But she's being debriefed…"

"I don't give a damn. She's in danger. Make up some bureaucratic nonsense about how the police need to question her about the shooting and get her here under police protection."

Sean took a deep breath.

"So, you are ordering me around now, is that it? Any more orders, Sir?"

'Yes. Get Salil and his family under protection. Ideally, get them to a safe house.'

He glared at me, hands on his hips, and then I stood up straight and stared him in the eye.

"Do all that now, or good people will die."

He stared back but he knew I was no longer his docile subordinate, and perhaps, if I give credit where it's due, he realized that what I was saying made sense. He quietly made a few calls and nodded at me.

Ten minutes later, Srini walked in. He sat down in front of me, and when I stared at Sean, standing in the corner, Srini asked him to leave us. Grumbling, but left with no choice, Sean left the room, closing the door behind him.

"Sir, are Salil and Amy okay?"

He smiled.

"Yes, Major. They are both fine. Murthy and his family are already in a safe house, and I've got a couple of our operations boys to step in and guard it instead of leaving it to the cops. Murthy just messaged me that he's on his way to the office. Ms. Khan is also on her way here right now."

He placed his elbows on the table and leaned forward, peering intently at me.

"I've known you for many years, Major, and you're a brilliant combat officer but a terrible liar. So, forget all the bullshit you fed Sean about some burglars breaking into your house and tell me what's going on."

"I'd prefer for Amy to be here, Sir."

Amy came in a couple of minutes later, and I stood up. She

came towards me hesitantly, and then I reached out and hugged her. My apartment had been swarmed by cops, and seeing the bloody mess, they had tried to arrest me. I had flashed my ID and got Srini to get the Police Commissioner on the phone to help, and Amy had called in her Embassy. When we were led off, the neighbors had peered out the window, seeing me covered in blood, being led out by the cops. Those geriatric retirees and young couples would have a lot to gossip about. I had showered and changed in the office and not had a chance to speak to Amy. I didn't care that I was in the office or that Srini was sitting just feet away, for now all that mattered was making sure Amy was okay.

"Are you okay? I was so worried something would happen to you at the Embassy or on the way there."

She looked up at me.

"I'm fine. I was so terrified back there."

"Thank you. For saving my life and for believing in me."

She held my hand and from inside her jacket took out my gun, handing it back to me.

"Thank you for trusting your life with me."

Srini coughed to get our attention.

"I can see you two have a lot to chat about, but care to fill me in on what the hell you've been doing tangling with all kinds of interesting killers all over Delhi?"

I told him everything. He just nodded at a couple of places.

"Sen, we checked out the attackers at your place and the bodies at Jama Masjid. As you'd requested, I didn't use the cops or our office boys here, but had a small group work with

MI."

Military Intelligence. I had expected Srini to trust me and to get this done right. I nodded as he continued.

"Two of them, the ones killed with the khukri, were known jihadis, of the sort you tangled with at Azfal's shop. Small-time crooks with delusions of being mujahideen, who used to post messages about waging jihad online and then became radicalized and trained. The four bodies at the hotel still don't have a positive ID, but I'm assuming they were like Munaf, boys trained in Pakistan and sent here for their mission. Two of them, the ones you encountered at Jama Masjid, the one shot there and the other, shot at your place, are much more interesting."

"What's interesting about them, sir?"

"They had both been in our forces."

That stunned me. I had never imagined those who had once worn the uniform of our nation and served the same flag I'd served would have been among my attackers and those who killed Pillai.

"Were they recently discharged or retired from the Indian army?"

Srini looked at Amy.

"More complicated than that. They were both in the infantry and both served together in UN peacekeeping missions in Congo together. The one killed at your home was the other man's commanding officer, a major before he left the army, someone who had undergone commando training. They both left the army under dodgy circumstances, supposedly allegations of corruption while in the UN force, and of sexual abuse against local women. Nothing was proven, but both left the army and disappeared."

"People who have served don't just disappear, Sir. They must have left a trail."

"That's what was curious. No trail. It is as if they had gone totally off the grid. That's when I cross-tabbed with others who had served with them in the Congo and found that three Americans and two Belgians had also resigned after that mission. All of them were involved in the same investigation our boys were facing. I couldn't trace all of them given the limited time, but the Americans had reports of one of them joining a Private Military Contractor firm along with some buddies. Don't know which one, or what they did, but it's been three years. Safe bet that our boys were earning their money in the private sector, earning good money for doing people's dirty work."

That explained the tactics and training. Suddenly, Amy stood up.

"Who did you check with about the American soldiers?"

"I sent in a standard request to our American intel liaison through an urgent mail and they responded pretty fast."

Then Srini stopped, blood draining from his face.

"Fuck."

I had never heard Srini swear before. He was the kind of guy who when really drunk and really angry at someone, would at worst call the person stupid. For him to swear was bad news.

"Yes, Sir, we are fucked but it's not your fault. You had no idea of what we've learned and been through, but if whoever among the Americans is behind this has access to our communication, which we should assume, then they know that you are not buying the official line and that you're investigating other angles."

"What do you think they will do?"

For the first time, I also saw fear in Srini's eyes. I could understand. He wasn't afraid for himself, but for his family. I knew he was married and had a college-going daughter. I had also seen how ruthless the men we were up against could be.

"Sir, get your family under enhanced protection. Easy to do that without ruffling too many feathers. Say there's a credible jihadi threat and get some good boys from SFF to come in and help. I know some of our boys who're chafing at sitting in Delhi and not being on active deployment. Someone like you would have the authority to call them up for duty as part of your shop."

Srini considered that.

"Sen, I'll need a plausible reason why I'm calling up operators into duty in Delhi."

I said the first thing that came into my head.

"Just say that you are expanding Unit 22 to deal with some new developments. Adding people to an existing operation will attract less attention and be faster than initiating anything new, which I'm sure the politicians and bureaucrats will sit on. If you're okay, you can get the paperwork moving and I can call the guys. That may help fast-track it."

He just nodded, already sending out emails asking for a short-term transfer of the operators I mentioned as I made the calls. I had not spoken to these men for over nine months, but they didn't ask me once why I hadn't called or what I had been up to. We were brothers in a way few biological brothers could be- we had lived together, we had shed blood together, and we had killed together as part of the Special Group. Within twenty minutes, four of them were in Srini's office. Unni, Kishore, Bahadur, and Pratap. All four of them had been in countless patrols and firefights beside me and had saved my life more times than I could remember, and I had watched their back in return. They were wearing jeans and t-shirts, but there was no mistaking that these were no ordinary civilians. They were not even ordinary soldiers. They stood at attention and saluted and I saluted back and then hugged each of them. I didn't have the time, nor did I want to get them involved in any broader conspiracy beyond the specific tasks they could uniquely help with, and I told them that Srini's family was under imminent threat and that was why they were being called into join Unit 22 to help. They were issued guns from the armory with Srini's authorization and two of them left to get his daughter from college and two went to his home.

When they left, I could see Amy smiling at me. When I asked her why, she grinned as she answered.

"Now I'm seeing you for who you really are, who you were meant to be. A soldier."

She was right. I had spent months dealing with the demons of my past, trying to forget, trying to forgive myself. Perhaps the best way of dealing with them was to confront them head-on again and defeat them. I wondered if Dr. Hadap would approve of the therapeutic value of all the men I'd killed in the last few days. I saw that Srini looked suddenly concerned.

"Sir, anything wrong? Your family will be fine, and then we

can sit down and think of our next steps."

"Major, you're a special officer and a special man, that's why I've always had a soft spot for you. You think of everyone else- Murthy, Amy, me, our families. My boy, you are the one who has caused them the most damage. The men you killed at Azfal's shop and your home, the disruption to their plans in Jama Masjid, capturing Munaf- you were behind all that. I realized we haven't thought at all about you and yours."

"Sir, I'm fine. I can take care of myself..."

Then I stopped myself in mid-sentence.

They would not come for me again if they really wanted leverage over me. They would have realized I made for a hard target. They would go for a softer target.

They would go after Ma.

***

I don't remember quite how I got to the hospital. Knowing that Ma might be in danger didn't leave much scope for me to think clearly, so I was happy to let Salil do the driving. He had got a gun as a well, and while Amy was unarmed, she had insisted she come along. Srini had asked for the police to step up patrols near the hospital, citing intelligence reports about enhanced jihadi threats to some of the senior retired generals who frequented the hospital for treatment. He also called up some of our operations boys to come by, but we knew all that would take time to organize. We needed to get there fast.

Salil glanced back towards me over his shoulder.

"Sen, don't worry, they won't hurt her at the hospital."

Amy was sitting next to him in the passenger seat and she looked back as well, concern in her eyes. She would later tell me that I had a murderous look in my eye and Salil had whispered to her that I needed to be calmed down. That was easy for him to say. Killers were likely going after my mother. He continued, noticing that I wasn't going to respond to his reassurance.

"You think like a soldier, not a spy. They aren't out for revenge. They want leverage over you."

"What the hell does that mean?"

I hadn't meant to snarl at him, but he smiled, perhaps happy that I was at least responding.

"They would want to know what you know and who you've shared that information with. So, they may take her and get you to come to them."

"Anyone touches Ma, I'm going to cut them to pieces."

More than my words, the look in my eyes made him quickly look away.

As I said, the rakshas was out, and there was no holding him back now. These people had killed some innocent people, had come for me, but if they were going after Ma, then they would not live long enough to regret what they had done. I was many things, but when you boiled it down, I was a trained killer, and I was good at what I did.

We rushed into the hospital lobby, flashing our badges to get past security. Salil pulled the two cops downstairs aside to brief them on a potential terror threat and get them to report on who had come through so far. I saw Ma's doctor in the hallway, and he was surprised to see me.

"Major, I thought you'd be meeting your mother at the specialty clinic she's being taken to."

"What clinic?"

He looked at the papers in his hand in some confusion.

"Am American man had come by, saying that they represented the company which was supplying the experimental drugs. His papers seemed to be in order, and he had a letter from the hospital director which approved his proposal. He said that your mother was being taken for some specialized checks and then would be brought back within a couple of hours. He just wanted to know if she was fit to travel and I said she could go in a wheelchair."

"Was he alone?"

He was surprised at my question.

"Him and an Indian attendant."

"How long ago were they here?"

"Just ten minutes ago."

My heart pounding, I pulled out my gun and ran up the stairs to the floor where Ma's room was, leaving the stupefied doctor behind, and shouted over my back.

"Amy, watch the elevator but do not engage. Watch and call me. Salil, take the other stairs."

I took the stairs two at a time, covering the three floors in a few minutes. As I entered the corridor, I scanned left and right. Nobody. I ran to Ma's room and found the door open. She was gone.

Where were they? I ran back out into the corridor and realized that there were at least three banks of elevators they could have taken. I remembered what Salil had said. I needed to think not like a soldier, but like a spy. They would not risk taking her out through the main door. Their bosses would have no doubt told them that we had our guard up, with the security around Salil and Srini's families. They may well expect me to come for them. So, they would likely take her to the parking level through the elevator meant for disposal and heavy equipment. I ran towards it, down the corridor, screaming as I went.

"Ma!"

Two nurses walking nearby stopped, shocked at my sudden scream but I was beyond caring. As I came to the elevator, I stopped.

They were there, right in front of me.

Ma on the wheelchair, shocked at seeing me, gun in hand. One man next to her, about to hold the lift door open so they could wheel her in, and a second man, the American, holding the wheelchair.

We stared at each other for a second, and then I raised my gun and shot the first man through the head. The second man had a thin knife out and I saw him take it towards Ma's throat. I turned, moving my gun towards him, wondering even as I did so, whether I'd make it in time.

That was when Salil grabbed him from behind and pulled him away. I ran forward and pulled Ma's wheelchair away from the melee as Salil grappled with him. The man kicked out at Salil's knee and as he recoiled in pain, he stabbed him in the thigh. He would have stabbed him again, this time a killing blow to the heart when I blocked his blow and sent him against the wall. He glared at me through his blue eyes and then, faster than I expected, threw the blade at me.

The blade hit me on the left shoulder. I dropped my gun and he was on me. A blow to the head with his right hand which I blocked with my elbow by raising my arm in an arc, another low blow following in quick succession with his left hand to my groin, which I blocked with a downward sweep of my right hand, and then a kick to my exposed midriff which sent me staggering back. He came at me without much delay, pulling out his blade and then swinging it back towards my neck. I screamed as the blade was pulled out and just managed to block his blow, with the blade inches from my throat. He was an inch or two taller than me and was using his height and weight to bring the blade down towards my neck as I used all my strength to hold him back.

Irresistible force meets an immovable object.

Well, then I changed the equation a bit by taking the object out of the equation. I took a deep breath and exhaled as I pivoted my left leg behind me and moved my body out of the line of attack, letting go of his hands at the last moment. He was fully committed and couldn't stop himself as his forward momentum continued and he staggered forward. He tried to recover and then turned towards me, pivoting on his left leg.

He must have weighed close to a hundred kilograms. The tibia, or in common parlance, the shinbone, is an interesting bone. It looks unassuming, 30 to 40 centimeters long and between 1 and 2 millimeters wide, but the tibias carry almost eighty percent of the body's weight. Now, with my American pal pivoting on one leg, his left tibia was probably carrying most of his weight.

See, simple soldiers like me know some fancy biology too.

Not to apply them in some classroom essay, but to know which bone to break. In short, when you break someone's tibia when they are standing on one foot, bad things happen to them.

So, when I shuffled forward and kicked his knee with the flat of my foot, his leg seemed to bend at an unnatural angle at the knee and he went down. He was a tough cookie and wasn't about to give up. He tried turning towards me, but then Salil hit him over the head with a fire extinguisher, knocking him out cold.

I ran towards Ma, hugging her tight as cops swarmed the area. Salil, despite bleeding from his leg, was taking charge, flashing his badge, dropping names of ministers and senior officers, and making calls, all to ensure that the cops didn't take away the American. No, there was no way our American guest was going to spend the night enjoying the hospitality of the Delhi Police.

We had our prisoner, and now we would find out more about who and what we were up against.

He was all ours.

***

Twenty-four hours later, I was back in Srini's office. Amy was there, having refused to fly back to the US, citing a misplaced passport, and Salil was there, a few stitches and bandages later. My shoulder still hurt a bit but had not required anything more than a few stitches. More guards had been placed outside the office and our homes and Ma was being guarded by two old buddies from the SFF. Srini seemed to have pulled strings to get as many of our men available in Delhi to join Unit 22 on an emergency basis and when they heard of the attacks on me and my mother, they didn't bother asking why we were being attacked or who was attacking us. They assumed jihadis were out to get us and rallied together to help. Sean was sitting in a corner, looking a bit overwhelmed. The very fact that he hadn't reacted, let alone chewed me out, for killing another man, told me he had come to accept both the situation and his relatively irrelevant role in it, as the new normal.

Shukla walked in, slamming the door behind him. For a moment, I wondered if he was pissed off at me.

"Sen, who the hell is doing this to us?"

Us? Well, seemed like I was out of the shit can and in the team. Srini had mentioned that there was no way we could get all the resources we needed without getting the IB on board, and he had reached out to Shukla and briefed him on everything we knew so far.

"Sir, I don't know. But whoever they are, they hire the best and they seem to be a step ahead of us."

He sat down, slamming his fist on the table.

"Well, they've messed with the wrong people. Thanks for all you've done so far. That takes initiative and balls."

He looked up at Amy and sheepishly apologized for his language. She just shrugged. She had killed two men in two days and was not about to be fazed by some mild swearing by a bureaucrat. I looked at Shukla as he poured himself some coffee.

"Break the bastard, Sir. If you don't want your boys to be dirtied again, get me in a room with him and he'll be singing like a fucking bird."

Shukla almost recoiled. I don't think he had ever seen me like this before. Well, it was about time he saw the real me. I wasn't the guy in the meeting room who took notes and made slides for the bosses. I killed people who needed killing. As much as the government hated to admit, it needed men like me. Some problems couldn't be solved by motivational speeches, political rallies, or summits in air-conditioned rooms. Some problems needed to be solved by a well-placed bullet or a cut throat. I think Shukla realized that he was no longer running an investigation involving reports and meetings.

He was in a combat zone.

He was in my world.

"Sen, we'll get to work on him, but he's already saying he's an American citizen and we can't touch him. He wants us to contact the Embassy."

Srini swore under his breath.

"He's right. We can't detain and torture an American citizen."

Amy spoke up and shocked everyone into silence with what she said.

"These bastards thought they could take Aaditya's Mom. We can't let him get away that easily."

Srini was the first to recover and ask her what she had in mind.

"He hasn't seen me. I'll go in and tell him I'm an American official sent to meet him and learn as much as I can about him."

"Won't you get into trouble?"

She looked at me, and I saw her eyes blazing. This was a totally new Amy I was seeing, and part of me liked her even more for it. Part of me was afraid. Afraid that the woman I had spent such intimate moments with had a dark side to her I had never seen.

"I'm already in deep shit. I've killed two men and now I'm officially absconding. I should be on a flight back to Washington. Instead, I'm here, having brought my service gun with me. Unless all this leads to something that actually prevents an attack on the President, it's a safe bet that I'm going to lose my job. So, I'm not worried about getting into trouble. Let's do this."

Two hours later, she was back, with a smug smile on her face as we all looked on expectantly.

"His name is Ryan Jameson. Former US Navy SEAL, got caught up in drugs while in Afghanistan, was discharged, and then joined the private sector, working for a PMC called Zeus. He has no idea who hired him, just that his company paid him big bucks to come here and do some dirty work."

"Who the hell is Zeus?"

Salil was already on his laptop as I asked the question.

"Private Military Contractor. Not much about them on the internet but it was founded by former SEALs. I'll get our boys to find out more about them."

As Amy sat down and I poured her some coffee, she relaxed and leaned back.

"He told me something else when I said that the only way I could help him was if he told me everything he knew. He knows that even if he's released into US custody, he's going to face trial, but he would prefer that to being here. He fancies his chances of arguing in a US court that he was just following orders, and after all, he didn't hurt anyone, and he has a point when he says that he hasn't been formally arrested or charged with any crime. He feels Zeus puts its people into all kinds of hellholes and conflict zones and knows how to get them out of trouble in court. He's probably right. Once he's back in the US, they will get him all lawyered up."

I looked at Srini and Shukla.

"Surely this bastard can't get away so easily."

To my disappointment and surprise, Shukla answered with a glum expression.

"He has a point. The letters he was carrying from the pharma company and hospital are legit. Someone hacked into their systems to produce the letters. He's claiming he was hired to move a high-risk asset from one location to another. He was given all his instructions by email and says that he doesn't really know who hired him. He was told the patient was at risk of being kidnapped and so he was prepared to protect her and thought you were kidnappers. He says all he had with him was a knife and not even a firearm. He says he knows nothing more."

I clenched my fists in frustration.

"Bullshit! Give me a few minutes with him."

Srini held out a hand, signaling for me to calm down.

"We've given him the polygraph. I know a trained man like him could beat it, but the papers are legit, and we can't hold or torture an American citizen without any proof."

I thought back to what Pillai had said, and it was evident once again that we were up against some powerful enemies, with resources and means at their disposal well beyond what any terror group would have.

"Who was the man with him?"

Amy answered that one.

"He has no idea. He was asked to meet a local driver who would take the patient to the clinic. That's all he says he knows. We checked him out. He's just a local thug hired with cash for the job. Looks like you may have thinned their ranks of trained operatives if they're using local thugs like him."

That did little to cheer me up.

"That doesn't mean much. We are up against some dangerous enemies and there are still two assassins out there."

***

EPISODE SIX

Gog And Magog

"Ma, are you sure you're okay?"

She ruffled my hair, and it broke my heart to see her, lying in bed, weakened, but still trying to be the one to take care of me.

"I'm okay. How are you?"

That was a good question. I don't know what Dr. Hadap would have made of it, but part of me felt better than I ever had. I had that familiar adrenaline rush of being in combat, the confidence of knowing that I was in a zone where I knew how to deal with my enemies instead of grappling with invisible demons inside my mind. However, there was a part of me that wondered whether that was a good thing. When I had been in the army, I wasn't just an uncontrolled killer. I had the discipline, the rituals of army life, the command structure, checks and balances that came with other officers and my superiors. Here, none of those existed. With the violence that had erupted, I could see Srini, Sean, and Shukla all look at me differently. They were all in a world now that was alien to them, my world, and when they looked at me, they seemed to be asking me what to do. I didn't know what to do, and I didn't necessarily like the way they looked at me, as if I scared them. As if they were looking at a wild, dangerous animal whom they had taken to be a friendly pet.

"I asked you, how are you doing? You haven't told me what's going on, but why would anyone come for me unless they were planning to use me to get to you? I can figure that much out. I just hope that killing these men who are after you is both for a good cause and doesn't burden your conscience too much."

I jerked up, looking at Ma in some surprise. Then again, she was the wife of a combat infantry officer and my mother, so she knew what combat did to a man and his soul.

"Ma, the problem is that this time the enemies aren't clear. I don't even know who they are. All we are doing is reacting to what they do and yes, they were after me. They came for me at home."

Her eyes widened, asking me the question she didn't need to ask.

"I wasn't hurt. They died, and no, hurting killers for hire like these men does not bother me."

"Just remember one thing. Don't let your emotions get the better of you."

"What do you mean?"

'When you were small, there were so many times I'd have to go to school when you got into fights, remember? It wasn't whether the fight should have been fought or not, the problem was that you got out of control with your anger. At times, I was told you'd one day kill someone and get into trouble. I worried a lot about you. I never told you that, but I did. That's when your Baba and I thought it may be a good idea to get you to learn martial arts and even before you brought it up after your Baba's passing, we had talked about you joining the army- to channel that anger and aggression into something positive."

I nodded. My Ma had never told me that, but I had sensed it, even as a child. When the blood was pounding in my head and I wanted to lash out at someone, I had seen the look in her eyes, and I had forced myself to calm down, not wanting to hurt her. Not wanting to scare her. However, what she said next did surprise me.

"It wasn't just about you being angry. Most of the time you got into fights because you were trying to protect your friends. When I say you were emotional, it isn't just that you were angry, but that you also went too far to help those you liked. With whatever you're involved in now, just be careful."

"Careful of what, Ma?"

"Be careful of who you trust and who you stick your neck out for."

***

The office was a veritable beehive of activity when I got there the next morning. Srini, Sean, and Salil were glued to monitors in the Situation Room. I had rarely been there before since that was where the bosses monitored and coordinated missions that men like me had gone out on. Amy was outside the room.

I stood next to her and gently squeezed her hand.

"You okay?"

She smiled at me, but I could see the strain in her eyes.

"I think they are going to fire me and ask me to return to the States immediately."

"Shit! We've made so much progress."

She looked at me plaintively.

"I just had a call with my boss. He said there's no real proof of any plot against the President and I'm wasting my time getting involved in what he says is a purely domestic Indian investigation."

"Well, he doesn't know anything about what we suspect as rotten apples in American intelligence and their involvement, does he? Why are you outside?"

She shrugged, the disappointment in her face clear.

"My bosses hate me and will fire me, and your bosses don't trust me enough to call me inside for whatever they're doing in there, so I'm just hanging around, drinking your coffee and waiting for you."

I knocked on the door and when the door opened, I whispered to Srini, asking what was going on.

"Something big, Sen. Something big. Good you got here in time."

"Sir, can Amy come in?"

He thought that over.

"Ordinarily, no. But then nothing is ordinary about what's going on. She's been in this deeper than any of us other than you, so bring her in."

On that note, Srini called her over. I saw black and white images on a screen, of small buildings in an otherwise desolate area. There was a vehicle moving slowly on a narrow road that snaked its way between the buildings. I guessed I was looking at drone footage. I had seen enough of these in after-action reviews, but what exactly was I looking at?

The vehicle, which seemed to be a pick-up truck, accelerated as it came into the open. There was a blur that emerged from the left side of the screen and then the vehicle exploded in a fireball.

"What was that?"

Srini looked at me and grinned.

"We all got lucky. Once we had word that Bin Azam was perhaps involved in a plot on Indian soil against the US President, we got our own friends involved without telling the Americans."

"Friends?"

"Iranians."

He smiled at the surprise on both mine and Amy's faces.

"The Iranians have a lot of skin in the game. They are keen to have the summit with the US President and when we told them Bin Azam was involved, they used their assets to track him to a remote village in Iraq. We passed on that intel to the US without telling them where we got it, and you just witnessed an American Reaper drone taking out Bin Azam and some of his men. If he was indeed involved in a plot, he's out of the picture. The Iranians want to keep their involvement low key for now, but at the right time I'm sure they'll let the Americans know this was a gesture of goodwill ahead of the summit."

I kept staring at the burning vehicle on the screen. Part of me felt the instinctive revulsion soldiers have for someone being killed by the push of a button by a kid sitting in a trailer thousands of miles away. Yes, he was an enemy, and enemies were to be killed, but this was different. This was war and killing reduced to a spectator sport, of people talking of seeing battles and counting enemy kills without realizing that the full picture wasn't revealed by the pictures on a screen, but by smelling the charred flesh, by seeing spattered body parts all around. If more people saw and smelled that, I suspect our leaders would be less trigger happy about starting wars they didn't have to fight and die in. But then, I had personally killed Bin Azam's father and the son had been a chip off the old block, beheading unarmed hostages for sport. Yes, he deserved to die, but I would have preferred if he saw his killer's eyes and knew at the end that he was the hunted, not the predator.

We were back in the conference room and Shukla joined us. He raised an eyebrow at Amy's presence but then settled down without saying anything about it.

"So, there may be two assassins still out there. We are doing everything we can to track them down, but we have learned something by shaking down some of our contacts. Whoever sent these guys, it wasn't Lashkar."

That got everyone to sit up and take notice as Shukla continued.

"Look, it could well be a splinter group, but to organize the infiltration of seven men with the kind of local resources they seem to have, would have taken leadership approval in Lashkar, and they haven't provided that."

"How sure are we of that?"

Srini looked at me and smiled.

"Actually, very sure. The Prime Minister's office called the Pakistani establishment, told them we had killed some terrorists and captured one who claimed to be Lashkar, and if that was true, then we would not hesitate to repeat air strikes of the sort we did at Balakot. They said they had no knowledge of any such plan, and the electronic chatter we intercepted between the ISI and Lashkar soon afterward makes us believe they had nothing to do with this."

Amy was now looking intently at Shukla.

"If Lashkar didn't organize this, how could someone like Bin Azam pull this off, sitting in Iraq? Maybe he had nothing to do with this plot after all. Maybe this was a local cell and, there was no threat to the US President."

Bin Azam probably deserved to die, but perhaps Amy was right, but then what the hell was going on? How were former special forces men hired as mercenaries in the picture, and why were the assassins who had been sent into India being killed? Who were these same unseen forces who were trying to kill anyone who was getting close to uncovering this plan?

Srini took a deep sigh, one which expressed the frustration we all felt.

"Some of our American friends no doubt know some of the answers, but we aren't sure who to talk to or not in the current environment."

***

I dropped Amy off at the US Embassy. As she got out of the car, I held her hand.

"Are you sure you'll be okay?"

She patted my arm reassuringly.

"This is probably the safest place for me. I don't want to be in my hotel alone, and while they're very welcoming, I can sense your bosses getting uncomfortable with me hanging out there all day, especially in the current circumstances. And I do want to keep my job, so best for me to go in, tell my bosses I was following up on an investigation into a possible plot against the President."

"What will you tell them about the events at my home and the hospital?"

She knew what I meant even if I had not put it into words. The crude question behind the question was simple- are you one of us or one of them? Anger flashed in her eyes for an instant before the smile was back.

"With all we've been through together, I'm hoping you trust me. I have no idea what's actually going on in terms of the players involved, and I will tell my bosses factually what happened. Don't worry and ask your bosses not to worry. I won't breathe a word about what you guys suspect about American involvement."

She began to walk off and then stopped and turned.

"Hey, be the soldier you are, don't start becoming a spy."

"What's supposed to mean."

"That means trust those who fight by your side instead of suspecting everyone."

Ouch.

My plan for the rest of the day involved checking up on Ma and making sure the security around her was tight, finishing some paperwork back at the office, and then meeting Amy in the evening when I hoped I could make up for having clearly hurt her feelings. I had hated myself for asking her about what she would tell her bosses, but Srini had insisted.

After meeting Ma, I was about to open my car door in the hospital parking lot when a powerful hand closed the door. I turned, ready to fight, and saw Bethune in front of me. Various scenarios whirred through my mind. Had he been the mole throughout as we had suspected? Had he come in person to finish me off? My gun was in the holster at my side and I could get it within seconds. Bethune didn't seem armed, but given his size, I didn't fancy my chances in unarmed combat with him, even though he was probably more than a dozen years older than me. My hand began to reach under my jacket when he smiled broadly and held out both his palms in front of him.

'Easy, Major. Easy. With what you've been through, I can't blame you for having an itchy trigger finger, but all I want to do is talk. Just let me buy you one cup of coffee."

Ten minutes later, we were sitting in a café, drinking coffee. I was still wary and when Bethune asked me how I was doing, my response was curt.

"If you wanted to know how I'm doing, you could come by the office. Why ambush me in a parking lot?"

He smiled and shook his head.

"Ambush? You are getting paranoid, Major. Your bosses

have for all intents and purposes declared me persona non grata. I don't know what the I did wrong. Maybe I was too hasty to walk out when that Munaf kid died, but I was given instructions to disengage and let the Indians manage it. It wasn't as if I wanted to leave Pillai holding the bag, nor that I enjoyed doing so. He was a good officer and I'm sorry for what happened to him."

I gripped the cup hard, finding it difficult to trust him.

"Why me? Are you trying to find out what our investigations show and since my bosses are shutting you out, you think the dumb soldier will open up?"

He glanced up sharply.

"What's with the anger, man? What have I done to you? Our guys are all over the investigation on their own, and they are probably as puzzled as your guys are. There are no real signs of a threat against the President, yet there clearly was some sort of plot, and then you have the assassins being killed."

I watched him, and he seemed genuine, but I was no spy, and I had no way of knowing if he was bluffing or not. In this game of cloak and dagger, I was well out of my league. Bethune took a sip of his coffee and continued.

"I wanted to check on how Amy is doing. I tried to help her with her bosses, getting people to understand the unique circumstances she's been caught up in. To be honest, with what she's been through, they were worried about her. They were ready to fly her out ASAP, worried about what being caught up in such a situation might trigger. Hell, I was worried about her and wanted to be sure she's okay. She seems like a good kid. She was seen as a rising star in the Secret Service and we had thought bringing her into what we thought was a routine investigation would be a good experience and if any real threat emerged against the President, we would bring in the cavalry. Things have gone all pear-shaped since then, and I worry about her being mixed up in this and how she might be dealing with the violence and stress."

I was about to reply when I thought back to something he'd just said.

"What do you mean, with what she's been through?"

He raised his eyebrow in surprise.

"You do know she was in Iraq?"

"Yeah, of course."

"Well, it's best if she tells you herself when she deems fit. I just wanted to be sure that she's okay. Give me your number and I'll text you mine. Let me know how Amy's doing."

That evening, I picked up Amy from the Embassy and took her to her hotel. We had dinner together and then went up to her room. She was quiet and tense, and I didn't press the matter, knowing she must have had a rough day with her bosses and dreading whether she would be ordered back immediately. Finally, she was the one who broke the ice.

"Anything interesting happen today?"

"Bethune came by?"

She sat up straight.

"To your office? What did he want?"

"No, he caught me for a cup of coffee."

She reached out for my hand.

"For a moment, you had me really worried. If he's involved in all this, I wouldn't want him to harm you."

I put my hand over hers.

"I don't know if he is involved or not, but he seemed to want to chat. In fact, he wanted to chat about you."

I felt her grip tighten on my arm and her eyes tense.

"What does that mean? What did he say?"

"He didn't say much, just that he was worried about you because of what happened in Iraq and how you would deal with the stress here."

Her grip on my arm tightened even more and I could sense her breathing quicken.

"You okay, Amy? Hey, you okay?"

She let go of my hand and suddenly lashed out at the bottle of water on the table, sending it crashing down to the floor, spilling water all over the carpet.

"Damn him! Damn him and whoever he's working for! He's using my past to make you doubt me, to drive a wedge between us."

I got up and held her shoulders and saw that she was crying. I held her close as she sobbed.

"Amy, it's okay. I trust you and you don't have to worry about me believing anything anyone says. He didn't say what he meant, and I didn't ask, and I won't ask you unless you choose to tell me."

She pulled back and looked up at me.

"You deserve to know."

Then she told me.

Her convoy had been ambushed by militants and her vehicle had been separated from the others. Her driver was killed; she had been taken captive. She had spent three days as their prisoner, during which time she had been sexually abused. When she was finally rescued by US Special Forces, she was dehydrated, severely injured, and near death. Then followed months of therapy as she limped back to normalcy and then, determined to get her life back on track, a second lease of life in the Secret Service.

She was crying freely as she finished telling her tale.

"So, that's who and what I am. Damaged goods. Weak. Someone who everyone will look at and feel sympathy for. Someone who still has nightmares every night. I cringed at the mere thought of physical contact with any man for a long time. Till I met you. I'm sure you hate me for what I've been through."

I held her tight and kissed her forehead.

"Amy, we are not damaged or broken. Perhaps we are like pieces of a puzzle who were meant to find each other. Alone we both feel something's missing; something's been taken away from us, but together, we complete each other. I love you even more for being as strong as you are."

She was crying as I picked her up and lay her down on the bed and lay down beside her. She put her head on my chest.

"Aadi, in the early days when I got back home, I just couldn't sleep. I'd wake up screaming every night. The doctor recommended I try and relax, but nothing worked. Then I chanced up something that seemed to work. Listening to music."

"What kind of music?"

She giggled, and I was happy to see her regain some of her spirit.

"Not classical music of the sort the doc ordered, but Ronan Keating. Specifically, that song of his from the movie Notting Hill. Remember it? It's called 'When You Say Nothing At All'."

I had seen the movie and vaguely heard it, and then Amy began singing it softly. I realized it was the same song she had sung to me to help me sleep the first night we had spent together. I joined in and she laughed at how bad my singing was. She kept singing and then she gradually fell asleep. I watched her sleep for a long time, and then I dozed off myself.

That night, I had no nightmares, no visions of dead and bloodied comrades. That night, I slept the peaceful sleep of a man who knows he has found the woman he loves.

***

The next morning, after dropping Amy at the Embassy, I walked into the office to find Salil wearing a suit with a tie.

"When did you start wearing a tie to work?"

He smiled as he looked at me in my jeans and sweatshirt.

"You clearly didn't see my message."

"No."

"Order from the boss. Dress up because we have a special

visitor."

Shit. It would give Sean another petty reason to hate my guts but I was beyond caring and I suspected that somewhere deep in his head, Sean was afraid that he would be added to the list of people I had put into the ground if he pushed me too far.

We entered Srini's office to see him, Sean and Shukla seated around the table with a man I had never seen before. He had a salt and pepper beard, grey hair that was combed back, a sharp nose, and eyes that betrayed a keen intelligence.

Salil was introduced and shook hands with him, and then he shook my hand. His hands were hard, the hands of a soldier, not an office-bound spy or a bureaucrat, and he stood with the ramrod-straight posture of a man used to giving commands, not sitting at his desk, but to men like me in the field. He smiled as he perhaps reached the same conclusion about me.

"You must be the famous major who has been single-handedly taking this terror cell apart."

Okay. I was prepared for many things, but being praised was not one of them, so for a moment, I was tongue-tied as he smiled and continued.

"Forgive my manners, Major. I know so much about you from your bosses, but I have not even introduced myself. I'm Arif Soleimani, Cultural Attaché at the Embassy of the Islamic Republic of Iran."

Cultural Attaché? One of the earliest lessons Srini had taught me when I joined his office was that most spies in foreign missions had as their cover assignments the most innocuous ones, the inside joke among the agencies being that if you wanted to catch all the spies working at enemy embassies, hold a music recital and invite the Cultural Attaches.

"Pleasure to meet you, Sir. I suppose before your interest in cultural matters, you've perhaps served in the field?"

He laughed, looking back to Sean.

"Mr. D'Silva, you sold him short. He is a thinker, not just a warrior."

That brought on a sheepish expression from Sean, and I wondered just in what other ways my beloved boss had tried to belittle me.

"Major, there are no secrets here between friends. That's why I am here. I served in the Revolutionary Guards and then in Military Intelligence before coming here."

We all sat down and when I realized that Srini had briefed Soleimani about our investigation so far, I wondered why we were sharing so much with the Iranians. I mean, India was trying to play a balancing act between Iran and the US, and the big planned diplomatic coup was to help broker a peace summit, not just because India was naturally peace-loving and wanted the good of mankind, but because it was in India's economic and strategic interest that Iran and the US not keep going at each other. Also, getting Iran on board even more strongly as an ally helped India put more pressure on our Pakistani pals who would have one more neighbor who hated their guts.

See, even a simple soldier understands that much about geopolitics. But why were we cozying up so much with the Iranians, including sharing misgivings about the potential role of American agencies? That was cleared up when Soleimani shared some transcripts and placed them on the table.

"Srini, here are the transcripts I had mentioned, and I will have soft copies sent over. For the benefit of the others, I'll sum up what I've shared with you. As I said, Bin Azam was a bad apple and deserved to die. We had been tracking him for a while since we tangled with him and his thugs when they were fighting with Daesh against our forces in Iraq. However, as we got his bearings and passed them on to you, we found evidence that someone was using his communication channels to pass messages to someone in Pakistan and Nepal. We had cracked his codes for some time and were looking to get a fix on him to kill him, but then the Americans obliged us."

Pakistan and Nepal? Someone hacking into communication channels? A connection to Bin Azam. I felt my hair stand up on end, realizing that this was bringing us closer to understanding the enemies we had been up against.

"Sir, sorry for interrupting, but what messages were they sending?"

Soleimani looked at me and nodded.

"That's precisely why we reached out to my old friend Srini here. They were messages about a terror attack planned in India against what they called a high-value target. Subsequent messages made it clear they were talking about a President being targeted. When I told Srini that day before yesterday, he brought me up to speed, and I realized that someone was making it seem as if Bin Azam was setting up a hit here, but someone else was doing it."

"Who?"

He smiled.

"That's the big question, Major. You see, politics is a

complicated business for soldiers like us. The Americans think Bin Azam was planning a hit on their President. We give them Bin Azam, and that, revealed at the right time, gives us leverage over them. Everyone's happy that son of a bitch is dead, and the Americans had at one time claimed that we were supporting Bin Azam. Hopefully, this lays that to rest as well."

"Didn't you fight Bin Azam and Daesh? Why would the Americans think you supported him?"

Soleimani laughed and continued laughing so much he began to cough. Srini handed him a glass of water, which he accepted. I could see that Srini was also smiling broadly.

"Major, this is a truly messed-up world. Do you know that when I was in the Revolutionary Guard, we actually worked with US Special Forces to coordinate force movements and attacks against Daesh in Iraq? We defeated Daesh in Iraq, and as thanks, in the popular US media and political narrative, we were just lumped with all their 'Arabs' and terrorists because it suited the US administration to have another war boiling to distract from their internal politics. Bin Azam was a genuine villain, but to paint Iran as a villain it becomes an inconvenient detail to mention that we fought the same villains as the Americans. Easier to lump us together with all the terrorists in that part of the world."

He put the glass down and looked me in the eye.

"I'm not naïve, Major. Politicians on all sides love to have a good war going. Keeps the unwashed masses distracted from asking too many tough questions, but someone was playing Bin Azam and bringing some assets into India to stage a real attack. What that was and what they were trying to achieve is anybody's guess."

He got up to leave.

"Srini, I'll be on my way. Let's stay in touch if our people learn anything new."

He turned to leave, pulling out his sunglasses from his coat pocket. His glasses caught on something and it came tumbling out onto the floor. I bent to pick it up and then froze.

A burgundy booklet.

With gold lettering on top and a curved symbol next to it.

A passport.

I had seen a bunch of these before.

At Jama Masjid.

In the hands of the man I had fought with there and who had died later in my apartment.

I looked up and realized that everyone was staring at me. Soleimani put his hands on the passport.

"Thanks, Major. Are you okay? You look ill."

I told them all where I had seen a bunch of similar booklets and it was then Soleimani's turn to look ill. He sat down heavily and took a deep sigh.

"Srini, pardon the language, but I think the Major here has stumbled onto some deep shit, which could drown us all."

"What do you mean, Sir?"

Srini had also made the same connection Soleimani had. I guess they both thought like spies more than I did and saw things I may have missed so Soleimani spelled it out.

"Here's what I make of it, Major. Someone sets up an attack

on the US President while he's visiting India. Supposedly ordered by Bin Azam, whom sections of the US media and political class have built up to be supported by Iran. Carried out by idiots who've been trained and infiltrated into India from Pakistan but carrying Iranian passports. So, if they succeed or not, anyone will think this was a hit ordered and supported by Iran."

Shit. That made sense, but that didn't make it any less scary for what it implied. Soleimani read my mind.

"The bloody peace deal is blown to hell; we're firing missiles at each other all over again. That's what would happen if this plan went ahead as it was perhaps supposed to."

"Why would the Americans want that?"

Srini looked at me sympathetically.

"Sen, given everything we know now, perhaps it's not as simple as whether the Americans are behind anything or not. It need not be the American government at all, or even an American government agency working on official orders."

Okay, but I didn't get it. This much intrigue was too much for a simple soldier. Soleimani helped out.

"Rogue elements in the CIA, oil companies, defense companies, private military contractors. Any or all of them benefit from more conflict and any or all of them could be involved. Lots of people in the world are happier and richer when there is a war on."

Srini picked it up, depressing me further with the odds ranged against us.

"Top of the line mercenaries who've served in special forces and the ability to hack into government comms would fit that pattern. I would definitely say there's some intel agency involvement along with non-state actors. It's much easier to wage war against a government. These guys don't obey any rules, can literally get away with murder, and have resources that no terror group would dream of having."

Soleimani had even better news to share.

"It may not just be for profit, though that may be a fortuitous side effect. There are enough people out there among the Americans and unfortunately among my own people who actually believe we are headed for an Armageddon, of the sort the Bible talks about, a final struggle between good and evil, between the armies of Gog and Magog, with a new world order emerging, in which of course they and their lackeys play a leading role. Armageddon is a real place, many believe it to be Megiddo, a Palestinian city. Ours is a part of the world that has known conflict for thousands of years and overlaying some ideological or religious justification often gets people committed to the cause more than just profits. The most dangerous adversaries are not just those with the best weapons or the best training, but those who actually believe in their cause. I fear those may be the kind of people we are up against."

I got the picture. In short, we were pretty screwed. Srini sealed that with his next statement.

"Clearly, Azfal's tipoff to Pillai got this on our radar screen. Otherwise, we would have just seen a terror attack against the US President, and everyone would think the Iranian government was behind it. They've been getting rid of all traces of the plot since then."

Soleimani interjected.

"It's not over, Srini. You mentioned there were seven assassins. So far only five are accounted for. So, there are two more out there who they will be trying to neutralize. We need to let the Americans know so that they don't find out through any other means and think we were behind it."

"Who can we trust among the Americans to share this? Bethune is our point person, but do we trust him?"

Srini thought that over.

"I have nothing against Bethune personally, but we need a direct line to someone senior in the US administration. At least one safe assumption is that the US President has no idea of what's going on since it's his life on the line."

"Wouldn't we still need to go through the CIA or someone who may be involved in the plot?"

"Sen, this can't be managed with anyone short of the very top. I'll get to the Prime Minister's office, brief them and then get them to help on how we get this information to the US President. Once he knows there may be rotten apples in the US system, he will know best how to manage this."

Soleimani got up to leave and as I showed him out the door, he paused.

"Walk with me, Major."

In front of the elevator, he turned to me and shook my hand.

"Major, be careful."

"Yes, Sir. I always am."

He smiled and shook his head.

"You are a warrior, but here you are not fighting against fellow warriors, but snakes who strike in the dark. They have no honor, no conscience, and will do anything to prevail. These are the people who topple governments, start revolutions, create wars. What you see on the news every day often has their fingerprints on it. Unfortunately, you have brought them into the open and you have disrupted their plans. So, my friend, as one soldier to another, be careful."

"You too, Sir."

He grinned.

"I will be careful, but you need to really watch your back till we get to the bottom of this. I have lived my life among such snakes, Major, plus here I am a diplomat with a lot more protection than someone like you has."

That was the last time I saw him alive.

***

"What's bothering you?"

Ma was sitting upright as I sat next to her hospital bed. Amy had joined us a few minutes ago, and Amy and I were planning to head out for dinner.

"Ma, it's okay."

"It's not okay if you're not okay."

That is how mothers are, I guess, or how mine is. She was lying on a hospital bed, going through experimental medication for cancer, and had nearly been kidnapped and killed in the last couple of days. Yet, her biggest concern was whether I was feeling okay. Amy ruffled my hair. I didn't know how much to share. For once, I didn't want to spook Ma with all that was going on, and as close as Amy was to me, it was clear that a lot of what I had learned from Soleimani was privileged information and not to be shared.

"Ma, it's just that everything going on makes me feel quite helpless. There are people out there much more powerful than I am and I feel like there's nothing I can really do to stop them."

She smiled at me.

"Sometimes you feel most empowered when you accept that you can't change everything. That's not something I made up. Your Baba used to say that when I used to ask him how he coped with all the chaos that came with some of his field postings. He used to say he would just focus on what was in front of him and do the best possible job there instead of wonderıng about the various things that were outside his control."

That made sense enough, I guess.

"So, Ma, you're saying I focus on the work I have ahead of me?"

She chuckled and gave Amy a knowing smile.

"Foolish boy. Always so serious about work. The most important thing you need to focus on is the beautiful woman next to you."

As we walked out of the hospital, Amy took my arm.

"Ma likes you."

She smiled and put her head against my shoulder.

"Do you have work tonight?"

Actually, Soleimani had called a late-night meeting at the Taj Man Singh hotel where he wanted to debrief on what he had heard back from his sources in Tehran. Srini couldn't make it as he had to take his daughter to the doctor, so Sean was joining. I had little value to add to an intelligence-sharing meeting, but Srini had messaged me to ask if I could join. He didn't say it, and he didn't need to, but in the current environment, all of us were potential targets and Sean may or may not have been a capable spy sitting in the office, but he was clearly not going to be able to take care of himself if men of the sort who had come for me came after him. I had messaged to say I'd be there, and Srini had said that he knew I was going to check on Ma and if in case I couldn't come by, it was okay and he would ask Salil to be there.

"Hey, are you busy or not? You seem totally lost? I thought we could do something special tonight."

"Any special occasion?"

She gave me an impish smile.

"Just my birthday."

"Shit. I had no idea. I mean, I never asked. I mean, I'm an absolute idiot. Of course, we'll do something."

I messaged Salil to take one for the team and babysit Sean for the meeting with Soleimani. Then I turned to Amy.

"I'm all yours, ma'am. Let's go celebrate in style."

***

"Did you do this to make me feel old?"

"Of course."

Amy was kidding, and she smiled and kissed me to make sure I knew she was, but as I looked around, I realized just how out of touch I was. Amy had said she wanted to go clubbing and asked which club I'd recommend. I had to sheepishly admit that I had no idea and then proceeded to google nightclubs in Delhi. Amy had found that charming and cute and asked me what I had done with my misspent twenties if I hadn't been clubbing with friends. Well, I had spent those years hanging out with friends, but friends with whom I'd go on missions to kill people who in turn were trying to kill us. I was snapped back to a far more pleasant reality when Amy kissed me again.

"Wake up and dance."

The dance floor at the Kitty Su nightclub seemed to be full of teenagers but we were two drinks down and Amy had kissed me again, so I really didn't care and didn't bother to remember just how much I hated dancing. Soon we were on the dance floor, lost in the music, lost in each other. When we got back to our table and ordered another round of drinks, I checked my watch. It was just after eleven. Sean and Soleimani would be at their meeting, I knew I'd have to buy Salil some drinks for pulling him out of home so late to go and babysit Sean.

"Do you have any other plans?"

I looked up at Amy and kissed her.

"No, tonight I'm all yours."

We were walking down the sidewalk, both slightly buzzed, and I had decided to leave my car at the hotel, not wanting to risk driving late at night with a few drinks in me. I might have been able to handle the car but being caught by cops would surely spoil Amy's birthday. It was now past midnight and I had celebrated her birthday at midnight by chugging two tequilas and then getting the DJ to interrupt the proceedings so I could go on stage and sing happy birthday for her and then, drunk and in love, had proceeded to sing a version of 'When You Say Nothing At All' which would have had Ronan Keating's lawyers after me for defamation for the way I had butchered his song. When I had gotten off stage, everyone had cheered and clapped and Amy had kissed me, and I had made a total fool of myself, and I had never been happier.

"Where to, birthday girl?"

"I'm all yours tonight."

I grinned and pulled out my phone to call an Uber and saw there were a dozen missed calls from Srini. My phone had been on silent, and I had been so lost in the celebration with Amy that I hadn't checked my phone even once. There was a text message from Srini as well.

Call me as soon as you can, Major. This is an emergency.

That sobered me up real fast. I dialed Srini's number and when he picked up, I could hear the stress in his voice.

"Sen, get to the hospital now. I'm there."

"What's up, sir. Not feeling well?"

"Just get here. There was an attack. Sean and Soleimani are dead and Murthy's barely alive."

Fuck.

Cops or not, drunk or not, I sprinted to my car, with Amy just behind me.

"What's going on?"

"I need to go to the hospital. Something terrible's happened. I'll drop you at your hotel."

"No, I'll come along."

I drove faster than I ever have, and thankfully no cops pulled us over, because I was sure I'd not stop for them and that would lead to an even more complicated night. I ran into the lobby of the All-India Institute of Medical Sciences and saw several cops there and a couple of our operations boys. The cops tried to stop me, but the boys waved me through and told me Srini was outside the ICU.

"What happened?"

I didn't wait for his answer because I saw Salil's wife, Bharathi, in a corner. Her eyes were puffed from crying and she was sitting there, her hands clasped tightly in her lap. I walked over to her. I had met her a few times when Salil had called me over but when she looked up at me, her smile was gone, and her voice was a bare whisper.

"They're saying he's barely hanging in there."

I knelt in front of her.

"He'll be fine. He's a fighter."

Amy had come up behind me and sat next to Bharathi, hugging her. Bharathi didn't know who Amy was but having a friendly and comforting face was enough for her to smile at Amy. Amy motioned for me to go talk to Srini. Yes, my friend was fighting for his life, but I was also a professional and needed to know what was going on.

Srini looked more worn out than I had ever seen him.

"Sen, they had just left the hotel and Sean was walking Soleimani to his car when the car exploded. Someone planted a bomb there. Both died, along with Soleimani's driver and guard. Twelve other hotel guests and staff suffered minor injuries. Murthy had forgotten his phone and had begun to turn back to get it when the car exploded. That's why he made it. Thank God he's alive."

I heard it all, but what was going through my mind was that Salil was fighting for his life because I had asked him to cover for me and go for the meeting. I had been enjoying the evening while my friend was close to death because of me. Then I thought of Sean, of all the times I had hated him, all the times I'd say flippantly to Salil over drinks, 'why doesn't some jihadi pick him up and get him off our face?'. Now he was gone. Not an ogre of a boss, not a bureaucrat who hassled me for paperwork, but a man. A man who left behind a family. A man who may have deserved many things, but certainly didn't deserve to die like this.

I sagged back against the wall, a headache coming over me. A rage coming over me. Not at those who had perpetrated this attack, but at myself. If I had been there, maybe I would have been able to do something. I grabbed my head in my hands and sat down. I felt Amy's hands on my shoulder. I had told her about skipping a meeting and asking Salil to take my place and she perhaps knew what was going through my mind.

"Aadi, there's nothing you could have done about it. Nothing. Don't beat yourself up about it. I'm the one who should be feeling guilty for keeping you from your work."

I looked up at her, tears forming in her eyes, and realized just what a mess we were all in. We were up against forces who were so far ahead of us that there didn't seem to be any way we could fight them, let alone prevail against them. Srini sat down next to me.

"How the fuck did they know?"

As I'd said, when Srini started swearing, he was under deep stress.

"About the meeting, Sir?"

"No, not just the meeting. About everything. About Soleimani meeting us, about us sharing intel, about the meeting. They knew everything, and they were able to set up a hit despite the security Soleimani would have had. How do you fight against such an enemy?"

"I have an idea."

We both turned towards Amy. The look on her face was intense, angry, but then she put a finger to her lips. She got up and motioned to a nurse and came back with a notepad and pen and began writing.

Bethune met you!

Are you sure he's not bugged your offices?

Are you sure he didn't manage to get a bug on you?

Shit. If a CIA spook like Bethune was one of the bad apples, we had thought we could cut him out by keeping him out of the loop in our communication. We had been naïve. If indeed someone like him was involved, working for masters who had both the resources and ruthlessness to act the way they had so far, what Amy said made a lot of sense. Srini took the pen and scribbled.

Back to the office. NOW! And no talking till we get there.

***

With the kind of work the R&AW did, there was often no concept of normal office hours, and somebody would always be in office, monitoring communications, heading off crises, or just ensuring the right paperwork got to the right people the next morning to have the right decisions taken. There was also a big technical crew, usually made of people who had served in the forces, experts at electronic warfare, signal intelligence, and other stuff which was well beyond the realm of expertise of a foot soldier like me, but whose expertise I had long come to trust and count on. We were outside Srini's office, having changed into hastily arranged shirts and trousers. They didn't fit well and were not very comfortable, but comfort and looks were the last things on our minds. The techies were sweeping all our offices and our clothes for bugs. They came up with nothing. Next were our devices.

It took them an hour to scour through our computers and phones and when they came out, one of them pulled Srini aside. I saw them looking at me and wondered what was wrong. Srini called me up to him.

"Sen, it was your phone."

Shit. How had Bethune managed to pull that off?

"There was an app downloaded on it, which you probably never saw as it was hidden deep in the menus. It used your phone's microphone to transmit everything that was said around it. To whom we don't know, but I think we have a good guess who may have managed that."

Something didn't make sense to me.

"Bethune? How would he get his hands on my phone to put a bug on it?"

The techie interrupted.

"Sir, they don't actually need to get hold of your phone physically. Did the person send you a link or a text you clicked on?"

Shit. Bethune had sent me his number and I had clicked on the message to save his number.

"Can you get rid of the bug? Sorry, sir. I messed up."

Srini laid a comforting hand on my shoulder.

"Son, not your fault. All of us have fallen prey to some trick in our career in this business and we have played our share of tricks on others who are pros at this game. This comes with the territory. The question is now that we know what we do, what next?"

We sat in Srini's office and first he apologized to Amy for having her scanned as well.

"No apologies needed, sir. With what's going on, it's better to be safe."

"Sir, what happened with the PMO call? Can they just ask the US President to cancel or postpone his trip?"

Srini looked downcast.

"I took it to them, but for them, this is more about the optics-how things look. Us asking the American President to cancel his trip because of a security threat here makes us look weak, and in an election year, the US President doesn't want to seem like he's weak, given we have no concrete intelligence or evidence. His own people have been telling him that there's no credible intelligence about a threat to him. According to them, this is normal domestic terrorism in India which we'll take care of."

That really set me off.

"What are they thinking? Why don't we tell them that someone in their own establishment is involved? Amy, can't you get to your superiors in the Secret Service and tell them about Bethune and what we suspect about him?"

She looked at me as if I was very naïve, a look of sympathy.

"What would I tell them? As is, they're pissed off at me for getting involved in two shootings when strictly speaking, I had no business being there. Now if I go to them with a conspiracy theory involving a senior and much respected CIA officer, what do you think they'll do? Go after Bethune and take him down or say that a junior Secret Service agent with a rough history has gone crazy after her PTSD acted up? They'll likely cart me off and suspend me and parade me before shrinks. In fact, even if I don't tell them anything, I suspect that's what they'll do anyway. They are probably waiting for the President's trip to get over, so they don't risk any media exposure about crazy Secret Service agents ahead of the trip."

She was infuriatingly right, but that didn't make it any easier for me to accept it.

"Are we really so helpless? Then we may as well just sit back and let these fuckers do what they want? Kill the US President, go right ahead? Start a war with Iran? Be my fucking guest.

There must be something we can do."

Amy was looking at me curiously.

"Lots of people would have given up. Not because they are cowards or don't care, but the fact is that in the world around us, there are things we can't do anything about. Wars do happen. Coups do take place, and yes leaders get assassinated. What makes you tick?"

I looked back at her and I could see her flinch at the look in my eyes.

"I care because these fuckers have decided to start their war in my backyard, by killing and hurting people I know, by threatening my family and those I care about. I don't care what wars and geopolitical intrigue they may be plotting, but whether they know it or not, I have declared war on them."

"What will you do?"

I looked at Srini.

"Sir, I don't know how to do this. I'm not the spy or the thinker, but you need to get a plan in place and then let me loose. I'll hunt these bastards down, whoever they may be, no matter how untouchable they consider themselves to be."

Amy was quiet.

"Amy, anything wrong?"

'These are extremely dangerous people.'

Once again, I looked her straight in the eye.

"I hope they've realized by now that I can be extremely dangerous. Sir, any ideas?"

Srini had been thinking, and when he stared off into space the way he was doing now, I had long learned that his mind was whirring, all his considerable intellect and experience coming into play. Finally, he snapped his fingers.

"Bethune doesn't know we know. As far as he and his masters are concerned, he's still got you bugged, and he thinks he will be one step ahead of us. So, we don't get rid of the bug."

"What do we do then, Sir?"

"We lay a trap and we reel that big fucker in."

Srini with a devious plan and a swear word.

This was going to be good.

***

I was as nervous as I had ever been before a combat mission, though I was sitting in a five-star hotel coffee shop. Srini had picked the Taj for a meeting, figuring only the way a spy can, that having the meeting here would signal to Bethune that we really didn't suspect anything. Otherwise, why would we call someone we suspected of murdering a colleague to the scene of the crime? Srini may not have thought it would have any impact on Bethune, but just two days after the blast, while the hotel was open again, cops were everywhere, and the blackened patch near the hotel gate bore testimony to the lives that had been taken here. I had texted Bethune saying I wanted to meet and that we had some news to share and while waiting for him, I sipped on a coffee, wanting something stronger, but knowing that I needed to be alert. If Bethune was indeed part of the plot against us, he was far more dangerous than I had imagined, and there was no telling whether he would use this meeting as a pretext to strike against me and take yet another one of our pieces off the board. Srini had wired me up with a bug, and I felt like a bloody lab rat, sitting there, bugged by both sides.

"Hello there, Major. First of all, I was so sorry to hear of Sean's death."

I stood up and shook his hand, working consciously to control my urge to stab him with the knife on the table there and then. The bastard had the gall to come and talk about Sean's death and to pretend to show sympathy. Perhaps he sensed my mood and withdrew his hand hastily and sat down opposite me.

"How can I help, Major?"

"We have a man in custody. An American called Jameson. Former Navy SEAL, now works with a PMC."

His eyebrows went up. He was a bloody good actor. Had to give him credit for that. If I hadn't known the games he was playing, I would have thought he was genuinely surprised.

"He came after my mother."

He looked straight at me and I held his gaze. Yes, he had come for my mother, and I was perhaps sitting opposite the man who had sent him. Bethune broke eye contact and ordered coffee.

"Why would your mother be caught up in this?"

I took a deep breath. Losing my temper was only going to mess this up.

"I think they were trying to get to me."

"Who?"

I took a sip of coffee and looked at him over the rim.

"The same people who took out the assassins in Jama Masjid, who took out Azfal and who came for me."

"ISI?"

The bastard was good. He was deflecting this in a totally new direction.

"Maybe. If Pakistan had set this up, would make sense for them to cover their tracks, but the ISI doesn't use American PMCs for their dirty work, at least they never have. We need your help to run this PMC link through and see if you can find anything more that would help us. And yes, we want to get rid of Jameson. He's of no use to us anymore, and we don't want the spectacle of an American citizen complaining later to the media or the lawyers of how we mistreated him. Can you get him off our hands?"

He growled in reply.

"I will get him off your hands, and if he's indeed a Navy SEAL who's mixed up in this shit, we will make sure he feels all kinds of pain. Pain of the sort you guys may have been coy about inflicting on an American citizen. Thanks for handing him to us and I'll be sure to let you know if our boys find out anything more from him."

As he left, I kept watching his huge frame. I had known all kinds of dangerous people in my life, but Bethune took the cake. To come and meet me, take in what I had to offer with a straight face, and then leave with a promise of staying in touch. Man, he had balls. You could hate an enemy and respect him at the same time. Bethune seemed like that kind of enemy.

The kind you would do well to be scared of.

The next afternoon, I was back in Srini's control room with him, staring at a monitor where a red, blinking dot was moving. Jameson had indeed been handed over to the Americans, but not before Srini's tech boys had given him a special cocktail, a glass of water with a tracker dissolved in it. They claimed we would be able to track him for over 48 hours, and we would know where the Americans had taken him. If he was nothing more than Navy SEAL who had made poor career choices, he would be off to custody, probably spending a lot of the rest of his life behind bars. But something like that would have to be done in a way that was above board, through the judicial system, and we would know. Indeed, we would have a right to ask the Americans about his sentencing given we had captured him. If he was however mixed up in some dirty business in which Bethune and his bosses were involved, chances were he would be taken somewhere else far from official channels and made to disappear. We would perhaps not know easily what had happened to him, but the mere fact of his going 'off grid' would signal that someone in the American establishment, in this case, the prime suspect being Bethune, was involved. Bethune had called me a few minutes ago telling me Jameson was off his hands as well, and some CIA boys had come to take him off in a chartered jet. We watched the red dot over the Indian Ocean, and Srini turned to me, asking me whether we should take a break and get some coffee since the flight would last for hours no matter where they were going.

"Sen, what happened? Did you hear what I said?"

"Sir, the dot has disappeared."

"What?"

We both looked at the screen and it was gone. Srini called his tech boys and had a rushed back and forth with them.

"Sen, they say this tracker can't be turned off or deactivated."

"So why has it stopped blinking? Would it stop if Jameson is dead?"

Srini looked at me, and I could see the confidence he had felt making this plan dissipate once he figured just how resourceful and ruthless our adversaries were.

"They say it would continue blinking for some time at least if he was just dead. It would stop blinking if someone bled him totally or if his body's structural integrity was suddenly compromised."

My expression told him what I couldn't put into words- say that in plain English, please.

"Sorry, that was what the tech guys said. It means that his body would have to suddenly explode or disintegrate."

Fuck.

Srini got a bunch of calls made, and it took us an hour to hear back from the Navy. One of their patrol aircraft had spotted a sudden flash of heat and light on its sensors that would be consistent with a mid-air explosion. They had gone in for a closer look and at the coordinates where we had last seen the signal for Jameson's tracker, they had found small pieces of wreckage. This aircraft had not just crashed due to a malfunction, it had been blown into smithereens in mid-air.

I kept staring at the screen. I had said I had declared war on these enemies. Now that I knew who they might be and just what they were capable of, I wasn't sure anymore this was a war I knew how to win.

***

EPISODE SEVEN

LAST MAN STANDING

"Don't look so glum. Wounds heal and chicks dig scars."

Salil began to smile and then grimaced.

"Don't make me laugh. The damn stitches in my back hurt if I laugh. By the way, did you just make that stupid philosophical shit up?"

I grinned as I adjusted his bed, raising the back so he could get to his breakfast. It had been two days since we had released Jameson, and Salil was much better. He was fully conscious, and the doctors said that there would likely be no long-term damage. He had just passed a pillar when the bomb went off, and the pillar had absorbed a lot of the blast wave. He had caught a bit of shrapnel on his back and side of his face, both of which were heavily bandaged now.

"I wish I had that level of deep philosophical insight. One of my COs told me that when I was hit by grenade fragments on my back- the first time I got seriously wounded. Seems it was from some Keanu Reeves movie he once saw."

Salil picked up some food with a spoon and then grimaced as he chewed.

"Does it hurt when you chew?"

"No, the food sucks. I mean, which sadistic bastard would serve tasteless oat porridge to someone who's already cut up and hurt and nearly died? Shouldn't the purpose of food be to cheer someone up and make them happy to be alive instead of making them feel even more miserable and wish they were dead?"

I laughed out loud.

"If you're complaining about the food, then you're back to normal. I asked the doctor if you could have stuff beyond the hospital fare, and she was a bit vague, so I interpreted that as wholehearted approval. Here you go."

Salil's eyes lit up as I took the packet that had been lying next to me and placed a couple of kababs, straight from Tahir's tandoor, on his tray. He took a bite and closed his eyes in satisfaction.

"Now I almost forgive you for sending me to that meeting."

He caught the look in my eye and patted my arm.

"Now, don't get all sentimental on me, Sen. I'm kidding. I don't blame you for anything. If you had gone, you might be dead now. I lucked out because I forgot my phone. And I lucked out because they used a pretty small bomb, one meant to kill those within a couple of meters of the car only."

When I asked him if he had seen anything unusual that night, he took a deep breath.

"My job was to protect Sean, so I had the driver stay with the vehicle all the time and I ensured I checked the car before we even left for the meeting. We were clean, and I spoke briefly to Soleimani's security guy. He seemed competent, but clearly not competent enough. Poor sod also died along with their driver. I don't know if Soleimani's people were sloppy, someone infiltrated them, or indeed if they managed to get one of the hotel staff to put the bomb inside."

As I brought him up to speed on all that had happened, he paused, kabab held in the air. And then he just stared at me, not saying anything, not eating.

"What's wrong?"

He took a deep breath.

"Sounds like we are seriously out of our league."

"Thanks for the vote of confidence."

He laughed, grimaced in pain, and then took a bite.

"Your phone? Are they listening in now?"

"No. The tech boys told me to just shut off my phone if I didn't want them listening in. I wanted to get rid of the bloody bug, but Srini told me to leave it. As is, the odds are pretty much against us, and as he said, perhaps the only card we hold is that they don't yet know that we know my phone is bugged."

Salil held out the kabab towards me.

"Share the kabab, man. When things are as fucked as they are now, you may as well enjoy the kabab. I don't fancy our chances of winning any mind games against the enemies we seem to be up against but keep the bug in your phone if the boss says so."

"Is that all the advice you have to offer, oh wise one?"

Salil grinned.

"I thought you'd come here for the company and to check on a dying friend, but if it's advice you seek, I do have one piece of advice for you. Screw what I had told you about thinking like a spy. Think like a soldier. The soldier you are. Don't try and think like the suits the rest of us are."

"What does that mean?"

"All of us- me, Srini, Sean."

He caught himself as he took Sean's name.

"Hard to believe he's gone. Hated his guts as a boss, but nobody deserves to go the way he did. Anyways, here's what I was saying. The rest of us have spent most of our lives in offices, so we think in a pretty linear fashion. Even Srini. He was in the army, but that was ages ago. Now, he thinks like the rest of us in office. We pass a file. It goes to someone; they pass it on and so on. We take the same thinking to deal with the sort of situation we have here. We try and find logical, linear solutions to problems we face because that's how investigative work is done. The problem is that the enemy is not acting linearly. They're not acting like a bunch of spies and bureaucrats shuffling papers and passing on files. They're acting like they're in combat- which they are. They're hitting us hard and fast where we least expect it, and we're scrambling before they hit us again."

"So, what do I do?"

"Go after Bethune. Now you know he's playing for the opposition. Take him out."

I leaned back. That made no sense and I told him so. Bethune was a senior CIA officer. Without any proof, we couldn't just attack him. Plus, R&AW was not in the business of carrying out rogue assassinations. We would all be crucified if we tried anything like this and the government found out. Salil just shook his head when I made all my objections known.

"Man, I don't mean kill him just like that. I mean you confront him in some way and see if you can get him to reveal his hand, something that gives you a reason to take him down."

"Any ideas on how I do that?"

Salil took a big bite of the kabab.

"That's all the advice a couple of kababs get you. Get me some more and a bottle of Scotch and I may come up with more ideas. But seriously, I have no fucking clue how to do that, but it can't be a good idea to keep ignoring the bloody elephant in the room. The fact is that the guy you suspect of being a key player in all this is sitting pretty in Delhi and will likely cover up the rest of the plot right under our noses. They've been taking our pieces off the board pretty well, maybe it's time we think of how we can take Bethune off the board."

"He's a veteran CIA agent. I can't win a battle of mind games with him, let alone come up with something that might fool him."

Salil looked at me.

"You're not alone in this, remember? You've got all of Unit 22 with you and more importantly, you have the one person I know who can think of something to take down Bethune. Srini."

***

"Aadi, can we chat?"

I had barely been able to spend time with Amy for a couple of days, having been caught up in sorting things out at work, checking in on Salil's family, and yes, going to Sean's funeral. So, when she landed up at my apartment that night, I wasn't surprised.

"I'm sorry, Amy. I've just been up to my neck in stuff."

She gently guided me to the sofa and sat down next to me.

"How are you doing?"

For the first time in a few days, I had time to sit down and relax, and I realized just how tired I was. I wanted to tell Amy I was okay, but I hadn't slept well, couldn't remember the last time I had a full meal, and had a headache that refused to go away.

"Lie down and I'll fix you some dinner."

I was too tired to object and Amy rustled up some pasta which I wolfed down as soon as she put it in front of me. After dinner, sitting with her, a glass of wine in hand, I finally felt as if I was able to relax, or perhaps it was just my lack of sleep catching up with me.

"I don't know if you heard about the President's trip."

I hadn't, but when Amy mentioned it, I hoped that he had canceled his trip. No such luck.

"He's coming. In fact, they advanced it by a few days, so they can spend more time on policy discussions before the Republic Day parade."

We really couldn't catch a single lucky break, could we?

"Amy, given the situation, why don't they postpone the trip? Given how screwed up things are, why does he want to come?"

Amy shrugged sadly.

"You and I know what the situation may be, but everyone he listens to is advising him that things are under control, that the supposed threat against him was a false alarm, and there's purely an internal terror threat the Indians need to deal with. The CIA is giving him that advice, by the way."

"Of course, they are, with Bethune there to help! What about the Secret Service? Wouldn't they listen to you?"

She took a deep sip of her wine.

"I'm totally discredited, by the way. Vet with PTSD gets involved in firefights where she has no business being, and yes, gets involved with an Indian intelligence officer. As I said before, they will want to avoid a spectacle ahead of the President's trip, but as soon as he goes, they'll bury my career."

I sat up straight and looked at her.

"How did they get to know about us?"

"Someone leaked that as well. Must be your friend Bethune."

Shit. Bethune had bugged me and had used that to not just compromise our operations and kill and hurt people around me, he had used it to go after Amy. I told her what Salil had suggested.

"Just be very careful. He's proving to be an extremely dangerous enemy."

I drained my glass.

"Do you think they're going to go after the President or is their focus now just cleaning up traces of what their plan was?"

She thought that over.

"It's always a bad idea to try and get inside someone else's head, but my guess is they are in clean-up mode. I think they began that once you showed up at Azfal's place, and since then, with so many of their assassins taken out of commission, I think they're just trying to clean up all traces of their plan."

I took another deep sip of the wine.

"The problem is that Srini, Shukla, me, and a bunch of others in the Indian establishment have an idea of what's going on. They can't realistically take us all out. Right now the politicians don't want to listen because they're blinded by the brownie points they will score with the US President's visit and the summit with Iran, but the moment we get some proof, whoever is behind all this will be toast."

Amy remained silent and encouraged by the wine that was now working its way through my system, I kept speculating.

"But I'm not so sure. We're up against some very smart people. People who are masters of, what was the word that spy with Bethune had used? Misdirection. They may have started with a real plan to carry out a hit on your President and blame it on the Iranians. When we got some hint of what was going on, they began to take out their assets in place. But those assassins we've encountered have hardly been the A-team. They've been a bunch of kids from Pakistan trained to pull triggers. They were the patsies, the fall guys, but the real enemy we're behind can afford trained men of the sort we've encountered-real special forces types. Why would they use these Pakistani kids when they could have used other assets who might be much better at getting the job done?"

I took another sip.

"Maybe these Pakistani kids would be used to stage an attack, knowing they would be killed or captured, and Iranian passports found on them, but the kill shot would be by someone else, someone much more capable, who would get away. Maybe they are taking out the Pakistanis because we got on their trail, especially after we captured Munaf, but maybe they will keep their real shooter in play because we'll get complacent and think it's all over when we have the Pakistanis off the board. Maybe the plot against your President is very much on. Or maybe you're right, if there ever was such a plot, they are just in clean-up mode, but with so many of us at least guessing what their plan was, they can't realistically clean up and leave all of us behind to talk about it. That still means a risk for all of us and our families."

I looked at Amy to see her reaction.

She was fast asleep, her head resting on the sofa. I picked her up and carried her into my bedroom and kissed her forehead before lying down next to her. I whispered, to nobody in particular.

"I wish we got a lucky break for a change."

As I drifted off to sleep in Amy's arms, I should have remembered what they say about being careful what you wish for.

***

When the doorbell rang, I thought I was dreaming. Then it rang again.

I looked at my watch on the bedside. It was 03:02 AM.

Who the fuck had come calling at this time?

As I got out of bed and began to head to the door, I stopped. Yes, assassins wouldn't normally ring doorbells before coming and after the last attack, two police constables were posted downstairs. But then, one could never be too sure. The bloodstains on the wall near my door, which had not fully come off despite all the scrubbing, bore testimony to that. I took my Glock in one hand, khukri in the other, and went to the door, looking through the eyehole.

It was Sharma.

As I opened the door, he took a look at the weapons in my hands and his eyes opened wide.

"Jesus, thankfully you check before you fire."

I let him into the drawing room.

"What are you doing here at this time?"

"I tried calling you, but your phone's off."

Tell me about it. I hadn't exactly wanted Bethune or his spooks to listen in on me and Amy and had kept it off. I had got a new encrypted phone from the office, but that number had only been given to Srini and Ma, in case they needed to get in touch with me.

"What's up?"

Sharma was the kind of guy who perhaps in another life, would have had a better fit as a software engineer or accountant than a spy. Whenever I had seen him, he had been intense, focused, and serious, but now he was literally hopping with excitement.

"We caught a big break!"

That was a welcome change. I asked Sharma if he wanted to sit down, but he said he wanted me to go with him.

"Where? At this time?"

"Just come with me. I'll tell you along the way. We can't waste too much time. I've already called Shukla Sir and he's coming, and maybe you want to tell your boss. We've got one of the assassins alive."

That jolted me fully awake. If we had managed to get one of them alive, then perhaps we could finally find a way of getting to the masterminds behind the attacks. I went back into the bedroom and Amy was awake, looking up groggily at me.

"Why are you putting on your sweatshirt and jeans? What time is it?"

I kissed her on the forehead.

"Hey, something's come up at work. I need to go. You sleep in as late as you want, and I guess I should be back by morning."

I don't know if she registered what time it was, or memories of the night of the attack came to her, but she sat upright, clutching at my hand.

"Don't go! Please, don't go."

"Hey, Amy. Sharma's in the living room and he says he's got a lead I need to see. We so desperately need a break given everything else that's happening. It can't take too long."

She refused to let go of my hand.

"I don't want to be alone here."

I sat down next to her on the bed.

"Hey, there are two cops downstairs."

"I'll come with you."

I shook my head and gently took her hand off me.

"Amy, I've got you into enough trouble with your bosses. No way am I taking you out on an operation at this time of night. There will be no reason for you being out there other than you being with me, and that would further damage you professionally."

"Aadi, please, I have an awfully bad feeling. With all the attacks, I don't want you to be hurt."

This was a very different Amy from the one I had seen shoot two men, who had dealt with the dangers we were facing with strength and courage. She seemed to be on the verge of tears, but I had a duty of my own. I had an obligation to get to the ones who had killed so many in the pursuit of their objectives and had come after Ma.

"Amy, they've captured someone alive, and I need to be there."

She was crying now, but I couldn't stay back just because of that. I knew she was concerned for me, but I could not hide in my home if there was a chance we were one step closer to getting to our enemies. I dressed, put on a jacket, under which I concealed my weapons, and headed out. If Sharma had heard Amy's voice, he was discreet enough to not show any reaction when I came out of the bedroom. On the way, I called Srini and told him what Sharma had shared. Srini had sounded grumpy and sleepy when I woke him up, but my words had the same effect on him that Sharma's had on me.

"Boss, this joker came into a small police post on the highway just an hour ago, said there were men out to kill him. They would have just kept him here and sent him on his way in the morning, thinking he was involved in some fight over drinks, women, or money, but then he said he wanted them to call someone senior in Indian intelligence, that he was someone sent on a terror mission through Nepal. He even has a bloody Iranian passport on him. They must have called the IB control room because Sharma got a flash message from them within minutes, knowing he was on the lookout for such fine young men."

"Who else knows, Sen?"

"Just us, Sharma and Shukla."

"Good, keep it tight. We've learned the hard way that when too many people know what we're up to, bad things happen. I'm on my way there as well."

That didn't seem right to me.

"Sir, at this time, you shouldn't be out alone. Get your security officer along, and your driver. Maybe come in the morning when we've got this guy secured. By then, I'll sort out who this guy is and what he knows."

He thought about that for a second.

"That makes sense, but I can't wait till morning. These bastards have caused too much damage. I'll get my gunman and ask him to drive, but I'm coming as soon as I can. I can't wait till my driver shows up."

"Sir, please don't rush. We're up against some pretty nasty people and I need to be sure you'll be safe. Get there when you can but don't come alone. We're headed to a small post beyond Noida, pretty much well on the way to the highway leading to Agra. No real milestones to talk about, but Sharma will send you a link on Google Maps."

As we continued on our way, it was pitch black outside. We had long passed the packed housing societies and markets of Noida and now all around us were fields and the Hindon river in the distance, just visible in the moonlight. I gripped my gun involuntarily. Sharma looked over at me.

"Everything okay?"

I kept looking at the road ahead. Salil had asked me to think like a soldier and everything I had learned as a soldier was telling me that the area around me, the time of night, the fact that we had so many of our key players converging on one place made it great for the enemy if they wanted to get us all together. So far, our enemy had proven to be resourceful, ruthless, and always ahead of us.

Fuck.

Were we heading into an ambush?

"Sharma, do you have a gun?"

He looked at me strangely.

"No, and I've never fired one after our initial training years ago. Even then, I wasn't exactly at the top of the class when it came to firearms. I'm an analyst, not a field agent."

Double fuck.

"Check with Shukla if he's bringing his guard along."

He messaged Shukla and then looked up at me.

"Actually, he's coming alone. He was so excited at getting a break after we lost Pillai Sir that he wants to see this son of a bitch as soon as we can."

Triple fuck.

"Okay, now this is important, so please listen carefully. This place we're headed to, this is a proper police station, right?"

"What does that mean?"

"I mean, with cops who have guns and presumably know how to use them. How many cops would there be in a police station, anyways?"

He thought that one over.

"To be honest, I have no idea how many are at this post, but in bigger stations, there could be over a hundred cops. Even if this is smaller, there should be a few around."

That was a bit reassuring.

"Just drive as fast as you humanly can. How much longer till we get there?"

"Ten minutes, I guess."

"Drive fast and tell Shukla to get there as fast as he can."

A couple of minutes later, I turned to Sharma.

"Are we there yet?"

He looked at me strangely once again.

"Now you're worrying me. Is everything okay?"

"Yeah. Just get there as fast as we can. I don't like the idea of any of us being out here in the dark, alone."

"This is just Noida, man."

I snapped at him, and the look on my face shut him up.

"We're at war and this is a combat zone."

He didn't speak after that.

"Hey, sorry for snapping at you, but are you sure there will be a bunch of cops with guns there?"

He took a deep breath.

"Yeah."

"Good."

If I'd known what we were actually headed for, I'd have added a quadruple fuck to the list.

***

The police station I had been hoping for turned out to be a small building with two rooms on the side of the road. As we came closer, I thought that my hopes of dozens of well-armed cops had just gone out the window. Waiting for us outside the post was an inspector and two excited-looking constables. Sharma announced who he was, and they saluted and when he whispered that I was an army officer, they saluted again. The inspector called me inside the post. The first room had a small table and two chairs, and the second room, while dark other than the light coming in from the front room, seemed to be a mixture of a storeroom and kitchen, with a couple of boxes, a stove on the side and the outline of a man in the corner.

"Sir, he's the terrorist we captured."

One of the constables had made the announcement with the pride and excitement that may have been more appropriate if he had engaged and captured a vicious, armed terrorist in single combat versus having him walk up to them and surrender. The inspector turned on a light and I got my first good look at our guest. He was young, perhaps in his early twenties, looked as if he had been roughed up, with a bloodied nose and torn shirt, and was handcuffed to a gas cylinder.

"How did he get here? He couldn't just have walked here from wherever he came."

The inspector shook his head.

"He got off a truck he had taken a lift in. Ran straight in, waking us all up, saying people were out to kill him."

I paused to get a better look at the cops. They were all pot-bellied, with their shirts half tucked in, and one of them wasn't even wearing his shoes. Well, I guess with the kind of duty they had, sitting by the side of the highway, watching for errant truck drivers in the biting cold, one could understand why they wouldn't exactly be parade ground ready.

"Just the three of you here?"

The inspector stiffened.

"Sir, the sanctioned strength is ten, but you know with the cold and the pretty light duties we have, some of the boys go to the bigger station nearby. We rotate who stays here."

I pointed to the prisoner.

"Did he get hurt by the guys who were after him?"

The man chained to the cylinder spoke up.

"No, these cops beat me up."

I looked at the cops again and the inspector had the look of a little boy caught with his hand in the cookie jar.

"Sir, here's a real terrorist, or so he says. We thought we'd give him a couple of slaps for all the boys in uniform these bastards have killed."

I took a deep breath and turned to the prisoner.

"What's your story?"

He shrugged.

"Get me to some senior intelligence officers and I'll tell them."

I took out the khukri from its scabbard and held it up in the light, inches from the man's face.

"You've obviously mistaken me for someone who will take any shit from you. Talk or I start cutting."

He spat at me, and I slashed him across the face. Not too deep, but deep enough. The idea wasn't to slice his face off but to let him know I meant business. I think he got the idea. His eyes were wide open in shock. I guess whatever he had expected and whoever he had expected to meet, he hadn't figured on meeting someone who would happily cut his face off. Bleeding freely from his cut cheek he began blabbering.

"I'm from near Mirpur."

"I knew a boy from there. Munaf. I caught him and broke his hand. Friend of yours?"

He shook his head, but his eyes said otherwise.

"He blabbered a lot before he died on us, so tell me something I don't know. Where's the seventh guy who's coming in?"

His eyes were wide in fear, but it was clear he had no idea what I was talking about. Munaf must have picked up that piece of gossip on his own.

"Who was trying to kill you?"

"Fuckers double-crossed me. A guy met me at the Old Delhi station where I had been asked to go and took me to a small hotel in Noida. Tonight, he and another man came to kill me. I managed to get away and got on a truck and kept hiding till I saw some cops."

I turned to Sharma.

"How far is Shukla?"

He made the call, but he didn't even need to finish his question when we heard the sound of an approaching car. Shukla came into the post, looking as excited as the constables. Looking at him, Sharma stood at attention, and the cops seeing an IB officer stiffen at the arrival of an older man, correctly surmised that the new visitor was a senior officer, stood and saluted.

"Is this the son of a bitch?"

"Yes, sir."

Shukla grinned at me.

"Finally, we get a break. I'll call the Home Ministry to get a good safe house organized where we can keep him out of harm's way and also call in some boys to take him away."

Meanwhile, I called Srini.

"Sir, where are you? Looks like we have a legit capture."

He whooped in delight, something so out of character for Srini that I hoped his driver wasn't startled enough to crash the car.

"Shukla Sir is here and is arranging a safe house and some boys to get him there."

"Google says I'm just ten minutes away, Sen. I guess Shukla's smart calling in reinforcements, but if he's alone, we have my security officer and you, and between the two of you, you could take him away to the safe house. Will be faster, and I don't like the idea of this guy being in the open any longer than he needs to be. If there were two men out to kill him, and they're still looking for him, they may well figure out soon where he is."

I told Shukla what Srini had suggested and he nodded.

"Makes sense. If Srini's got his gunman with him, we should be okay. Plus, this man doesn't look like he'll be much trouble with you holding that bloodied khukri at his face."

Sharma laughed, and the cops joined in. Just then, Sharma's phone beeped. He looked at it with a confused expression.

"What is it?"

"It's a flash message from the Control Room saying that some local cops have a man they believe I may have interest in."

I took his phone and looked at the message.

"I thought they already messaged you. How long ago was that?"

"About an hour."

The Inspector chipped in.

"He landed just over an hour ago and after we figured he wasn't just another drunk, I called the IB Control Room. With all the terrorists running wild, we were instructed to call the Control Room if we saw anything the IB may have interest in."

"Why would they send two messages, Sharma?"

He looked at his phone and opened up the previous message.

"Beats me, but the timing of the second message is normal. The guy taking the call would call the Duty Officer, who would figure out based on current investigations who should get the message, so it normally takes half an hour, and at this time of night, might take a bit more. It's strange how fast the first message came in."

He looked at the messages in more detail.

"Something's strange. The second message just says there's a person of interest related to my investigation. The first message has more details like the Iranian passport."

I noticed the prisoner doing something peculiar. He was staring at the pocket of his shirt and muttering something.

"What the hell are you doing?"

The man looked up and began to protest his innocence when I grabbed the pocket and tore it off cleanly. What I saw inside it made me freeze. I pulled out the object inside the pocket and stamped on it with my boot, breaking it. I turned to the inspector in anger.

"You guys didn't even check what he was carrying! For all you know he could be wired up with a bomb!"

He sheepishly shrugged his shoulders.

"Sir, we checked for weapons…what is the matter?"

I held up the shattered black object I had stepped on.

"He was wired. Someone was hearing everything we said."

I took a deep breath and tried to control myself. These were poor street cops who had no experience of such things. No point in taking out my frustration and anger on them. Shukla was looking puzzled.

"Why would they wire him?"

Our prisoner now had his eyes closed, his palms turned upwards and he was muttering, his head swaying back and forth. Sharma shook him, but he just shrugged him off and continued.

"What the fuck is he doing?"

Sharma had never seen something like this, but I had. Just before a suicide bomber detonated his vest. Just before a cornered jihadi came out, aiming to go out in a blaze of glory. Just before I had slit Mullah Azam's throat. I knew the answer, and I dreaded putting it into words because I knew only too well what came next.

"He's preparing to die. He's declaring his faith and reciting his last prayers."

Shukla was looking at him, eyes wide open in shock.

"What does that mean?"

"That means, Sir, that we've been set up. This guy was the bait and we fell for it. They'll be coming for us now and he is praying because he knows he will die along with the rest of us."

The quiet of the night outside was shattered by the sound of what I immediately knew was automatic weapons fire. The deep, rattling sound of an AK-47 being fired on full auto, soon joined by several other rifles. Then the sound of a car screeching and a loud crash. I ran out of the post and saw the lightning-like muzzle flash of a Kalashnikov being fired on full auto, pouring its bullets out at 600 rounds per minute at its target. Then there was silence and darkness again. I called Srini, but there was no response. Shit, they had ambushed Srini's car, knowing he was coming with a guard armed with an automatic weapon of his own. It was hard to judge perfectly given I had seen only one muzzle flash, but I guessed our attackers were still five minutes away if they were driving towards us, perhaps longer if they were coming on foot.

I went back in and told everyone to gather around. I first addressed the cops.

"How much firepower do you have?"

The inspector took out his service revolver from his belt.

"Sir, I have this. With six bullets."

"And your men?"

He looked down at the ground.

"They don't have guns. The rifles are normally kept at the bigger station."

"Call them and ask them to send reinforcements now. We will be hit in no more than ten minutes."

His eyes widened as one of his men made the call.

"Sir, they will take at least thirty minutes to get here. I know how lazy these bastards are."

I turned to Shukla, and he shook his head.

"Sorry, Major. I'm unarmed."

Fuck.

I noticed some movement in the corner.

"What's that?"

One of the constables grinned.

"We have three chickens."

As if things were not messed up enough, why were there chickens in a police post?

The constable looked sheepishly at his boss.

"Sir likes eggs."

Our prisoner had stopped praying and looked at me and smiled.

"You will all go to hell."

I took a piece of cloth lying on the side and gagged him with it.

"Strip the bastard, put a police uniform on him, free him from that cylinder and handcuff his hands behind his back."

"Free him, sir?"

I glared at the constable.

"We're about to get into combat, so do as I fucking say, and you may yet live."

He shut up and got to work.

I asked Shukla and Sharma to hide in the back room and call whoever they could call for help.

"I want to help."

I patted Sharma on the shoulder.

"You have a family?"

"Yes, wife and two sons."

"Well, then help by staying alive for them. Call anyone who'll listen- the NSG, the Home Ministry, IB, R&AW, the bloody Pope. Get someone to come here fast. And stay back here. Whatever you do, whatever you hear, don't come out. You can't run from our attackers and there's no help to be had anywhere close. Our only hope is to delay them long enough till help gets here."

I turned to the inspector.

"Your chickens just got drafted into my army. Free them."

Our prisoner was beginning to kick and struggle and I walked up to him and cut off three of his fingers with the khukri. His eyes widened in shock, and if the cloth had not been wrapped around his mouth, I'm sure he would have woken up societies in far off Noida with his scream.

"I've had it with your shit. You want to die and meet houris in the afterlife, right? Well, I'll let you die and then go fuck those houris. The question is whether I cut your heart out here or I give you one last chance to run for it. What will it be?"

He quit struggling after that. I asked the constables to do what I told them and then get back into the post and join Shukla and Sharma. No point in them getting massacred. I looked at the inspector.

"Ever killed anyone?"

His hand was shaking as he replied.

"No, sir. Haven't fired the gun in years."

"Just remember that the fuckers coming for us are the same sort who kill our boys in uniform. Same breed who slaughter unarmed civilians. Same bastards who behead people on TV. We may die, but let's get some payback for all of them, and take a few of these bastards to hell with us. You with me? You don't need to kill anyone or even fire your gun unless these bastards get through me and get close to the post, but you can help me a lot."

He nodded as I gave him his instructions.

And then we waited.

One soldier with certified mental health issues, a pot-bellied inspector, two terrified policemen with sticks, and two unarmed spies who spent their careers sitting at desks. Armed with two handguns, a khukri, three chickens, and a gas cylinder. Up against an unknown number of highly trained killers armed with automatic weapons.

If I were a betting man, I wouldn't have bet on us.

But then, I wasn't a betting man. I was a man who had walked into Tibet and walked back with a Chinese helmet. I was a man who bit off the ear of a Chechen mercenary in hand-to-hand combat. I was a man who cut off enemy heads when they took my brother's heads. I was a man who sang at night with my comrades about those we had lost and those we had killed. I was a man who still had nightmares about the brothers I had lost and the men I had killed, but I was no longer scared of those nightmares. I took strength from them because when you had seen what I had seen, done what I had done, and still were able to carry on, you became more than just a man.

You became a warrior.

And tonight, I would fight for all of us. Gurung, Thapa, Pillai, Sean, Soleimani, Azfal, and many others. People who had died because they were doing what they thought was right. Killed by bastards who thought that they could get away with it because they had power, they had money, they had connections and they were willing to kill to have their way.

I walked out of the post and as I heard the sound of approaching footsteps, I felt a peace I had never felt. The peace that came with accepting the fact that I might well die, but that I would fight and die to try and keep alive those with me who were unarmed and unable to fight back.

I had lived a warrior's life, perhaps it was time to die a warrior's death.

***

I still couldn't see our attackers clearly, they were mere shadows in the darkness, but I could hear them clearly enough. Whoever they were, they perhaps weren't the former Navy SEALs and Special Forces men I had gone up against. They were walking down the road with pretty poor noise discipline. Their shoes or sandals scraped the ground, their rifles brushed up against the ammunition belts around their chests. Maybe they were trained as trigger pullers but never really learned the finer points of tactics. Maybe they were overconfident. Or maybe they knew just how hopeless our situation was. They had set this up carefully, and I had no doubt they knew the lack of men and firepower at this station. They would guess I would be armed but they would have figured they could send enough firepower to take care of me easily, especially since they would have thought they had an element of total surprise on their side.

That pissed me off even more. The fact that these men, these half-educated louts, these apes with Kalashnikovs, could think I would be easy prey. I tried hard to control my rising anger and channel it into rage. Anger was like a flame that burned out of control, burning everything in its path, burning you. Rage was something you could hope to control and direct against the target you wanted to turn to ashes. I had walked some twenty feet along the side of the road away from the post, towards our attackers and then I knelt on the ground and whistled once when I judged our attackers were close enough. The Inspector did his job well, and the door to the post opened and a man in uniform stumbled out, walking wildly from left to right. At a distance, you might think he was drunk or had just woken up and was disoriented. Two separate muzzle flashes erupted just ahead of me as two of our attackers opened up on what they took to be a policeman out on patrol. The idiots fired on full auto, missing with most of their shots, but enough hit home to send their target spinning like a rag doll to the ground. The tourist from Pakistan who had arrived with hopes of martyrdom and glory had just been shot by his own side. I took aim at the nearest muzzle flash and fired again and again, till the flame of the muzzle flash suddenly jerked up and then was extinguished.

One down.

I ran on as fast as I could, lest the fallen man's buddies target my own muzzle flash, but no shots came. These men had come expecting easy hunting, and it took time for them to process that they were the ones being hunted. I whistled again and phase two of our operation unfolded as the inspector let loose his three precious chickens. Our feathered warriors ran off here and there, panicked by the sounds, and one idiot began firing at them. Someone shouted at him to stop, but in war, it's the stupid who die first. I aimed at his muzzle flash and emptied my clip, bringing him down. This time, his buddies were firing back at me and I slipped and dove down the slippery slope beside the road as bullets careened off the ground near me.

Two down.

At least two more left.

I replaced the clip in my gun and crawled back towards the post, hoping the men would stick to their mission- of taking out helpless senior intelligence officers stuck inside the post, and not come hunting me. I flattened myself against the ground and whistled again and a third time the inspector held his nerve and didn't fail me. If you ask me, he was the bloody hero of the night. It's easier to fire a gun at an enemy when you've trained for it for much of your adult life and done it countless times. It's much harder, and much braver, to hold your nerve and do what you're supposed to under enemy fire when you've never been shot at before. I vowed to buy the inspector as many drinks as he wanted and to buy him a bunch of new chickens if any of his precious flock had been hurt. Provided we all made it out alive, that is.

A rolling sound. The gas cylinder sent rolling down the slight slope towards our attackers.

Shit. This part of our plan didn't quite go as I had hoped. Nobody fired at the cylinder and I had no new targets. The dumb ones had fallen for our feints and died. The ones left standing were smarter, better trained, or just wizened up by what had happened to their buddies and they kept going towards the post. I could see them now. Two men, wearing black, holding AK-47s, both walking in a crouch on the opposite side of the road from me. One of them reached into a pouch at his waist, pulled something out, and threw it.

A grenade.

Well, so much for me thinking through a plan. I had counted on being up against men with automatic weapons and those odds were bad enough. I emptied my clip into the man, and he spun and fell to the ground as his buddy dove to the side of the road and opened fire at me. I lay down flat to take cover and then looked up to see an explosion rock the front of the post. The door was hanging open askew and I could see a leg sticking out from behind it. The Inspector had perhaps paid for his heroism with his life.

I could hear multiple footsteps now. Just as I had used the idiot jihadi prisoner and chickens as feints, they had used their cannon-fodder to go in first and be the first to fall. They would have known they were not attacking defenseless civilians but a bunch of trained intel officers and cops. They may not have known just how poorly armed we were but would not have sent in their A-team first, without finding out what they were up against. I kept myself flattened against the ground. I thought I could make out three separate patterns of footsteps. One paused and proceeded again, the sounds getting progressively louder. Okay, so one had made his way towards me to finish me off while the others went on to the post. Perhaps they had thought there were armed men inside, so they had been a bit cautious. With no resistance forthcoming from the post, perhaps they had begun to understand the reality of just how helpless Shukla, Sharma, and the cops were, and if I were in their shoes, I wouldn't even bother firing. I would just lob grenades into the post till everyone inside was finished.

I heard the thud of a grenade exploding and realized they had done as I had feared they would. I wondered how the men inside the post were holding up and prayed that they would have taken cover behind the table at least. I knew what a grenade could do to soft human tissue in a confined space like that only too well, and also knew that without any combat training or experience, the men inside were ill-prepared to deal with such a threat. I couldn't do anything to help till I dealt with the threat approaching me.

The footsteps came closer and then stopped. I stilled my breath, keeping myself flat against the side of the road. I felt gravel cascade down over my shoulders and head as the man stood just above me, kicking the ground in frustration. He had been rather good to guess where I was and had come straight to my position. His problem was that he had assumed I would be trying to escape, and he was peering into the distance, trying to see where I was. Ahead of us were bare, open fields, and if I had been making a break for it through them, he would have spotted me in the moonlight and shot me down. Of course, unfortunately for him, I had no intention of running. As I heard his feet move, perhaps as he was turning around to signal something to his buddies, I bent my knees and elbows and brought myself leaping out from my hiding place. I grabbed his waist and tackled him down to the ground and before he could fight back, I had slashed him across the throat with my khukri. He screamed once before he died, but that was enough to get the attention of his buddies and they began firing at me, not the spraying and praying their first line had done, but carefully aimed single shots. One bullet hit the man below me as I pulled him up as a human shield, and then as I tried to roll out back to the side of the road and return fire, I felt a searing pain on my left shoulder as a bullet grazed me.

Then someone else was shooting.

Sharma. Holding the Inspector's pistol, standing at the entrance of the post, firing away at the two attackers. He seemed to be walking unsteadily and was perhaps already wounded by the grenade, but he kept firing.

'No, get back inside!'

He either didn't hear me or didn't want to, because he kept coming. In real life, when a heroic, untrained man with a revolver takes on two trained men with AK-47s, there can be only one outcome. Unfortunately, real life is not like the movies and the heroic, good guys don't always win. One of the men turned towards Sharma and fired three shots at him. Sharma staggered back as the first round hit his chest and the second took him in the shoulder, felling him. I was so pissed off at a good man dying trying to save me that I forgot about taking cover and emptied my clip at the man who had shot Sharma. I don't know how many of my shots hit him, but he was dead by the time he hit the ground. The last attacker was now facing me, his rifle raised, and for a second, I felt a clarity I had never felt before.

I knew I was about to die.

I could have tried to bring my gun around, but I was out of bullets and out of time. Instead, I thought of Ma, and how she would have to deal alone with the death of another person in her life. I hoped she would be as brave she had always been. Then I thought of Amy. A relationship which perhaps had no future, yet one I would miss terribly. She was a lover, a friend, and perhaps more than all of those, a soulmate- someone who had finally understood and accepted me for who and what I was. I sighed, closed my eyes, and lowered my gun as the man pressed the trigger.

The bullet whizzed past my ear as I heard several more shots different from the harsh, guttural bark of a Kalashnikov- the duller sounds of a handgun being fired repeatedly. The man fell as his unseen attacker kept firing at his prone body. When I dove, opening my eyes, confused at what had happened, relieved at being alive, wondering who had come to my rescue, I heard police sirens on the road ahead. Several vehicles came screaming in, lights flashing, coming to a stop around me.

The cops were shouting something, and I just sat there, staring at the police post. At Sharma's body in front of it. One of the cops grabbed my ID which I had held up without realizing it, and more cops seemed to have come out of nowhere. It was like a scene out of a bad movie, where the cops come when all the fighting's done and take the bad guys away. Except here there was nothing to be taken away other than a bunch of corpses. I don't know how long I sat there by the side of the road, but a couple of ambulances came by, one of them speeding up ahead to the site of where Srini's car had been ambushed, and the other dropping medics who began to check for signs of life among the many bodies scattered around me.

I heard someone say that everyone was dead other than Sharma, who was barely alive.

Everyone. Except me. Once again, cursed to live when other, better men with me died. I had failed miserably. I should have listened to my instinct that we were headed into trouble and called off our trip. I should have asked Shukla and Srini to turn around and not come to this place. I should have made a better plan for dealing with our attackers.

Instead, I had failed, and good men had died as a result.

I was sick of it all. I gripped my gun tight, wondering what it would feel like to put it in my mouth and end it all. Just then, a cop came and sat next to me, asking a medic to come and dress my wound.

"Sir, you'll be okay. The bullet seems to have just grazed you. You are lucky."

No, just cursed.

When he didn't get any response from me, he tentatively continued.

"We checked the IDs and there are two IB officers in there, one dead and one barely alive and one R&AW officer down the road, seriously injured, but his driver or gunman is dead."

I exhaled loudly as I processed that at least Srini was still alive.

"Anyone else made it?"

His voice was low.

"No, sir. All the policemen are dead as well."

"What was the Inspector's name? I never even asked him his name."

The cop looked at me and smiled sadly.

"Sir, that was Balwant Singh, a good man."

I lowered my head.

"Not a good man, a hero."

The cop's tone was hesitant as he continued.

"I checked who you are, Sir. I don't know what happened here, some undercover operation, I suppose, but from everything I can see, you killed six terrorists all on your own. I'd seen your photo in the papers when you won the Ashoka Chakra in Kashmir. It's an honor seeing you in person."

I didn't say anything. There was nothing heroic about failing the men you were supposed to protect. Then something the man said cut through the fog in my mind.

"I didn't kill the last guy. I think one of your men shot him. Thank whoever that was. He saved my life."

The cop looked bewildered.

"Sir, none of my men got a chance to fire. When we got here, all the terrorists were dead."

I sat up straight, turning to stare into the darkness from where had come the shots that had saved my life. I kept looking at the blackness as my shoulder was bandaged.

Who had just saved my life?

***

EPISODE EIGHT

CHECKMATE

I got home after more than an hour at the police station, answering questions, identifying the dead, and in general, feeling numb. The cops dropped me home and I walked into the bedroom, peeled off my bloody shirt, dropped it on the ground, and lay down on the bed. Amy turned to face me immediately and sat up, her eyes full of concern.

"Are you okay?"

I had no energy left, I had nothing left in me.

I fell asleep.

When I woke up, I smelled coffee and something cooking. As I sat up, I felt a bit of a tug in my left shoulder. The bullet may have just grazed me, but I would feel its effects for a long time. My clothes had been taken off the floor and when I checked the time, it was past ten in the morning. Amy came in, fully dressed for work and carrying a tray with coffee, eggs, and toast on it.

"Eat. After what you've been through, you need to eat

something."

I began to wolf down the food and then looked up at her.

"Last night..."

She just pointed to the food.

"Keep eating. The news channels are full of stories about a big shoot-out in which several cops and terrorists died. Not much by way of details, but is that where you were?"

My voice was a low whisper.

"They ambushed us. They killed everyone at the post other than Sharma, though I don't know if he made it. Srini is in hospital as well. Only I got away relatively unhurt."

She felt my left shoulder and when I winced, she kissed me.

"Thank God you made it out okay. What will you do now?"

That was a good question. I had never felt this defeated and helpless before. I had no idea what I would do.

"I really don't know. This is too big for me. I don't know what to do."

"Aadi, you've done more than anyone else would, more than anyone else would expect. What happened to the guy you said was caught?

"He's dead as well."

"Doesn't that mean six of the seven are gone? Isn't the terror plot pretty much finished then?"

I didn't share her optimism.

"Maybe, but who are these guys taking all of them out and now taking us out? The plot involving the guys coming in from Nepal may be more or less over, but whatever else was cooking could still be on."

She sat down next to me on the bed.

"I don't know. If they had some sort of plot they were trying to remove all traces of, they seem to have done so, other than the one guy left. Given what they've done, they'll take care of him as well. Look, I have no idea who else is involved and whether Bethune is actually involved as you suspected, but if there are rogue CIA officers involved, they don't do things just to keep some vendetta going. They've sent the message they wanted to send- that you guys shouldn't come in their way, and when it wasn't heeded, they struck in a pretty serious way. You have no proof of their involvement so you can't threaten them in any way. Maybe they'll just leave if you leave them alone."

I put down the coffee and stared at her.

"Amy, I can't leave it alone, not after last night. Those bastards killed a whole lot of good men."

She looked disappointed in my reply.

"Aadi, I don't want anything to happen to you, and you can't fight this war all by yourself."

I had no answer to that. As it was, I had pretty much reached the same conclusion myself. Perhaps it was just my pride, my stubbornness, and my desire to avenge fallen comrades that were keeping me going.

"Hey, I need to go to the Embassy. My bosses have called a meeting later today to talk about the President's visit and once that show gets on the road, I'll be really busy. Why don't you take a couple of days off and we can spend some time together?"

She kissed me again, but this time, I was so worked up that her kiss was not enough to mollify me.

"Amy, I can't let it go. I have no idea what to do, but I can't let it go. I'm going to go to the office and see what I can think of."

She was visibly disappointed and left for work, asking me to call her when I was done at work.

***

I had once hated sitting in the office, but now, sitting alone in the office, I missed it all. I missed Salil coming up and asking if we could sneak out for a kabab or offer to buy a drink when I had a particularly bad day; I missed Srini's ability to cut through issues and get to solutions and somehow, despite all my issues, have faith in me; I also missed Sean. Yes, I hated him as a boss but seeing his empty office didn't feel right. Srini's secretary, Betty, peeked into my cabin and knocked.

"Sir, here are the printouts you wanted."

When you're in the line of work I was in, you were wise to keep your will updated and signed and your insurance payout beneficiaries updated. I signed a couple of the insurance forms and handed them to Betty. I didn't have much in the world, and what I did would of course go to Ma, but I wanted to make sure that my insurance payout would be enough to help pay for the experimental drugs she was on and to have clear instructions so that Ma knew where all my savings and few investments were so she would not have any trouble accessing them. It was morbid work, as I suppose planning for your own death must be, but it needed to be done. That didn't mean it did anything to improve my mood. After everything that had happened, I needed to take seriously the possibility that I might be the next to fall to our enemies, and I had to keep things in order if that happened.

There was another knock on the door. It was the cop from the previous night, the one who had sat with me on the road and along with him, DCP Niladri Banerjee. Both sat down in front of me, without being invited in, and Banerjee offered his hand. As I shook it, he took out a sheaf of papers he had.

"Major, first of all, accept my condolences for the losses among your comrades. We too lost three men last night, and I know how hard it is to lose men."

I wanted to get going with what I had in mind, and my impatience must have shown for he quickly moved on to what he actually wanted.

"We're trying to understand what happened last night. Clearly, a terror cell attacked you when you had gone to take into custody the man who had come to the police post. We have already got mails from the IB saying that the man was part of the cell you were tracking. That man had an Indian passport on him, and we checked your previous files and hypotheses, and it matches. Same date of issue as the others you'd tracked coming in from Nepal. We've also got an ID on the five attackers you killed last night. Three of them are known local jihadis. We have their social media posts talking about unleashing jihad and so on. Clearly, they took their jihad further than typing on their keyboards. The two others are more interesting. No ID on them, and their fingerprints don't show up on any of our databases. Both have many scars on their bodies, indicating hard men, who had been in battle before."

More of the trained mercenaries our friends had been sending our way, I guessed, as Banerjee continued.

"What we can't figure out, Major, is what caused the man to get there. You've told my men what that terrorist said, but there was no such attack reported in any hotel in the area."

"Sir, that was a setup. I think he was sent as bait to lure us in and then the plan was to have the kill team come in and finish us."

His eyes widened as he took that in.

"Well, it has been a tragic loss of life, but the Home Ministry is pleased. Of the seven attackers who you thought were coming in from Nepal, six are now known to be neutralized. Whatever their plan was, it must be impossible to carry out."

"What do you and the Ministry make of the men who killed the four at Jama Masjid, came for me and then hit us last night? Who do you think they are?"

Banerjee seemed confident in his reply.

"Their jihadi friends and handlers, I suppose. Once they learned you were on their trail, they were trying to clean up their tracks and also stop you. I suppose they couldn't afford to risk having their men captured alive. After all, a live capture of a terrorist who was trained by Pakistan and sent here would be a disaster for their masters across the border. That's what the official IB report says, by the way. We just got that sent our way from the Home Ministry."

Pillai wouldn't have written that, and Shukla knew better. Unfortunately, both were now dead and in no position to contradict whatever rubbish was being passed up the line by the IB. So, who was providing the official IB report that was convincing the Ministry that all was under control?

As Banerjee got up to leave, something he said struck me.

"Sir, did your men find an Iranian passport on the terrorist who had come to the post?"

He looked puzzled.

"Iranian? No, there's no mention of that."

Sharma had mentioned that the guy had an Iranian passport. That was part of the reason I had been so ready to go there, why I had not pushed hard for Srini to hold off. Getting our hands on an Iranian passport on the terrorist would have been our first real proof of the plot we suspected. If there had been no Iranian passport, why would the cops tell the IB there was one?

The IB.

Balwant had called the IB Control Room, and they had sent on a message to Sharma. I remembered that Sharma had got two messages from the Control Room. The first had been unnaturally fast and had mentioned the Iranian passport. The second had come much later when we had been at the police post and had made no mention of the passport. If our enemies had penetrated our systems, chances were that they could have done the same with the IB. Also, if Banerjee was right and the IB was passing on memos that gave a nice, sanitized, and palatable view of what was happening, not what we actually suspected, then perhaps it went deeper than just hacking into systems.

Could there be an insider in the IB working for the enemy? One who had the message sent to Sharma that got us to the post in such a hurry, and one who was also passing up a version of events to the political bosses which ignored all the concerns we had.

***

A few calls established that Shukla reported to an Additional Director called Ravindran. An Additional Director in the IB was a big deal and before I did anything else, I went to see Salil. He was well on his way to recovery and thanked me for the kababs I took for him.

"How long before you're discharged?"

"Maybe a day or two. What's up? You look glum."

When I told him what had happened, he left the kababs uneaten.

"Fuck."

"Yeah, fuck. Srini's alive but severely injured. I checked on Sharma. That now is a real hero, and he's lucky to be alive, but he's hooked up to a ventilator and will take a lot of time to recover. These guys have really got our number."

I told him about my suspicion about someone in the IB helping our enemies.

"How likely is it that a senior officer is working for the enemy?"

He wasn't as shocked as I thought he would have been.

"It's happened before. In the nineties, an IB Additional Director called Sehgal was suspected of spying for the CIA. He disappeared, probably spirited away by his handlers, and settled down in the US. A few years after that, one of our own, an R&AW Joint Director called Rabinder Singh, was caught spying for the CIA. He escaped to the US via Nepal using a fake passport and lived there before dying in 2016 in an accident."

"Accident?"

He shrugged his shoulders.

"Hey, maybe it was a real accident, maybe he was becoming too much of a liability for his hosts, but this shit happens."

I put a folder next to his bed.

"What's in that, Sen?"

"Ma's medical files and details. When you get out, please do me a favor and look after her."

He sat up straight.

"What are you saying?"

"I'm just going to take your advice. I'm going to be a soldier, and sometimes soldiers don't come back."

Srini was fully conscious though a bit drowsy from all the painkillers and sedatives they had given him. As far as I had been able to understand, his personal guard had saved his life. When the attackers opened up with AK-47s, he had turned the car off the road. He had been hit by several bullets and killed but Srini had not suffered a single gunshot wound. With Srini having his seat belt on and the airbags deploying, he had still suffered fractures and a broken arm when the car had traveled several hundred meters off the side of the road down the slope towards the river and then overturned. Their attackers, in a rush to get the main ambush site and knowing we would have heard the gunfire, would have moved on, not having the time to go down to the car and ensure that Srini was dead.

He smiled at me as I sat down next to his bed. His neck was in a brace, and he winced as he moved his head to look at me.

"Fine mess we're in, Sen."

The TV was on behind me and the news was still covering the dramatic shoot-out near Delhi. Srini looked at me questioningly and I knew then that he still hadn't heard of what had actually happened at the post.

"Shukla, the cops there, all gone, sir. Sharma's alive, but in bad shape."

He closed his eyes and gritted his teeth.

"They really knocked us out, didn't they? Good to see you're okay. Did you do some damage to them?"

"All the bastards who came for us are dead, Sir."

His eyes were hard as he nodded.

"Good. What do you plan to do now?"

"What makes you think I'll do something?"

He smiled as he responded.

"Because you're a troublemaker at heart. Because you're the best operative I've seen in my career. Because you want to ensure these bastards don't get away with it. What's your plan, son?"

I told him what I had learned and asked how I could conceivably go after someone like Ravindran.

"You set a spy to catch a spy."

And then he told me what I needed to do. To be honest, it was well beyond what I thought I was capable of.

The next stop was Ma.

She looked much better than I'd seen her in months, and before I entered the room, the doctor told me that her recovery had been great, and she could perhaps go home in a day or two, continuing treatments once in a couple of days, with a nurse coming home. I closed my eyes in relief. The doctor was still not willing to commit to saying that her cancer was gone or under remission. I could understand that. In matters like this, no doctor would want the family to get their hopes up unless they were sure. However, this was big progress. Ma would be coming home, and with the treatment continuing, she would win this battle again. Then I stopped myself before I entered the room.

She might win the battle and be back home, but would I be there with her?

Sure, I had asked Salil to look after her, but that wasn't the same thing. Was it fair to leave Ma alone, just because I wasn't willing to let go? As Amy had said, perhaps many others would have just accepted that things sometimes were outside their control and would have let things be. Why was I so obsessed? Yes, I was pissed off that many good men had paid with their lives. I was pissed that they had dared come after Ma. But was that all that was driving me? If I was honest with myself, had they hurt my pride, my ego, by getting the better of me, and like a stubborn old soldier, was I refusing to give up once the enemy had bloodied my nose?

"What happened to your shoulder?"

"Nothing, Ma. I'm fine."

"Shut up and come here."

As I sat down beside her, she opened my shirt a bit and saw the bandage covering my left shoulder. I had hoped that with my jacket on top of my shirt, she would not even have noticed it.

"What happened? I saw that you were moving with your left side looking a bit stiff."

Trust mothers to see it all and know it all. I figured there was no point in lying to my mother, not if I might not even make it through the day to speak with her again. She listened in silence to everything I had to say. When I stopped, she had her hand on mine.

"Ma, I don't know what to do anymore. These enemies are powerful, and always ahead of me. They have killed or hurt so many good men that I want to hunt them down, but I'm scared. I'm scared of dying, not because I'll die, but because I'll leave you behind to deal with life all by yourself. Scared that I'll die without even getting a chance to tell Amy just how much I care about her. Scared that even if I die trying, it won't matter. These men are too powerful and will probably do what they want anyway."

I sat there, spent, exhausted, on the verge of breaking down.

"Maybe this is too much for me, maybe they are too much for me."

To my shock, Ma slapped me.

I couldn't remember the last time she had hit me. Maybe when I was in my early teens, after I had beaten up some kid and broken his tooth. I just stared at her in shock.

"Major, now you listen to me. Maybe you like sitting and wallowing in self-pity while your brothers are being killed around you, but I won't allow a son of mine to do that. What do you think you see when you look at me?"

I didn't know what to say. She spat out the words.

"A poor woman with cancer, battling for her life? Spare me the drama and sympathy. I don't want to die any more than the next person, but if I die, I won't fear it, because I've lived a life worth living. I've looked life in the eye, told it to go to Hell when it looked like it was not going my way. I was married to a man I loved, a hero who won the Maha Vir Chakra and gave his life for the nation. I brought up a boy who became a man, a soldier, a warrior. The Ashoka Charka and Kirti Chakra you won don't define you as a man in my eyes. The way you held me at your father's funeral told me all I needed to know about the man you would one day be."

My eyes were misting over, but Ma's eyes were blazing. I had always thought I was the one being strong for her, the one protecting her. Maybe I had been wrong all along.

"Son, remember that movie you liked so much and told me about? American Sniper or something like that, right? You said there was a line in there about there being three kinds of people in the world, sheep, wolves who prey on them, and sheepdogs who protect their flock. Let me repeat what you had said about how that made you feel about doing what you did. About how it inspired you to help others who couldn't protect themselves. Well, my son will never be a sheep to blindly do as others say and I'll be damned if he becomes a wolf who preys on the weak. You have no option but to be a sheepdog, to protect those who need protecting. Do you understand that?"

I just nodded.

"Major, your duty calls. Your brothers have fallen in combat and the enemy is out there. Now, are you going to sit here and ask for sympathy or will you go and do a soldier's duty? I am not your mother, but the wife of a soldier and the mother of a soldier. I know how my heart broke when your Baba fell and how I died a little every time I spent sleepless nights knowing you were in harm's way during operations, but we, all of us, whether we like it or not, have chosen to serve. Now, will you do your duty? These men you talk about may be powerful, they may be ruthless, but I know my son. I know what he is and what he is capable of. Forget what all those doctors told you about adjusting back to civilian life. Imagine you're in the field again. Imagine that these men have killed Gurung and Thapa all over again."

I sat up straight, looking into Ma's eyes, seeing them blaze with a fury I now felt rising inside.

"They have cut off your brother's heads. Will you hide and slink away or will you bring me their heads?"

I looked at my mother, a frail woman battling cancer with an IV drip attached to her arm. Yet, at the same time, wife and mother to warriors, and perhaps something I had never realized, a warrior herself.

I stood up. I had hugged and kissed Ma countless times.

For the first time in my life, I saluted her.

I was going to war.

***

In the real world, villains didn't lurk in underground lairs, surrounded by dangerous henchmen. They sat drinking wine with their family at the Delhi Gymkhana Club, the place where the capital's elite gather to socialize. A couple of calls made and favors called in had told me where Ravindran might be, and while I wasn't a member of the elite club, I had called an old general who had once told me that if I never needed help, he was one phone call away. He was a member, and I asked him to join me for a drink at the Gymkhana Club. Srini had suggested I call him and as Srini had predicted, the general came when I reached out.

Major General Rathore was now retired, but he was as sharp as ever. I poured our drinks and he raised his glass in a toast.

"To the poor fools who think they can kill you."

I raised an eyebrow as if asking what he was talking about and he chuckled.

"I read the papers, my boy, and I hear the chatter. A bunch of jihadis showing up dead all over the city, talk of an army major now in R&AW being involved, and then that shoot out at the hospital where your mother is undergoing treatment. I connected the dots and I'm sure you didn't call me after all these years to reminisce about the old days. I can see it in your eyes. You're up to no good, and some poor sod is going to learn the hard way not to mess with you. What are you up to, Major?"

"Sir, I need to apologize to you. I needed to get into this club to check on a potential bogey and I wanted to use your credentials as an excuse to spook him."

He finished his glass in one long swallow and poured another and then laughed out loud.

"Well, that's a new one. Me being taken for a ride by one of my boys. Won't be the first time that hanging with me was an excuse used by you or your buddies when you were up to some mischief, is it? Well, what are you waiting for? Happy hunting. Just don't blow up the club or something, I do enjoy my drink here."

Ravindran was sitting in the main dining hall, with his wife and son and I walked in and sat down on the vacant fourth chair.

"Yes, how may I help you?"

Ravindran was lean and looked like an erudite professor with his glasses and grey hair that was neatly combed back. But he was not a professor, he was a veteran intelligence agent, and he knew trouble when he saw it.

"Sir, I'm Major Aaditya Sen. I work for Srini Iyer and we were working closely with Shukla in your team."

He dabbed his lips with a napkin, not taking his eyes off me.

"Shame about Shukla. A good man, and a good officer."

I held his gaze.

"Yes, a real shame. I was there when he died. I killed the men who killed him."

His eyes widened as he made the connections. He must have heard my name but had never seen me. No reason for a senior officer like him to see someone like me. His wife started saying something, but he put a reassuring hand on her arm.

"Major, we are here to celebrate my son's getting a scholarship to go to college in the US. Why don't you see me in the office tomorrow and we can talk then?"

"We can do that, Sir, but there are a couple of things bothering me about the circumstances of Shukla's death that I needed to get to someone senior in the IB. I was told by an old contact in Military Intelligence that they had been monitoring a potential leak in the IB for some time. A leak they suspected of giving out secrets about defense installations. They monitored someone interfering with the Control Room messaging last night and sending a message to Sharma well ahead of the actual message. That message was used to lure us into the trap."

I could see his hands tighten on the glass he was holding, but other than that, he showed no other visible reaction. You didn't become a senior IB officer without having ice in your veins. I was skating on thin ice, making this up as I went along. Rathore had indeed been in MI, and if any of Ravindran's handlers were watching, they would have seen me with him that night, and that would if nothing else, give some credibility to my claims.

"As I said, Major, this is all shop talk, and it's bad form to discuss work when I'm trying to have a quiet evening with my family."

I began to get up.

'I apologize, Sir. It wasn't my intent to disturb you, but if I could have a word in private before I go."

He got up and walked a short distance with me towards the main door.

"Sir, I really respected Pillai and Shukla, and they both spoke of you in glowing terms as such an honest and capable officer."

He smiled, as anyone who has just had their ego stroked would. Of course, Pillai and Shukla had never mentioned him, but he had no way of knowing that.

"So, when my contact at MI mentioned that you were one of the people they were monitoring, I was surprised. I told them it wasn't possible, but I also thought I'd let you know so that you don't get taken by surprise."

He stopped and I could see his mind working through it all, processing the danger he faced. I pressed home my advantage, handing him a piece of paper.

"Sir, this is my number. Call me any time after eleven tonight if you think I can help share any more details of the MI investigation which may help you. Enjoy your dinner."

I left him and walked to the bar to meet Rathore.

"You seem happy enough, my boy."

I poured myself a large peg.

"Sir, for once it feels like I'm doing the hunting instead of being hunted. Srini Sir told me that you could help. I'm hoping you can help me because I'm in way over my head."

***

I called Amy but didn't get an answer. I didn't know if she was pissed with me for having gone into harm's way the previous night, but there was little I could do about it. So, after another drink with the General, I had gone to Ma, and checked on her. She had been sleeping so I just sat there and looked at her. I was now well and truly committed to my course of action. By going to Ravindran, I had taken a big risk, and I'd know soon how that had played out. At eleven, I stepped out and sat near the coffee machine in the hospital, and got myself a coffee, both to keep myself awake and to pass the time.

My phone rang at 11:05. I didn't recognize the number but when I answered the call it was Ravindran.

"Major, you have a very unorthodox way of working, but tell me what I can do for you."

"Sir, I am only trying to help an officer I respect and have a lot of regard for. I would hate for MI to draw the wrong conclusions without you being able to get your side of the story out first. I can arrange for you to meet my senior contacts in Military Intelligence. Your family looked wonderful. I'd hate to imagine how they'd cope with the adverse publicity that any such affair would bring."

I didn't like being a blackmailer, and I wasn't very good at it, but I had very few cards to play. Salil had asked me to be a soldier, and back in the day when I and my buddies would head out to tangle with all sorts of enemies, my natural inclination was to go in hard and fast, but my officers had taught me that sometimes the best way to prepare for a strike was to launch a diversionary attack elsewhere. I had wondered if Ravindran would take me for a genuinely well-meaning officer or someone who was out to shake him down. Also, whether Ravindran was a bad apple was a hypothesis, one which I hoped to validate through this. He made that clear with his next question.

"What do you want for this help you will provide me, Major?"

Bingo.

No clean officer accosted with the offer I had would ever ask that. He would have laughed it away and said there was some misunderstanding or at most ask to see what I knew or had. He would never ask about a quid pro quo. Or so Srini had said, and I was leaning on his judgment and experience to pull this part of the operation off.

"Nothing as of now, Sir. Just let me know if, in light of what we've talked about, you'd be willing to meet up again. I have the files MI has on you and I can show them to you. If you deem them to be of value, then we can talk about some suitable compensation."

He laughed.

"Well, that sounds fair. Where and when?"

"Tomorrow morning. At the Old Fort Boat Club, at five in the morning. Come alone."

The next morning, I was there at the Boat Club. I had used my bugged phone while talking to Ravindran and so Bethune and whoever he worked for knew that Ravindran was meeting me and what we had talked about. This could play out two ways. If Ravindran was loyal to his paymasters, he might just contact them and tell them of the meeting. In that case, they would come for me in force. If he was in it just for the money and wanted to save his own skin and reputation, he would come alone, but his masters would likely come for him as well.

Either way, I had to get my plan in motion before that happened.

As I said, Salil had asked me to act like a soldier, and I was doing just that. As a soldier, it was stupid to go on missions all alone. You always have buddies to cover you, and this time, I was prepared. They had taken me by surprise all too often, but this time I was ready for them. Jogging around the lake was Bahadur, packing a handgun of his own under his sweatshirt. Pratap was pretending to do Yoga a few hundred meters away. Kishore and Unni were in a car parked near the entrance to the Old Fort. I had called them at night and told them that I might be running into the men who had ordered the hit on Srini and my mother, killed Sean, and put Salil in hospital. All four were old buddies from my days in the SFF; all four were like family, and all reacted with the same rage as would be appropriate if anyone had violated their family. I had told them that this was dangerous work and not strictly sanctioned as such, that I was doing this on my own to get some payback at those who had hurt us so much. I had told them that if they got into any official trouble, I might not be able to help them. They had basically told me to fuck off and that I must be getting soft sitting in an office to tell them that. I had gone to the office late at night and used the authorization I had got from Srini to check out some firearms for all of us. At least this time I would not get into trouble for checking out firearms. Srini had helpfully sent out a mail that Unit 22 was authorized to check out firearms at my discretion given the security situation.

This time, I fully intended to be prepared for whatever our enemies had in store for us.

Ravindran showed up five minutes late, wearing track pants and a sweatshirt. I knew he lived just across the road in the government colony of Bapa Nagar, home to many senior officers. With many of them having cops providing security outside their homes, our enemies would not send a large force like the previous night. Too messy, too likely to get caught up in a firefight with the cops around. If they came, they would hit hard with a small team and get away fast. I didn't like standing there, exposed in the open, but I didn't have too much choice. My buddies had swept the area and so far, they had all sent all-clear messages on my encrypted phone, but I knew that could change very fast.

"Good morning, Major. Show me the files."

Ravindran was nervous and in a hurry. I walked up to him.

"How much are they paying you? Is it just cash or did they also get your son admission and the scholarship? What's the exit plan? Have they promised you they'll get you and your family to the US as they did with Sehgal and Singh in case you get compromised?"

He just stood there, staring at me.

"I have no idea what you're talking about."

I took out my khukri.

'Sir, I don't know much about all this cloak and dagger shit, but I do know how to cut people's heads off.'

He took a step back.

"Nonsense. You can't kill me."

I slapped him. Hard. With my left hand. He had been watching my right hand with the khukri and he never saw it coming. He may or may not have been a good spy, but he was no fighter, and he went down to the ground.

My encrypted phone buzzed. It was Kishore. I put the speaker on so Ravindran could hear.

"Boss, two men just came. They're hanging around at the entrance and they look like they're overdressed for early morning exercise."

"Establish if they are a threat and if so, take them out."

That was all. I didn't know if these two newcomers would be found with their throats slit or a bullet in their heads. I didn't care. Kishore and the others knew their business, and they were carrying handguns with suppressors to do their business quietly. Ravindran was looking up at me, real fear in his eyes for the first time since I had met him. I knelt before him, the khukri inches from his face.

"Your friends will think you're working with me now, especially after the two men they sent to kill you are found dead. I reckon they will repay that disloyalty by paying your family a visit. What do you think?"

He just stared dumbly up at me, processing the situation he was in, perhaps concluding that he wasn't going to talk or bargain his way out of this.

"What do you want?"

"I want you to confess what you've done."

"They'll kill me."

The khukri slashed out, nicking his face. He howled.

"I'll kill you as well. Look at the bright side- if you confess, the government will protect you and your family, and the best way of protecting your family is to help us take down those you're working for."

"I don't know much. They pay money into an offshore account, and they had some photos of mine from an overseas training trip to the US. Photos with a prostitute, which they used to keep me quiet. I've never met them, and they send all their instructions via encrypted mail. All I've done is relay messages they asked me to pass on."

"Messages that have got people killed, you bastard. Like the message last night which got Shukla, Srini, and Sharma rushing to that police post. Did you send that message?"

He bowed his head.

"Yes. I have access to the admin account in the Control Room. Got that from someone in IT by telling him I wanted to do some investigating on potential double agents."

I hauled him up and slapped him again. It was purely my anger making me lash out, but it felt good.

"I swear I don't know anything more about what they intended. All they wanted was some information on files, and for me to transmit some messages once in a while and to tailor my reports on the investigation you were doing to fit a certain narrative. I thought it was for some political points they hoped to score. I had no idea how far they would go, but I'm trapped."

I slapped him again and he collapsed again. This time, I kicked him in the ribs, perhaps breaking one or two, and he screamed in agony.

"Do you really think I will have any sympathy for you? Just because you couldn't keep your pants zipped in some whorehouse, just because you got greedy, many good men are dead. Now go and confess to what you've done and hope the government you've betrayed will protect your family."

"They'll lock me up. I'll be disgraced..."

I kicked him again. It was no more heroic than kicking a dog on the street, and I admit part of me felt low for doing it, but part of me, the one I was straining to hold back, wanted to tear apart this traitor in front of me with my bare hands.

"You should have thought of that before you betrayed the trust so many people had placed in you. If you confess, maybe you can spin a more sympathetic tale. I have recorded this conversation. If you don't turn yourself in within the next couple of hours, I'm sending the recording on to some TV channels. Trial by media will destroy your reputation more than any government inquiry. I'd like to see your family deal with that shame. At least the government will deal with this more discreetly since publicity of this sort about a senior officer will not look good for the government either."

I began walking off, leaving him on the ground. I turned around to him one last time.

"Hurry, motherfucker. They'll probably send more men after you and next time, I and my buddies won't be around to save you."

I spent the next couple of hours at the Starbucks in Khan Market, drinking coffee, and reflecting on what I had needed to do. Hurting and blackmailing an unarmed man was not what I had signed up for as a soldier, though Srini had told me this was the way to get to a spy like Ravindran. I closed my eyes, craving something stronger than the coffee, craving the simplicity of my days as a soldier when there were armed enemies out to kill you and you had to kill them first. Damn this cloak and dagger shit, damn this intrigue, damn these enemies who fought in the shadows. I must have cursed aloud because a young girl sitting close to me picked up her cup and moved a bit further away.

The boys had gone back to their guard duty at the hospital. With Ma, Sharma, and Srini all there, if the bad guys wanted payback, it was a compelling target. Yes, the cops were there in force, but I would trust our boys more to deal with the kind of attackers who might come for revenge.

I had been thinking of the next move when I caught a breaking news item on a newspaper's website.

Senior Home Ministry official commits suicide in Delhi. Breaking reports say that an Additional Secretary in the Ministry of Home Affairs, identified by some early reports as A. Ravindran, has committed suicide by jumping off a balcony at the India International Centre. Further details are awaited.

The coward had taken the easy way out, but either way, I had taken a significant enemy piece off the board.

Now, on to the next enemy piece I needed to get off the board.

Bethune.

***

"Major, I didn't expect to see you here."

"I thought I'd drop by for breakfast."

I had come to Bethune's hotel the next morning and parked

myself in the coffee shop, overlooking the lobby. Either I'd see him leaving for work or I'd catch him as he came for breakfast. Bethune put his bag near the table and went and got himself breakfast. My mood was foul, not just because of what had happened the previous day, but because Amy still wasn't taking my calls. I had sent her a few text messages, and she had just replied saying she was busy and would call back.

When Bethune sat down, to my surprise, his plate was piled with what looked like more than half a dozen croissants, muffins, and cakes. He caught me staring and answered a bit sheepishly.

"I have few weaknesses, but a sweet tooth is one of them. By the way, I heard about the ambush and the losses you guys took. Deeply sorry to hear but am glad that Srini is okay."

I sipped my coffee and waited for him to put away a couple of muffins before I got to the point.

"Bethune, I've been thinking about something."

He raised an eyebrow as he stopped smearing jam on a croissant.

"We've identified a leak in the IB. A senior officer who was passing on information to some elements in US intelligence. We have reason to believe that this whole thing was a false flag operation of some sort. The terrorists had Iranian passports which were perhaps meant to be left at the site of the attack on the US President. Not sure if they were intended to succeed or not, but the passports and the trail back to Bin Azam would make it look like an Iranian sponsored job."

He put his croissant down and stared at me for a full five seconds before he said anything.

"Do you realize what you're saying? This sounds like something out of some fringe conspiracy website."

I resisted the urge to stab him there and then. I hadn't tried to get my khukri and gun through hotel security, but I was holding the knife that had been laid on the table in my right hand and for a brief moment of madness, I contemplated what it would feel like to drive it through Bethune's eye. He caught the look and sat back, visibly concerned. The smile was gone, and the croissant would remain uneaten.

"How long since you've been handling Ravindran?"

"Who?"

I was losing patience at his insistence on playing dumb.

"The IB Additional Director who confessed to working for you."

He leaned forward; his palms held out in a conciliatory gesture.

"Look, Major, you'vc had a rough fcw days, but this is crazy. As per protocol, the CIA works with the R&AW, not the IB, as the first line of contact. Secondly, I have no idea who this Ravindran is, and third, if you're so sure, let's go have a chat with him and you'll soon see that this is a mistake of some kind."

"Nobody will be chatting with Ravindran anytime soon. He committed suicide once he was confronted with his treason."

"What do you want with me then?"

"I want you to lead me to whoever is masterminding this. I want more evidence so we can bust this open. Military Intelligence already has Ravindran's confession and while

Srini is badly hurt, as we speak, he is talking to the PMO about what we suspect. One way or the other, this will blow up in your face."

I saw something change in Bethune's eye. He had been trying to be friendly, but now he perhaps realized the danger he was in.

"Major, you have no proof of me being involved in anything of this sort. I am here as a diplomat with immunity and I will walk out of here and you can't stop me."

As he began to get up, I grabbed his left hand. He was bigger and stronger than me, but I was fueled by rage and I twisted his hand, holding it palm up while I placed my left palm on his wrist.

"You were a Marine, Bethune. You're big and I'm sure you can handle yourself, but you know I can break your wrist right here, and believe me, I will. Sit the fuck down and let's continue the conversation."

He sat down, nursing his sore wrist.

"What is wrong with you, Major? Why do you think I have anything to do with this?"

If he was still playing dumb, then I'd lay it all out.

"My phone was bugged, and we found that out soon after you met me and sent me your number."

"Come on, I came to meet you because I was concerned about Amy. She seemed really stressed out and withdrawn and her boss is an old buddy of mine who had asked me to look out for her when she was here. Only an idiot couldn't see the chemistry between the two of you. I was just afraid that she'd do something silly under the stress she was in and so thought I'd tell you to look out for her. She seems to be a good kid and I didn't want her burned by what's going on."

"You met Munaf soon before he committed suicide."

"So what? So did a bunch of other people, and I didn't meet him alone. Come on, Major, this is getting preposterous. You have a bunch of assumptions you're making and you're making a major leap from what is just circumstantial evidence to concluding that I am some kind of villain who's been pulling the strings in this crazy conspiracy theory."

"Okay, humor me then. Here are the facts- not circumstantial evidence. Someone paid off Ravindran to pass them info and to lead us into an ambush. Someone bugged my phone. Some of the men we've encountered have been veteran mercenaries, not the kind of men ordinary jihadis hire. One of them, Jameson, was bugged by us, and his flight disappeared over the ocean. Those are cold, hard facts. Care to explain any of those without concluding that you're involved in this?"

"Fuck, Jameson? I put him on that plane. It was an Agency flight that came in as a private charter. I knew one of the men on the plane. He and I served together in the Marines. Did you say it disappeared?"

Something wasn't right here. I may not be a spy, but I knew how to read people, and Bethune wasn't faking this.

"We were tracking Jameson. Yes, the flight disappeared over the ocean and our Navy spotted signs of a mid-air explosion and wreckage in the water."

Bethune took out his phone and called someone. I saw his face, anxious and intent.

"It's saying the phone's switched off."

He made another call.

"Hey, Lucy, this is Donzel here. I was wondering if Ron is stateside."

"Okay. No worries, I'm sure he's fine. You know how it is when he's in-country."

He hung up and faced me.

"Ron told me that after that flight, he was going home. He had taken time off to be there for his son's graduation."

He sat back; his big hands clasped together.

"Shit."

"Bethune, if you're involved in this, I hope you realize you've been party to your friend's murder along with all the other people killed."

He slammed his fist down on the table, startling everyone else around us. His voice was low, but came out in a dangerous growl, tears coming into his eyes.

"Fuck you, Major. Fuck you. I didn't have anything to do with this. If Ron is dead, then those who've done this will pay. I served my country with honor when I was in the Marines, and I continue to do so. I will not have you come here and accuse me of being a traitor, of conspiring to kill my President, and of killing my friend."

My mind was racing. Bethune was either the best actor in the world, or he was indeed behaving like a man who had learned an old friend was dead, and he was being accused of the crime.

"Someone is involved. Someone very close to everything

we've been doing. If not you, who?"

Bethune sat back, his chest heaving, trying to get himself back under control.

"I don't know, Major, but I will find out. That I promise you."

He got up and I walked with him. I still wasn't fully sure if he was indeed innocent or not, but then I'd kept my phone on. Whoever was running this had been listening in. Either Bethune was leading me into an ambush, or he was going to be in grave danger. He continued walking out of the lobby when my instincts started screaming again. This time, I was going to listen to them. I turned off my phone.

'Bethune, stop!'

He turned towards me.

"My phone was on. The one that's bugged. They would have heard everything and if you are indeed innocent, you are a dead man. They will come for you. They've been particularly good at cleaning up loose ends."

He began to say something about diplomatic immunity and then stopped, realizing just how stupid it was to talk about diplomatic immunity when you were up against trained killers who were taking out senior Indian officers in the middle of Delhi and killing them in their own homes.

"What do you suggest?"

I called Kishore on my encrypted phone and within minutes, he was in the lobby. I had brought him along in case I needed backup.

"Kishore, sorry man, but you should get to the hospital and join the other boys. I think I may have stirred up a hornet's nest and I need to be sure everyone at the hospital will be safe."

As he got out of the car, he asked me if I'd be okay. I assured him I'd be fine as I opened the boot and got my gear ready. A Kevlar vest over my shirt, a double shoulder holster. On the left side went my personal Glock 17, on the right side went the Glock 18 from work, set on full auto. An extra clip on each side was inserted below the holster and additional clips were stuffed into my jacket pockets. The khukri went into the scabbard on my left hip.

Bethune was looking at me, wide-eyed.

"What are you planning, Major? You look like you're preparing for war."

"We are already at war, Bethune. Srini is calling the PMO and I need you to come with me to someplace safe and then I need you to get to someone senior in your government, someone who won't be involved in this for sure."

"Who?"

"Somehow get to the President. He can't have set up his own assassination."

"I can't just call the President."

"Get in the car. You can figure out how to do it while I drive."

As he got in, I turned to him.

"And you're not off the hook, Bethune. You make one false move and I'll kill you without a second thought."

I began to drive towards one of our safe houses which I knew was nearby. It was tempting to head to the office but if anyone was listening in and planning an ambush, they would cover the office. The safe house was located in Golf Links, something Srini had passed on to me, saying that if I got into trouble I should go there. It was supposedly regularly scanned for bugs, had a safe inside with additional arms and ammunition and secure comms equipment. I'd take Bethune there, and then call Srini for further advice. Srini had asked me to take Ravindran and Bethune off the board and I had succeeded in doing that. With all that had got messed up around me recently, these had been a rare couple of days of unmitigated successes.

Bethune's phone rang and he began to reach inside his jacket. Keeping my right hand on the steering wheel, I took out the Glock 18 with my left hand and pointed it at him.

"Bethune, this is set on full auto. It'll make mincemeat of you, so don't try anything."

"Cool it, Major. I'm just taking out my phone."

I saw him answer the call and a puzzled expression come on his face.

"Pull over, Major."

"Why?"

"This guy wants to talk to you."

Keeping the gun pointed at Bethune, I pulled over to the side of the road and took his phone in my right hand. The voice over the phone sounded garbled but was clearly male. Salil had told me the spooks did that electronically to mask their real voices at times. I put the phone's speaker on both so that Bethune could also hear what was being said and so that both my hands were free if Bethune did try anything.

"Well done, Major. I am impressed."

"Who is this?"

"For someone whom I took to be a mere trigger-puller and foot soldier, you have achieved a lot. Clearly, I had underestimated you."

"Thanks for the compliments, but who the hell is this, and what do you want?"

He chuckled.

"Now, now. You've played this game really well so far, why lose your composure? When I began playing this game many years ago, I thought of it like chess. I used to play chess competitively in college, and I could see the similarities. You have your pieces on the board and so does your adversary, and success comes down partly to anticipating moves, partly to planning ahead, and partly to misdirection- doing something while you signal something else."

"Have you called to lecture me on chess?"

"Major, yes indeed. I think you could still learn a fair bit about how to play this game. You see, great chess players often must sacrifice some pieces for the greater good. I think you struggle to do that or to live with that because you get attached to the pieces. I, on the other hand, do that easily. It comes naturally to me. That gives me an edge over someone like you. Second, great chess players always play the long game. You are a true soldier in the sense that you're focused on the mission, winning the here and now. I, on the other hand, am always looking ahead, always seeing how I can keep my edge, how I can stay on course for my long-term goal no matter what you may do."

"If you've had enough of complimenting yourself, why the

fuck are you calling me?"

"Why indeed, Major. Because I have made another move which I think will be of interest to you. One which you may not have any counter for."

I had a bad feeling about where this was heading.

"Ms. Khan is our guest. While you were out and about taking out our pawns and rooks, I went for your queen. I'll send a location on the map to Bethune's phone. Come there now and come without alerting anyone else. Believe me when I say that the moment I get even a hint that you're bringing anyone else other than yourself and Bethune, I will first rape Ms. Khan and then cut her into little pieces for you to pick up when you get here."

My throat was dry, and I couldn't think of anything to say.

The man hung up with one last word.

"Checkmate."

***

EPISODE NINE

Female Of The Species

The location that had been sent to Bethune's phone was a farmhouse in an isolated, forested area near Mehrauli, well outside of Delhi city. It took us close to forty-five minutes to drive there and throughout that time, I kept thinking of whether there was any realistic chance of me getting away alive.

Halfway there, I concluded that I was driving to near-certain death.

"Sen, should we call anyone?"

I snapped at Bethune, keeping my eyes straight ahead.

"Shut up. Your friends have caused enough trouble already and I don't want Amy to get hurt."

He turned towards me and I picked up the Glock that was lying next to me. He held out both hands in front of him.

"Relax. I'm not going to try anything. Do you still believe I'm involved in all this? Come on, man, I had no idea of what was going on. I was just trying to do my job."

"Why did you get Pillai to lean so hard on Munaf and then abandon him when Munaf died? For that matter, how did Munaf die? Pillai maintained till the end that Munaf had not been tortured so badly and he was too young and fit to suddenly have a heart attack. While we're on the subject, how did Pillai die? Too convenient for him to commit suicide, isn't it? A man like him, who was so committed that he kept reaching out to those who'd listen even when he'd been sidelined, he wouldn't have just killed himself. So, who the hell killed him?"

I screamed out the last words and Bethune sat back, deflated.

"Add to that Ravindran, my phone being bugged, so someone at your end was running all this. So, don't give me crap about you being innocent. If not you, then who?"

Bethune was quiet for a while as if thinking things through. Then he sat bolt upright.

"Walker."

"Who the fuck is Walker?"

"Charles Walker."

I so wanted to blow his brains out, but I struggled to control myself for Amy's sake. Bethune whispered the next few words.

"The Ghost Who Walks."

That did it. I turned towards him, holding the gun inches from his face.

"What are you talking about? Make sense or I swear I will blow your brains out."

He took a deep breath and sat back in his seat.

"Sen, I'm not your enemy. I'm nobody, just another dumb guy doing his job. Just another guy who's been set up. I think I have an idea of who could be doing this. The man who came with me to your office. That's Charles Walker."

I remembered the man who had been with Bethune. Dark suit, thin, thinning hair, glasses. Had looked like a spy, and the few times he had opened his mouth, it had seemed like he was ordering people around.

"Who's he?"

'A CIA legend. One of the first men into Afghanistan after 9/11, the brain behind a lot of the Black Ops we conducted around the world. His work is so shrouded in secrecy that most of us in the Agency just hear rumors. An Iranian general taken out in a bomb attack; a terror financier killed while on holiday in France. That's why he's called the Ghost Who Walks behind his back, not just because he works in the shadows, but because people are scared of him."

"Why was someone like him in Delhi for the investigation?"

"He's been up to his neck in the Middle East, so when we heard Bin Azam might be involved in a plot against the US President, he was sent in to assist me, because he knows all the groups there. Hell, he's probably run some of the same jihadis whom we're trying to kill today! I found it curious at the time, but I just put it down to the fact that a plot against the President would get the Agency to send in heavy hitters."

A man with a reputation like that, a man who was deeply involved in the Middle East. I could see him plausibly being involved, or was Bethune just implicating him to save himself or buy time? Perhaps Bethune saw that I doubted him, so he kept speaking.

"If you remember, he also spoke up about Pillai leaning more on the prisoner. In fact, he had whispered to me in the meeting that the Indians should not be soft on the guy. He went with me to meet Munaf, and he asked for a few minutes alone with Munaf. He could have slipped something to him or injected him."

I stole a glance at Bethune. He was speaking, not so much to me, but giving voice to things he was working through in his mind, making connections, and as he kept speaking, he got more and more animated.

"The PMC some of the guys you got worked for was a company called Zeus. Founded by a former SEAL. Walker told me he'd check on that connection because he had used Zeus before in the Middle East for some of his ops, and he was the one who sent in a report clearing Zeus of any involvement and reporting that Zeus had said that all the men mentioned had been fired from Zeus and were working as lone wolves."

We were about ten minutes out, and I turned to Bethune.

"Assuming it's him, the question is why and how? Why the hell would he do all this and pulling off an operation like this would require millions of dollars. How would he fund it?"

"I have no idea about the funding and why he'd do something like this, but he could pull something like this off with the connections and expertise he has."

I kept driving, thinking of the strange world I found myself trapped in. One where your enemy was often not the man shooting at you, but someone wearing a suit having coffee with you. A world where the most dangerous enemy is often not the man holding the gun, but the man hiding behind him in the shadows. This was a world that was alien to me, and it left me disoriented and afraid. Afraid not just for myself, but for Amy. Against enemies like this, I had no idea if I could protect her. They would kill me for sure, but that didn't mean they would let her go. I smashed my fist against the steering wheel in frustration and swore aloud.

"Sen, it is remarkable what you've done so far, do you know that?"

"A fat lot of good that's done. A bunch of good people have died and more may die."

Bethune turned to look at me.

"Sometimes all you can do is fight the good fight. Sometimes that's enough. Remember that I was a Marine before I put on a suit, and you remind me of the best of the Marines I fought with. Men of honor. Warriors. I don't blame you for coming after me. I can see why you'd reach the conclusions you did."

I took a deep breath.

"Why are you telling me this? It's a bit late and honestly, it doesn't matter a bit anymore what you think of me. Your pal may be the Ghost Who Walks, but I'm a dead man walking here."

"I'm telling you because my dad, who was also in the army, told me that before you go into combat, you shouldn't leave things unsaid. You never know if you'll get another chance. He was a man of faith, and he instilled that faith in me. Forgive those who have trespassed against you and ask for forgiveness when you have the chance. So, I'm sorry I wasn't able to do more to help Amy. She came to the Embassy yesterday, looking stressed. I asked her if she was okay, but maybe I should have called you. Maybe I should have done something to help her."

We were now just a few minutes away from our destination. I could understand why Bethune was saying the things he was.

He was readying himself for death.

At that moment, I knew that he was innocent.

"Bethune, I'm just sorry I stayed alive when so many good men around me died. I don't deserve to live any more than them. I'm sorry I won't be around to take care of Ma, and I'm sorry I may not be able to save Amy. My shrink told me I had PTSD, that I was grappling with survivor's guilt. I'm sick of being a survivor. Maybe it's better if it all just ends. Maybe it's better this way."

We came up to an opening in the forest with a narrow road leading right. As we turned, after a few hundred meters, we came up to a gate. I could see CCTV cameras mounted on the side of thc gate. As our car approached, the gate swung open. Bethune tapped on my arm.

"Don't give up on yourself, Sen. Perhaps you lived so you could avenge them, so their deaths wouldn't be in vain. Maybe you're not just a survivor, you're an avenger."

***

We drove through another inner road, which had CCTV cameras at regular intervals before turning into an even narrower road, into which the car barely fit, ringed by a high concrete wall topped with broken glass and barbed wire with the forest all around us. A few minutes more of driving and we were well and truly in the middle of nowhere. The road widened a bit and we entered a driveway leading to a large farmhouse. From the outside, it looked fairly run-down, but given that someone had gone to the considerable expense and trouble to create the roads leading into it, I'd assume the unpretentious appearance was deliberate.

Two men came out, both white men, both tall and well-built, both wearing wraparound sunglasses and both packing body armor and automatic weapons. I would guess both were former special forces and alumni of the same private contractor which had produced some of the men I had bumped into recently.

I got out of the car and they walked towards me, their AK-47s held high. One of them raised his gun toward my chest.

"Lose the weapons. Gently place them on the ground in front of you."

I put both Glocks on the ground and took a step back. The man grinned at me.

"The knife as well."

I took out the khukri and laid it beside the guns. The second man came up and patted me down, not roughly, but thoroughly and professionally. Then he did the same with Bethune.

"Give me all your phones and follow us inside."

We walked into a living room that was sterile and spartan yet betraying a modernity that was totally incongruous with the building's outer appearance. Its walls were metal-lined. Lead, I'd assume, and I filed this away as another evidence of just how well-prepared and paranoid my enemies were. The military normally lines high-value equipment with lead to prevent them from being susceptible to electromagnetic pulses in case the enemy uses EMP weapons to fry their electronics. There were just four chairs in the room, modern office chairs of the sort which spin around and with adjustable heights, around a low, wooden table. A door to our right opened and I caught a glimpse of monitors and blinking lights inside. Their communications room. The man who stepped in was Charles Walker. The famous Ghost Who Walked.

"Sit down, Major, and Bethune, don't look so glum, sit down."

Bethune reluctantly took a seat, but I kept standing, observing Walker. He was wearing the same suit as he had in the office and his eyes were twinkling, as if in amusement.

"What's so funny, asshole?"

He tut-tutted and sat down.

"Just because you want to kill me, and I will kill you doesn't mean we can't be civil. Sit down, Major."

The last words were barked out as an order and one of his men nudged me in the back with his gun to indicate that sitting down was not optional.

"Now that we're all sitting down like reasonable men, let's get to your speculations. First of all, Bethune, not blindingly brilliant but still competent enough of you to get me as the link. Now as to your questions, Major, about the why and the how."

He could perhaps see the baffled look on my face. I had kept my phone off. How had he heard everything we had said? He chuckled and asked for Bethune's phone which he proceeded to smash against the ground.

"No use for this now. Did you really think your phone was the only one we were bugging, Major?"

Bethune began to say something angrily when Walker cut him off.

"Oh, spare me the betrayed look. You've been in the Agency long enough to know better. Now back to the why and the how. The how is easy. All one needs are the right sponsors willing to fund and benefit from an op. I don't need to go into who they are. My men also don't have a need to know but suffice to say, interested parties who would stand to gain from an event like this and have money to spare. The rest I could manage given what I've done with most of my adult life and the kind of connections I've formed through those experiences."

Bethune shouted out; the fury obvious in his voice.

"Why would you do it, Walker? Why would you kill your own President? For money? That makes you nothing more than a mercenary."

That got to him, and for the first time, I saw a crack in his otherwise civil veneer.

"You think I did this for money? I've been there, in the darkest corners of the fucking wars we wage, where the media won't go, where we officially aren't even there. I grappled with the Taliban in Musa Qila, I called in airstrikes against Daesh when their boys in pick-up trucks were all around me, and I played cat and mouse with the Revolutionary Guards in Yemen, Iraq, and Syria. The enemy is not one we can negotiate with or have peace talks with. We need a war to end it all and end the root cause of it- the Iranian regime. I lost a brother in the

1983 Beirut bombing, planned by the Iranians, and have lost many brothers to their bombs in Iraq. Our President talks a big game but then chickens out when he can strike. He is a coward and a politician who will withdraw our troops because body bags before the elections make for bad PR. We need decisive action and our plan would have put the Iranian regime in our crosshairs, subject to the kind of righteous rage that followed 9/11. No double guessing, no waffling, just decisive action."

I was watching his eyes. This was a man who believed in what he was saying. That made him even more dangerous.

"War with a nuclear-armed country sounds like a really smart move, Walker."

He chuckled.

"They wouldn't dare use nukes if our President was hit, Major. The whole international community would back us. We would hit their strategic targets and the regime would be overthrown and those dogs would face justice."

"And I guess your sponsors are driven by the same ideological zeal you are or is it oil and weapon sales and share prices that interest them more?"

"You're a smart one, Major. Let's leave it at that. It would all have worked out if that idiot Azfal hadn't heard things he shouldn't have and not had a sudden attack of patriotism or conscience. And of course, if you hadn't insisted on sticking your nose where it didn't belong. After Azfal's killing, we would have just cleaned up our loose ends and prepared for the operation at another time and place, because it was obvious that given the chatter about a plot against the President, security would be heightened here, but you messed things up time and again. You are perhaps responsible for many of the deaths that occurred."

"Why are you telling me all this. Do you plan to talk me to death? What the fuck do you want with me and Bethune, anyways? Where's Amy?"

Walker got up, put a glove on his right hand, and took my Glock 17 from one of his men.

"Too many questions, Major. Way too many. Let me take them one at a time and start with the easiest one. I have no real use for Bethune, but with what he now knows, he is too much of a liability to leave alive."

He turned and fired a single shot into Bethune's head. Bethune's head rocked back and then lolled forward on his chest. Adrenaline was rushing through my system at the sudden violence, and I saw that Walker was smiling. I had known many men who had killed others, I had killed my share, but we had done so for our duty, and we had all struggled to live with what we had done. Walker seemed unaffected, indeed even slightly flushed. This man was a psychopath who seemed to get off on killing. He turned towards me and smiled.

"Why don't I just kill you? Why am I telling you all this? Because, Major, I am a good judge of people and in you, I see potential. I had you put on the team through my contacts in the Agency because I saw someone who would be relatively ineffectual- a vet with known mental health issues. Instead, you surprised me. Your kinetic abilities were to be expected for a man of your background, but your lateral thinking and strategic planning are to be lauded."

I was still dealing with Bethune's sudden killing and had little time or patience for Walker's bullshit. I spat at him when he came close. He wiped the spittle off his shirt and looked at me, his eyes hard.

"This can end in a couple of ways. I was hoping you'd join my crew. Get paid far better than what your government can ever pay you. Looks like you may have issues with that. Well then, it'll make for a tragic story. A former war hero with mental health issues starts a relationship with a US agent when they work together in a task force. When she tells him she has to leave back for the US and their relationship can't continue, he kills her. He then kills a colleague of hers who tries to intervene and then grief-stricken, he puts his gun in his own mouth and blows his brains out. The news channels will lap it up, don't you think?"

"Where's Amy?"

He sat back down, still holding my gun in his right hand.

"That's the irony isn't it, Major? You came here to save her but if you accept my offer, you can in fact work with her."

"What are you talking about?"

"Major, when you learned there were seven assassins, you made an error of judgment. You assumed they'd be seven men, coming in from Nepal, just like the one you captured. Six of them indeed were. But the most important assassin, the first assassin, was someone very different. John, bring our guest in."

The door to the communications room opened and a third armed man walked out, pointing his rifle at a figure who emerged beside him, hands tied in front, tape across the mouth.

Walker seemed to be enjoying this very much and he grinned

at me.

"Say hello to the first assassin, Major."

It was Amy.

***

I just kept looking at Amy, not sure of what Walker was saying, not really hearing the words, as if my brain was trying to block them off.

"John, take off the restraints and tape. I think she'll be better behaved now that we have the major here."

Amy sat down on a chair next to Walker. I could see her cheek was puffed and red and her eyes were bloodshot. I glared at Walker.

"You shouldn't have hurt her."

He laughed aloud and I saw the man he had called John grin.

"Major, you are in no position to tell me what I can or cannot do. Especially to someone who is in my employ. I do find your chivalry touching, though misdirected, as you're feeling sympathy for the one who has been an integral part of our plans."

I was looking Amy in the eye, and to my disappointment, she avoided eye contact. I thought back to how I had suspected her, and then how I had trusted her fully. Perhaps that had been my error- I had let my emotions get in the way. I had let myself believe that someone I could connect with so much at so many levels, someone who was supporting me along the way, someone who had bonded so well with Ma, could be nothing more than a very special person I had been lucky enough to meet. That betrayal hurt more than anything Walker could have done to me physically.

"Why, Amy? Why? Did none of it mean anything? Was I just someone you were using?"

She looked up and I could see that she was crying.

"No. It meant a lot. I didn't want it to, but it did. I tried to save you so many times- the night when I came to your home with Salil, knowing they would attack you; that night when I said it was my birthday so you wouldn't go for the Soleimani meeting; that night of the ambush at the police post, I tried to keep you from going and then came there to help out."

Realization dawned on me. My unseen savior that night had been Amy.

Walker turned casually and slapped her. I began to get out of my seat but felt a gun digging into my back.

"Ms. Khan has been a very disobedient employee when it comes to you. In other respects, she did what she was expected to, like bugging your phone, like keeping you suspecting that Bethune might be the one who was working against you, but her weak spot for you has made her a liability. So, we will need to get rid of both of you and then wrap up the operation. Shame we couldn't pull it off the way we envisaged, but there'll always be another time."

Two strong pairs of arms grabbed me from behind and began to haul me up. If I was to die, I needed to at least know why Amy had done it.

"Amy, why?"

Walker beckoned for his men to hold me up but wait. He stood up and walked closer to me.

"You deserve to know that before you die, Major. Ms. Khan came back from Iraq seriously damaged- physically and mentally. Three days of abuse and degradation at the hands of that local militia will do that to you. Our fearless President hesitated to order a rescue mission because it could be politically sensitive to lose men- something his generals told him was inevitable given the secure location they were holding her. He kept asking for a foolproof mission and then finally chickened out and asked the Agency to use local assets and PMCs to rescue her- so that even if there were casualties, the American voters wouldn't have to see coffins draped in the Stars and Stripes on national TV. While she was being raped, he was hosting corporate bigshots and giving speeches. My men and I were on the ground and together with some contractors went in and got her out. She owes me, Major, she owes me big time. That's part of why she signed up for this mission."

He held Amy's shoulder and then looked at me.

"But there's more. The militia holding her was run by the Iranian Revolutionary Guard. Our leaders and theirs posture, lob an occasional missile and Tweet, but poor soldiers like her suffer on the ground. Our plan was a rare opportunity to get rid of this feckless President and take out the Iranian regime. You, Major, came back damaged from war as well, but as someone suffering from guilt, seeking redemption. Ms. Khan came back seeking revenge, self-destructive, lashing out at others. I harnessed that rage; taught her we could get revenge for her, and others like her. Being in the Secret Service was a perfect place for her to be, to give us plans and locations for where we could get to the President most easily, and communication codes for us to stay ahead of the Secret Service. She thought we would stage an attack on the US President and lay the blame on the Iranians and then bring down the full wrath of our forces on them. She would be avenged; my bosses would be happy, and I would get a payback of the sort our political establishment has been too weak to contemplate. Of course, Ms. Khan didn't know it all. Perhaps fitting she finds out now."

At that, Amy looked up sharply at Walker. The surprise in her eyes was genuine, and I realized she had been played like so many people. Walker laughed, though there was no humor in his eyes.

"A Lee Harvey Oswald for the post 9/11 generation. Muslim immigrant, a PTSD sufferer, showing her true loyalties to the Iranians and her faith over the American flag. Chances were always high that those six Pakistani idiots would be taken out by the Indians or the Americans. However, with the passports we'd planted on them, they would put a direct link to the Iranians even if they failed. Our insurance policy was Ms. Khan. We would have drugged her and used her gun with her prints on it to kill the President in the fog of war. Enough of a paper trail had been created- bank transfers to offshore accounts, encrypted messages from Iran. The narrative of a Muslim immigrant gone rogue also suited some of my clients well enough."

"You bastard!"

He casually slapped Amy as she shouted at him and then he held Amy's chin up so that she was forced to face me.

"Major, I had no great desire to kill you. This could have all ended differently. Ms. Khan was to fly back to Washington, we would kill those six idiots we were bringing in and clean up this op, and then we'd plan another op later which wouldn't be compromised. We would have figured out how to use the backstory we had built on Ms. Khan, but no doubt she could be sacrificed in another op. But then you fucked things up by being such a pain in the neck and Ms. Khan made things worse by getting involved with you."

He nodded to the two men behind me and one of them bent my left arm behind me with one hand, his other arm encircling my neck. The other man grabbed my right hand and held it out. Walker came up to him and handed him my Glock 17.

"Now, Major. You will shoot Ms. Khan and then shoot yourself. We'll clean up and we'll be back home by tomorrow."

The man on my right side put his knee on the back of my leg and both men bent me down to a kneeling position. He was holding my right hand with both his hands as Walker put the gun in my hand and moved to the side. The man on my left was continuing to hold my left hand behind me but had moved his other hand from around my neck to support his other hand so that I couldn't pull my left hand free. He also put his knee against my back, so I wasn't able to get up. I looked up and saw that the third man was holding Amy from behind. He was wearing a vest and even if my shot went through Amy, he would live.

Walker had thought through everything.

I was in over my head. Betrayed by the woman I loved. Outthought and outmatched by my enemies.

The man's hands were closing over mine, forcing me to point the gun towards Amy.

I was defeated. I would die. I would die disgraced as a man who had killed his lover and killed himself.

I was a failure. Even in death, I would fail and would leave behind disgrace for Ma. I was trying to move my hand away, but the two men were strong, they were putting their whole body weight on me, and my hand was steadily moving towards Amy.

I looked at Amy, into her eyes. I saw not a villain, but just a woman. A woman who had been through unspeakable horrors, who had not been as lucky as I had been to have people around me who could keep me from going over the edge. Someone who was still capable of love in her own way. Someone who had tried to save me, going against her ruthless masters, for nothing more than love. Perhaps there were no heroes or villains the way we see them in the movies. We are all damaged. We are all dealing with our own demons. Some of us are lucky enough to have those who love us enough to heal those scars and prevent us from succumbing to those demons. Others are not. I had also learned that revenge didn't heal scars, love did. I wish I had known Amy longer to tell her that, to try and heal her. I was crying now, but I wasn't ashamed of my tears. I wanted Amy to know now because I might never have another chance.

"Amy, I still love you and always will. I will always remember you as the best of who you were. Thank you for helping heal me. I wish I had been there to help heal you."

She recoiled as if I had struck her and then she put her head back and cried out loud- a sound of deep anguish. My heart broke to see her like this and then all those thoughts crystallized into something else. I had fought for many things in my life- for flag, for country, for my brothers in arms, for duty. I had been ready to die for all of those.

Today I would fight and die for love.

***

The men holding me were young, strong and no doubt well-trained. They had me covered on all fronts. Both hands subdued, pressure on my back to prevent me from bringing my body weight to bear in any offensive motion. However good these guys were, I suspected they hadn't seen much, if any combat. The kind of men I had danced with at Jama Masjid or Jameson were. There's something you learn once you've been in combat, especially if you go up against guerrillas and ruthless terrorists of the sort I had for a living.

You can be taught all sorts of rules and techniques, but nobody ever can really teach the one golden rule about combat. Once you're up against a bastard who is willing to die and has nothing to live for, there are no rules.

They had my hands under control. They had my back under control. They had my legs under control.

I was a sheepdog, but sometimes to fight the wolves, sheepdogs must bare their teeth. I bent my head down towards the arm of the man holding my right hand. He was so intent on getting me to shoot Amy that he didn't notice till I had my teeth around his forearm. I bit, and I bit hard. That fucking Chechen whose ear I'd bitten off will testify to the fact that I was a sheepdog who didn't just bark but had a bite to match. The man screamed, a piercing, high noise as I took out a chunk from his forearm and then spat the bloody flesh into his face. He recoiled in horror, letting go of my hand.

The guy holding me on the left had obviously taken a fancy to my khukri and had kept it tucked into his belt. I grabbed it with my right hand and swung it out, slicing through the neck of the man on my right who was grabbing his mangled arm. The khukri cleanly cut through his neck and he fell back, his head almost totally severed from his shoulders.

Gurung would have been proud of me.

I didn't have an apparent or easy target on the guy holding me from behind, so I stabbed down, impaling his foot through his shoes with the khukri. His grip on me loosened and I half-turned, pulling the khukri out and bringing it up in a ripping motion, cutting him upwards through the groin. I left the khukri in him as he screamed and staggered back, his midsection a bloody mess, both of his hands clutched around it, trying to hold his intestines in.

I turned around to go for the third man, who was holding Amy.

I was too far, and I would never make it in time and there was no way I would risk taking a shot with Amy in the way.

But at least I would have gone down fighting.

That's when Amy rocked her head back, smashing the man's nose with the back of her head. As his grip on her loosened, she dove to her right. The guy I had decapitated was lying just feet away, my Glock 18 at his belt. I dove, pulled it out, and came back up in a crouch even as the man in front of me was bringing up his rifle. He was wearing a vest, so I aimed low at his hips and fired. The Glock 18 had been set on full auto, and in one depressed burst, seventeen bullets tore his hips and midsection apart, and what was left of him collapsed on the floor.

Walker was moving to my left, but my gun was out of ammunition. I dropped it and looked for my other Glock which had fallen a couple of feet away when I had bitten the man who had been forcing me to hold it.

Walker had a gun, a suppressed pistol, which he was bringing up towards me, when Amy barreled into him, trying to grab his gun. I saw them struggle briefly and then Amy's body went slack as Walker fired a couple of shots into her. As she fell, he began to aim at me, and I picked up my gun and emptied my clip into him. A couple of shots hit him in the stomach, a few more on the chest, and the last couple of shots blew his head away.

"Amy!"

I ran over to her and sat down by her side, cradling her head in my lap. There was an expanding pool of blood under her and by the sucking sound she made when she breathed, I knew she had suffered a lung shot. I hated the part of me which told me from long experience that she would not survive. I found my phone on the floor and called Salil, screaming at him to send help to the location I was sending him, but in my heart, I knew that no help would come on time.

"I'm sorry, Aadi. I'm sorry for all I did."

I didn't know what to say or do. When you have seen the life I have, when you have led the kind of life Amy had led, do you still retain the right to judge anyone? Perhaps we were well beyond needing to explain ourselves to each other, to apologize for what we had done. Perhaps, at this moment, with minutes for her to live, she just needed to know one thing.

"Amy, I still love you. I love you."

She smiled and blood pooled out of her mouth. I wiped it away and kissed her forehead.

"Aadi, don't give up. Keep fighting."

I looked up at her eyes, wondering what she was talking about.

"You know I won't make it, but I don't want you to give up on yourself and on others. Be the sheepdog, for there are many wolves out there, and sheep who deserve to live more than I do."

I smiled and nodded. We had watched American Sniper together one evening, both of us reliving what it meant to serve in combat, and I had told her about what that line had meant to me. She raised her hand to wipe my tears, though her grimace told me just how painful even that simple action was for her.

"Aadi, help me sleep. Sing for me, please."

I was crying, my voice breaking as I sang the song that she used to help her fall asleep during her darkest nights. The song she had sung for me when I had revealed to her the demons that kept me up at night.

"You say it best when you say nothing at all."

I kept singing, kept stroking her hair, kept crying, my eyes locked on hers. I saw a peaceful, content expression on her face. She had known a hard life, but now she smiled. Then she went limp.

Amy had finally found peace.

***

EPILOGUE

Back in the Hunt

"Sir, I just hope something came out of it all."

That wasn't the first time I had asked Srini the question that evening. I had been asked to take some time off after the events at the farmhouse, both for me to recover and for the powers that be to clean up the colossal mess that would have resulted from the discovery of the involvement of a CIA agent like Walker in an assassination plot against the US President. Two weeks had passed, and we were both standing in front of Rashtrapati Bhavan, the official residence of the Indian President.

"It was quite something, wasn't it? It's not every day that you get invited for dinner by the President."

I nodded, but realized he was trying to change the subject. Yes, it was not every day that one got invited by the President, and after the dinner, in a small, private ceremony, she had handed me a medal, in her capacity as the Supreme Commander of the Armed Forces. I was sure Ma would insist I put it up along with the other medals at home, but like so many of the medals I'd won, it would never make the papers, and very few people would ever know why I had won it. Also, like so many of the other medals I'd won, this would forever be tainted by memories of those I had lost.

I began to walk away, and Srini must have sensed my disappointment.

"No, my boy, your efforts and sacrifices were not in vain."

He knew I wanted more. I didn't care how the politicians dealt with the mess, but I did care about how Amy would be remembered. Srini knew that as well, and he reached out and placed a hand on my shoulder.

"First of all, Amy's legacy will be protected. I have given a detailed report of how she and you uncovered the plot, leading to the showdown, and how she died a hero."

I exhaled and looked away, feeling tears form at the corner of my eyes. When I looked back up, Srini was still looking intently at me, a warm smile on his face.

"Thank you, Sir."

He shook his head.

"I can only imagine what she went through, and in the end, she came through for you, and for the mission. No point in dragging her name through the mud along with scum like Walker."

Srini's phone buzzed and he answered the call, telling his driver to get his car.

"Sir, I know you can't reveal everything to me, but I just hope those behind the plot got some payback."

Srini smiled, this time the grim smile of a veteran intelligence agent.

"I don't know it all myself, but if I were to be particularly imaginative, I would read something into the fact that a couple of Wall Street CEOs were fired last week amidst scandals regarding sexual improprieties and corruption. It could of course be a coincidence that all these scandals erupted overnight."

Of course, it was no coincidence. I didn't read the business news much, but even I had caught mention of a couple of the scandals. Most likely the US authorities had dirt on them, as they perhaps did on many people, and when they ended up revealed as being part of the plot involving Walker, they were cut loose.

Srini leaned forward, his voice a bare whisper.

"Of course, if you're given to conspiracy theories, you might read something into the fact that two private planes crashed last week. One went down over the US, and another in Europe. Three senior retired US officers died, all of them having served with Walker."

I stood up straight. The US government was playing hardball, but then their President had been directly threatened. The cynic in me told me that the real brains behind the plot were perhaps still out there, but then some payback was better than none.

As his car drove up in front of us, he smiled at me.

"Well, your break's over. Join office on Monday for your new assignment. Give my regards to your mother."

As he began to get into his car, I asked him what my new

assignment would be.

He turned towards me.

“Enjoy the weekend. We can talk shop on Monday.”

Then he smiled as he added,

“There’s plenty more hunting to be done, Major. I need you back in the hunt.”

***

AUTHOR'S NOTE

THE REAL-LIFE UNIT 22

While all characters and actions depicted in this novel are fictional, the Special Frontier Force does indeed exist and does indeed report into India's external intelligence agency, the Research & Analysis Wing. It was set up in the aftermath of the 1962 Indo-Chinese war, to conduct covert operations behind Chinese lines. It was initially staffed largely with Tibetan exiles and with officers from elite units in the Indian Army like the Paras. Much of its operational history is shrouded in secrecy to the extent that the SFF is mentioned separately in the 2nd schedule of the Right to Information Act, 2005, which exempts the government from having to furnish any information on it. Over the years, details of some of its exploits have come out into the public domain, including cross-border operations like a daring climb up the 25,645 feet high Nanda Devi mountain in 1965 to install a nuclear-powered transmitter to keep watch on Chinese nuclear and missile activity and the pivotal role it played in operations such as Meghdoot, the capture of the Siachen Glacier in 1986. Today, the SFF is deployed in several operational roles, including counter-terror operations.

Like Major Aaditya Sen and his comrades depicted in the series, the SFF has long enjoyed a fearsome reputation for seizing the initiative and taking the fight to the enemy. Perhaps as a result of cross-border missions which rattled the Chinese, in 1975, the SFF was prohibited from being deployed within 10 kilometers of the Indo-China border unless it was explicitly ordered to do so. Such restrictions, usually placed on fighter planes and strategic assets, being placed on a special forces group, speaks both to the SFF's capabilities and to the strategic and psychological impact it has on adversaries.

The Special Group, which the fictional Major Aaditya Sen served in, is one of the elite elements in the SFF and is often its sword arm for conducting the most hazardous and daring operations. The inspiration for Unit 22 comes from the fact that the SFF is also sometimes known as Establishment 22 or just '22' in honor of its first Inspector General, Maj. Gen. Sujan Singh, who commanded the 22nd Mountain Division in Europe during World War II and later commanded a special forces unit in North Africa. He was a legendary figure in the British Indian Army and won the Military Cross. He and others who followed him created the ethos that has led the SFF to be one of the least known, yet most deadly, of India's special forces, whose men serve in the shadows, to keep us safe.

As Winston Churchill said, "We sleep safely at night because rough men stand ready to visit violence on those who would harm us."

ABOUT MAINAK DHAR

Mainak Dhar wears many hats. He considers his most important job to be the best possible father and husband he can be. An MBA from the Indian Institute of Management, Ahmedabad with over two decades of experience in the corporate world, his 'day job' involves leading businesses and teams as a CEO. A self-described 'cubicle dweller by day and writer by night', when he's not with his family or at work, he loves creating and sharing stories. He is the author of over twenty books, many of which have been bestsellers, including the Alice in Deadland series, 03:02, and Sniper's Eye. His books have been translated into Turkish, Vietnamese, Japanese, French, German, Portuguese and Hindi, with close to half a million copies sold worldwide. He is also a passionate student of Karate and holds a Black Belt. Learn more about him and contact him at www.mainakdhar.com.